FATED GODS

SUMMONERS
BOOK THREE

A.M. YATES

For Nae,
first friend,
reader, and fan.

PROLOGUE

ONE MONTH AGO

THIS IS THE DAY I DIED.

Simone crashes into me. "Oh gods, Josie. Oh gods!" She's sobbing.

I don't sob. Dead people don't sob. I'm glaring. At another corpse. He glares back at me. He looks like an athletic eighteen-year-old with fire-blue eyes and gold-blond hair and a sharp brow that once spoke to me. But I can't read anything on his face now. I don't want to. He is not Judah. He only wears Judah's body. Inside, he is a fire god. Judah's soul is gone—to the realm of Death.

My dad races down the back steps. "Josie, where have you been? Are you all right? What happened?"

I disengage Simone, only to be gathered up by my dad. He smells like leather portfolios and expensive soap and worried sweat.

"Lily," I say. "She kidnapped me."

My dad pulls away from me, tear-filled hazel eyes bulging behind his rimless glasses. He touches my hair, my cheek, my chin. He sees me—standing, breathing, talking—and he probably thinks I'm okay. But I'm not okay.

"How—?"

"She has her mask back," I report. "I had to repair it because she—*kuso.*" I jam my fingers into my forehead. "Russell. She had Russell. We need to find out where he is, if he's all right."

Caroline has appeared behind my dad. It's her yard we're standing in—a perfectly green stretch of trimmed lawn under a perfectly clear expanse of summer blue sky behind a tidy yellow craftsman-style house in a quiet Portland neighborhood. She doesn't know her son is dead. Judah—the Fire God in Judah's body, that is—stands there, silent and unmoving, but by all appearances, alive.

Caroline reaches for him. She and Judah look so much alike, the same golden complexions and sharp features.

He is not your son, Caroline, I want to say. But the words don't come.

I suspect Simone knows the truth because she leaps between her mom and the Fire God before Caroline's hand touches him.

"We have to find out if Russell is okay!" Simone practically screams.

My thoughts are turning towards Death. I'm remembering what Death told me the last time I saw him in the pathways of the gods.

"Once you find what you've been missing," he'd said, "don't let it go, even if it seems irrevocably lost. Don't stop looking. It will be returned to you, I promise."

At the time, I hadn't understood, but I feel like I might be starting to.

"What is going on?" Caroline asks. "Josie, you were kidnapped? From the party last night?"

"No," I say, only half hearing her.

As soon as I'd found Judah behind the fire god mask, I'd lost him again. His soul had been pushed out by the god.

Had Death known? Was that what he'd been promising me? That he would return Judah's soul to me? If only I kept looking . . .

"Josie was taken from here," Simone says.

"That's not possible. The house is protected," Caroline says.

"Not from here exactly," I say. "From the pathways. Somehow the Fog God found me in the paths of the fire gods . . ."

But how? And if he'd found me once, could he find me again? If I went back . . . *when* I went back . . . because I had to return to the paths of the gods, those routes between the mortal realm and the Beyond, to find Death again.

I would give Death whatever he wanted for Judah's soul. And I didn't need the Fog God interfering.

Caroline gives my dad a look I know too well these days— incredulity. But that's okay. I don't care if anyone believes me anymore. Nothing matters but Judah's soul. Nothing.

"Josie," my dad says in an annoyingly gentle voice, "what are you talking about? You can't travel the—"

"Yes, I can," I say. "That's how I've been repairing the tribe's masks. I've been taking the pathways to the Beyond and pulling the masks from the immortal realm. I was . . ."

I stop myself from telling them why I was in the paths of the gods.

I glance over at the Fire God. He's holding position. The woven leather necklace around his throat is deceptively simple looking, considering it's one of the sacred devices of the gods.

I clench the spear of quartz in my hand. So long as I have it, I have control over the Fire God. I hope. The quartz and the necklace are part of the same godly tool—the Chain of the Gods. I'd retrieved it for Judah, to give him mastery over the Fire God, but again, I'd been too late.

My dad clamps his hands on my shoulders, redirecting my attention to him.

"Josie, you need to explain to us—"

A deafening boom interrupts. The ground begins to quake. We stumble—all of us except the Fire God. He continues to stand there, unmoved, scowling at me. He doesn't like being chained.

I hold tight to the Chain's pendant. I won't let it go. I won't let him go. When I find Judah's soul, I'll have his body ready and waiting.

My dad and I are able to keep our balance for a moment, clinging to each other, but the quaking continues to intensify. We topple to the ground. A deep rumble seems to shake the air itself. Car alarms sound. Glass rattles and then cracks and then crashes. Wood splinters and snaps. Concrete explodes. Birds squawk and protest, taking flight from the cedars and poplars. Distant screams and shouts from across the neighborhood break through the cacophony.

Dark-bellied clouds roll into the calm blue sky like black-hulled pirate ships, blotting out the sun.

I force myself up to my elbows as a frigid wind shoves against me, raking icy fingernails across my face.

I have to give it to that crazy bitch; she doesn't waste any time.

Caroline tugs Simone up, flicks her wrist, and retrieves her mask. She brings it to her face and is subsumed by a guise of restless blue waves, a slender figure sculpted of water. In possession, she's much steadier on her feet, like the Fire God who hasn't moved an inch. Cracks appear in the siding of Caroline's house.

"We have to go!" Caroline's voice is echoed by that of her ocean goddess's—Caroline's, screaming and panicked; the goddess's, deep and roaring.

My dad goes into possession. He, too, is a water god. A sea god. His guise is deep gray with curls of frothy white churning over it. He rises to his feet, pulling me with him. We're about to translocate.

I turn towards the Fire God, squeezing the pendant so hard its edges cut into my palm.

"Follow me," I command, though I'm not sure he can hear me over the shrieking wind and thunderous destruction. Or that he needs to hear for the Chain to exert its power over him.

He bares his teeth in a menacing snarl. I guess he hears me.

An ear-shattering crack and a deep groan precedes Caroline's peaked roof shifting and then sliding off the house and crashing into her driveway, crushing her SUV.

"Mom!" Simone screams.

They translocate away.

My dad draws me into his arms. In a swish and swirl of water, we translocate out of Portland.

This is the day the war begins.

CHAPTER 1

AUGUST 28TH

JOSIE WATCHED THE FINAL EVACUATION of Portland on a computer screen. Muted.

Images of residents torn from their flood, earthquake, and fire damaged homes, sobbing and clinging to the last scraps of their possessions—tattered clothes, cherished scrapbooks, half-burnt stuffed animals—spoke for themselves. One woman clutched a cast iron frying pan to her chest, as if cradling a child.

The young woman had once been a professional. Josie could tell by the tasteful gold hoops in her ears, the manicured arches of her eyebrows, the bold indigo jacket she wore— ready for the office, not the disaster zone. Her eyes were wide, shock-flattened, two tarnished green pennies that had been abandoned on the tracks and repeatedly squashed.

The reporter, clad in a helmet and flak jacket like he expected bombs to go off, turned towards the camera. His lips fired off words at Gatling gun pace. Josie didn't need his commentary. She knew more than he did. The series of apocalyptic disasters—starting with the earthquakes, followed by three successive hurricanes, interspersed with fires and more earthquakes, and ending with twenty sinkholes that had swallowed neighborhoods whole—weren't natural. At least not in the way most people thought of as natural.

The gods had destroyed Portland. They'd blown it down, swept it away, burned it up, and at last, devoured it. Gods under control of Lily and her minions. A little sand in the eye of her former tribe. Crazy witch.

The downloaded newscast ended. Josie took the drive from the computer and held it out to Kai, who'd been watching grimly over her shoulder. Simone clung to his side, tears running down her pixie face.

"Thanks," Josie said flatly.

"You know me," he said with that half-smile of his, "always here to bring a little sunshine to your day."

Josie wished she could appreciate Kai's self-deprecating dark humor like she once had. Not even Kai seemed to enjoy it. He looked almost as shocked and pale as the frying pan woman.

"Want to hear the latest on Osaka?" he asked.

"Not really." She pushed out of her chair. "But tell me anyway."

"Gone."

She glanced out the rough-hewn hole that passed for a window on the Triune's Island. One floor below, in the adjacent courtyard, a tent city sprawled, packed with weary summoners. Ty, Kai's former bandmate, lay flat on the ground, passed out cold. His blond hair was dusty, his long frame skinnier than ever. People stepped over him, carrying boxes of food and batteries, jugs of water, sacks of laundry.

Beyond the sounds of murmured conversation and movement in the courtyard, she could hear the grumble of the far-off ocean. Under the rush of waves were the voices of the primordial gods. One of them was bellowing curses. Stuff about humans being the offspring of pigs and insignificant as beetle dung, but above all, demanding to be worshipped. No one could hear them but Josie.

Simone wiped the tears from her face. Her hair was no longer spiky and bright blue like it had been a month before. The drab peroxide yellow clumps hung, dispirited and uncombed, around her face, souring her complexion to a color akin to yesterday's rations of instant oatmeal.

"When do you have to go back?" Simone asked Kai.

Kai glanced down at his watch. "I'm supposed to meet your mom at Outpost East Coast in a few hours."

Simone burrowed closer to him. "You should sleep."

Kai kissed her forehead. "What about the two of you? Any luck?"

Josie wandered away from Kai and Simone and over to her dresser. Carved figurines littered the surface. Taking her pocketknife from her jeans and opening it, she picked up one of the many unfinished pieces—Billy the Cat, part of her foreign cat cartoon series. Billy looked like an ordinary kitty boy, but he was really a human soul reincarnated as a cat.

"We haven't found anything," Simone answered softly.

"You can use my mask again." He flicked his wrist.

A delicate, porcelain white mask appeared in his hand. An ancient ocean god. One she'd repaired last month. Had it only been last month? It seemed like lifetimes ago.

Josie worked the edge of the knife along Billy's stripes. "Thanks."

She didn't move to take it. She'd broken and repaired so many masks over the last four weeks; she'd lost count of how many.

"But, 'The pathway to Death's realm travels apart from the gods,'" Simone quoted.

A passage they'd both been ruminating over since they'd found it a few days before.

Over the last four weeks, Josie had translated dozens of ancient texts, which she and Simone had been poring over. They searched for a charm, an invocation, a myth, anything that could help them reach the realm of Death. She'd gone to the edge of the Beyond and screamed, pleaded, begged. But no whisper, no glimmer, no trace of Death. Or Judah.

Death's realm was separate from the gods', and she hadn't figured out how to reach it—except by dying herself.

"Yeah, but Death didn't seem to have a problem finding you when he wanted to, right?" Kai asked.

Josie deepened the curve of Billy's mischievous kitty grin. "Maybe he's afraid Tessa will find out he's been sneaking around behind her back."

"I don't think you have to worry about Tessa finding out anything," Kai said. "She's the walking dead these days—"

Simone slapped his narrow chest. "Word choice."

He rubbed the spot where Simone had smacked him, grimacing. "What I'm saying is she's tapped. Tessa's half a

Triune, at best. We have one pissed off earth bitch wielding some super badass devices of the gods with a squad of ancient gods at her back, you know, reducing old Stumptown to Old Hole-in-the-Ground town. We need a real Triune. Tessa can barely summon the Tripartite. When she does, she loses control, and afterwards, she's useless. We were trying to save Osaka from burning down and sinking into the floods, but Tessa accidently turned the wind Nancy had under control and ended up fanning the flames instead."

Josie plunked Billy down on the dresser. "I know you're telling the truth, but don't let anyone else hear you saying anything like that, okay?"

"I won't," he said. "And I won't let anyone else hear me say I think we would've been better off if you'd been the Triune."

"Tessa is the Triune," Josie said. "And we're behind her. Right?"

"Of course we are," Simone said. "You know we are."

Kai didn't look so certain.

Josie tapped the body jewelry hidden under her shirt. Two belly button piercings, one on the left and one on the right, held a spear of quartz between them. She'd had Simone craft a special mounting so Josie could wear the quartz that controlled the Fire God. No matter how cold she was, the stone was warm.

"But what about Death, Life, and the Other?" Kai asked. "Are they behind her?"

"The Tripartite doesn't have a choice," she said. "So long as the Covenant is intact, they have to serve her."

"Or kill her, whichever happens first," he said. "There's already plenty of talk at the outposts about who will be the next Triune."

Simone hit him again, on the arm this time. "Shush it."

Josie didn't hate Kai for telling the truth. In fact, it's one of the reasons she liked him. So few people she knew were willing to speak to her at all, let alone in the blunt, unintimidated fashion that Kai did. That and the fact that he worshipped Simone and loved her as much as Josie did. Plus, he'd taken her dirty clothes to the mortal realm to be washed.

But Josie hated that she couldn't deny what he'd said, not even as a show of loyalty to Tessa. The Three-Faced God, the Tripartite—Life, Death, and the Other—were under Tessa's command. Or they were supposed to be. As the Triune, Tessa was supposed to lead the Core—the Corpora Deorum, summoners of the gods. Except no one had expected her to be the Triune. Josie was the one who'd spent her life training to wear the mask of the Tripartite.

Tessa had been struggling since day one. And ever since Lily had started her bid to end human civilization, Tessa had been pushing herself to do more and more. If she lost control of the Tripartite, she risked losing her life. A thought that was almost as unacceptable to Josie as allowing Judah's soul to remain lost. Though she was beginning to fear that if there was anything she could do for Tessa or Judah, she was running out of time.

Josie ran her hand over the grooves of Billy's stripes. She'd gone too far, too deep, but it was too late now.

"How bad is Tessa really?" Josie asked.

Kai's dark eyes seemed to darken. "Don't you know?"

Simone lowered her manga eyes, pressing her pale cheek to Kai's chest.

"I haven't seen her for . . . a while," Josie said.

Not for almost two weeks, since Josie had tried to convince her little sister to take a break and let everyone else handle the brunt of the battles. Tessa had accused her of not having faith and had stormed off.

"Go get some rest," Josie said to him, leaning against the dresser, feeling like she could use some sleep too. She wasn't sure when she'd last slept. Night and day didn't exist on the island, and Josie didn't bother wearing a watch.

Kai held out the mask again. "Are you sure you don't want to give it another shot?"

Josie traced the surface of the Fire God's quartz with her fingertips. "There's no point. Like the lady said, Death's pathways are separate."

"We'll figure it out, Josie—" Simone started.

Someone rapped on the wall outside the dark curtain that served as Josie's door.

"Come in," she said.

Daisuke pushed by the curtain. He, like everyone, looked thinner, sleep deprived, and older. But his eyes remained warm, his expression, open.

"Kai," he said, smiling. "When did you return?"

"About ten minutes ago," Kai said. "You?"

"Just now."

"Where are you headed next?" Kai asked.

"Tokyo. You?"

"New York." Kai glanced at Josie. "Hurricanes. Want to hear about it?"

His dark eyes told her everything she wanted to hear. "Not really."

"Me neither," he said. "I think I'll pass out now."

Simone hugged him closer. Together, they started towards the door.

"Simone," Daisuke said, "I require another access charm."

Simone's lip protruded in a weary way. "Another one? I made you one two days ago."

All the summoners who were translocating to the Triune's Island required an access charm. Josie hadn't even known it was possible for anyone but the Triune to translocate to the island. But when Portland had come under siege, Tessa had given Simone instructions for a charm that allowed others to find the way. At the moment the safest place in the world wasn't in the world at all, but between worlds. Not encouraging.

"I apologize if it is difficult—" Daisuke started.

"Don't apologize," Simone said. Kai lifted the curtain for her. "Come find me before you leave. I'll have another one ready for you."

When Kai and Simone were gone, Daisuke turned back to Josie.

"What's wrong?" she asked. She knew Daisuke too well to pretend she didn't understand the look on his face.

Daisuke's broad chest expanded beneath his fitted gray thermal. Even on an interdimensional island without power or running water, he managed to look well dressed.

"Earlier we spoke about your sister." Like always, he seemed to give each word consideration before speaking it, which may have been because English wasn't his first language, though he spoke it perfectly. But even when they spoke Japanese, he never seemed to say precisely what he wanted. Rather he skirted around what he actually meant, speaking towards it. Maybe, if he'd been capable of directness, Tessa would've realized he was in love with her.

"I tried to tell Tessa to take it easy," Josie said, opening up the bag of clean laundry—the scent of fabric softener wafted out. Kai had taken her clothes to be washed, somewhere in South America that had escaped Lily's attention for the moment. She began pulling the laundry out.

"Tessa is the Triune," Josie said. "I can't make her listen to me."

"Yes. I spoke to her," Daisuke said, running a hand over his short crop of black hair. "Her duties weigh heavily on her," he said. "Perhaps this is why she wishes to spend her free time with old friends."

Josie stopped sorting her laundry. "Old friends? What do you mean?"

"I went to her room a moment ago to discuss the latest reports." His gaze moved evasively towards the corner of Josie's room. The plush rugs and brightly hued pillows did little to soften the chiseled edges of rough limestone. Living on the Triune's Island was worse than living in a castle. It was living in the ruins of a castle—the damp, depressing and, now, overcrowded ruins. "Allison suggested it would be impolite for me to interrupt."

Josie tossed her fluffy clean sweater aside on the bed. "Interrupt what?"

"I believe she was meeting with Judah—"

CHAPTER 2

AUGUST 28TH

JOSIE STORMED DOWN THE HALL. Slipping through the narrow spaces between boxes of supplies, she charged up the dilapidated stone stairs to the third floor. She bowled by Allison, who was seated on a folding chair, scrolling through her tablet. The blond teen had taken it upon herself to act as Tessa's personal secretary.

"You can't go in right now!" she called after Josie.

Josie shoved aside the purple flowered curtain into Tessa's room.

Tessa sprung back from the Fire God. Her cheeks were pink, her hazel eyes like a dewy lawn under moonlight. The Fire God smirked at Josie. A ghost of blue flame flared in his eyes. Josie's hands balled so tightly her knuckles felt like they might burst through the skin.

He'd been kissing Tessa. He was in so much trouble.

"Josie, is something wrong?" Tessa asked.

"Daisuke needs to speak to you," Josie said as calmly as she could. "It's urgent."

The glowing flush drained from Tessa's cheeks. Her skin took on a translucent pallor. Every blue vein seemed visible under the tight, pale layers. She was worse than the last time Josie had seen her. Something had to be done. Someone had to convince Tessa to stop summoning the power of the Tripartite, at least for a few days, so she could rest.

Tessa didn't argue or whine, like she might've done a few months ago. She only nodded.

Josie felt bad. If Tessa had been kissing anyone else on the island, in the whole world, this one or the next, Josie wouldn't have interceded. Gods knew Tessa needed some outlet for all the stress, but the Fire God was not the answer.

Josie, Simone, and Kai had all agreed to keep the truth about Judah's death a secret for the time being. But the Fire God wasn't making it easy. He tested Josie's control over him at every turn.

Josie knew the only reason he was here kissing her sister was to provoke her. And it was working.

"I'd better go," Tessa said to him.

The Fire God cocked his head in apparent disappointment. "If you have to."

He had matched Judah's voice almost perfectly, but Josie could hear the difference. Where there should have been warmth and depth, there was nothing but hiss and burn.

Tessa gave him a weak and hopeful smile—one that stung Josie, even though she knew it wasn't really Judah her sister had been kissing—and then left. Josie held the curtain back for her. She watched as Tessa descended the steps, her blond ponytail swinging behind her. Allison scrambled to her feet and followed, the obedient hero-worshipper.

When they were gone Josie let the curtain drop. She rounded on him.

"I don't suppose I need to tell you that whatever just happened isn't going to happen again. Judah broke up with Tessa. She doesn't need you making her think that he might be interested in her again. Not now. Not ever."

The Fire God flopped onto the low bed. "Jealous?"

"That is not going to happen ever again. Is that clear?"

"You could join me." He patted the bed invitingly. "I'm certain if your sister saw us in bed together, she'd stop begging for my attention."

Josie's fingers itched to slap him. "The Triune doesn't beg for your attention."

"If you say so." He flashed Judah's teeth at her in a mocking smile.

"You will not touch Tessa again, unless you're saving her life. No hugging, no kissing, no sex, nothing that could be in any way construed as amorous or affectionate or intimate. Is that clear enough?"

The Fire God shrugged. "You tell me."

Tacky sweat broke out over her body, as it did every time she exerted her will over his. The pendant was supposed to give her control over the Fire God, but actually managing him was a daily test of fortitude. A toddler Godzilla would have been more compliant.

He toyed with the Chain, pouting. Not for the first time, Josie found herself wanting to kiss those lips. She forced her gaze away, to the desk in the corner. Messages from the Core spilled over the surface and onto the floor—requests, warnings, pleas for help.

The Fire God wasn't the one she wanted to kiss; it was Judah. She wanted to kiss Judah so badly that in her darkest moments, she thought that kissing him in the realm of Death would've been better than never kissing him again. But she wasn't giving up yet. Death had told her to keep looking and she would.

"You're thinking about him again," the Fire God said darkly.

"Now who's jealous?"

Godly fire leapt into his eyes again.

"I told you not to do that," she said.

"Did you?" he asked as if he'd forgotten.

Josie held herself rigid and expressionless, but in truth, she was worried. This wasn't the first time he had defied her command. The Chain should've prevented him from acting against her instructions. But sometimes, usually when they were alone together, he managed to creep over the lines. Thankfully, around other members of the Core, he seemed to be held, for the most part, in check.

The Fire God inspected his fingernails. He took care of Judah's body as she'd instructed. He was the only one in the Core who'd put on weight over the last month. Prior to his death, Judah had been straining to keep the Fire God from ousting his soul. Now that the Fire God had complete control, Judah's body was back to the lean, athletic perfection that Josie remembered from her first meeting with Judah—before she'd made a mask that had granted the god entrance into Judah's body and had set Judah on the path towards death.

"Aren't you supposed to be helping in the infirmary?" she asked.

"Ah, yes, putting to use all those handy skills young Judah spent so much time learning." He pushed off the bed. "Alas, the injured have been tended, and your sister has decreed that the severely wounded should be sent on to hospitals in the mortal realm. After that last one . . ."—he rolled his eyes—"all that screaming. What a lot of noise for someone who was only going to die in the end."

Josie let out a measured breath and stalked into the dim hallway. The corridors were stone, wide and barrel vaulted. But even on the Triune's floor, the halls were packed tight with supplies. The island didn't have any natural resources, being that it wasn't entirely real. The light was perpetually hazy. No sun. No stars. The plant life was inedible and at times vanished altogether, like a mirage. Only the sprawling compound, the ocean full of primordial gods, and the crabs that inhabited the beaches were constant. Everything else could, and would, vanish without warning.

The Fire God followed close at her heels. "I know what you need."

"Spare me the sexual innuendo."

He hooked her arm. In a rush of heat and flame, they translocated off the island.

The moment they came through to the mortal realm she shoved him away.

He grinned, flashing Judah's perfect white smile at her, and stretched. "This is better."

She squinted. Heat and humidity poured down on her like boiling oil, leaving her knees weak in their sockets.

He had brought them to a mountainside, which dropped steeply away from the rutted dirt path where they stood. Below, the slope was coated in lush tropical fronds. In the distance, a breathtaking lake sprawled, surrounded by green ridges. Further, on the other side of the water, a peak—a volcano. It reminded her of Crater Lake back home, except Oregon had never been so sweltering, even when the Fire God had set half the state's national forests ablaze.

"You can't translocate me off the island."

"No?" He tapped his chin thoughtfully. "I don't recall that being one of your orders. You instructed me to translocate you off the island in instance of emergency."

"And what was the emergency?"

The heat around them grew until Josie could barely breathe. His white T-shirt and fashionably ripped jeans stirred, as if by a breeze. Though there wasn't any. Josie would've killed for a breeze. The stagnant air was pooling in her lungs.

His eyes spilled over with blue flame, from his pupils to his sharp brow.

"What are you doing?" she demanded.

"Blowing off some steam."

A boom issued, rattling her eardrums. A cloud of smoke erupted from the far-off peak.

She started to reach for him, but the faint pink scars on the pads of her fingers twinged, stopping her. The last time they'd argued she'd slapped his face. Her fingers had been burned where they'd touched him. He was under strict instructions not to hurt her, but he'd been able to anyway—somehow. He'd offered to remove the burns if she slept with him. She'd kept them.

"I told you, you're not allowed to—"

"This mortal form cannot contain my powers," he said. "I must release them, or I might inadvertently damage this body you care for so very much."

She wanted to argue, but then maybe this was part of the reason he'd been defying her so much. Unlike all the other summoners in the Core, the Fire God had been stuck on the island with her and Simone. Since neither of them could translocate—not being summoners—they needed someone to stay with them, just in case. In case no one else came back.

The Fire God, Judah, had volunteered to babysit. There had been arguments. Judah was a powerful summoner; he was needed. But Josie had made certain the Fire God had answers for all the objections. He had to stay with Josie because everyone knew that Lily wanted Josie to build her an army and that Josie couldn't be left unprotected, even on the island. What everyone didn't know was that the last time Josie had seen Lily, the evil hippie had tried to kill her. Lily was no longer interested in using Josie. Now, she wanted Josie dead. Too much trouble, Lily had said. Only her son, the mysterious Fog God, had stopped Lily from murdering Josie, an act of compassion that Josie couldn't explain, considering all the other crimes Fog God had perpetrated.

Josie stepped back from the Fire God's radius of drumming heat. Wiping the sweat from her forehead, she retreated to a nearby palm tree and sank down to the ground.

She ground her teeth each time the volcano erupted, hoping that he'd remember he wasn't supposed to hurt anyone, not even inadvertently if he could help it.

Each deafening boom caused itchy palm fronds to fall on her. In spite of the sweltering temperatures and the volcano thundering in her ears, she found herself dozing.

Josie had been on the Triune's Island for almost four weeks. That was almost as long as she'd ever stayed without a break—even though she'd been raised there from the age of seven to seventeen. Growing up, she's spent as much time off the island as on it. As the Triune, her mother had been expected to attend to all the tribes, hundreds of bands scattered around the world.

A Triune's duties were endless and often trivial-seeming. Her mother had insisted that the tasks which appeared the most mundane—naming ceremonies, witnessing contracts, inducting a new elder or matriarch or member of the Eye— were the most important. To those involved, they were paramount. These were their big moments.

You can never separate yourself too much, her mom had told her. *You cannot risk forgetting that you are human.*

Except Josie had never really felt human, not until after her mother's murder had forced her to flee to Portland.

Her mother had told her to remember her humanity, but she hadn't raised Josie to be one. She'd raised Josie to be a Triune, subjugator of the Three-Faced God and leader of the Core. Not a glad-handing politician, but a dictator absolute.

Duty to the Covenant and the Core before all things, including her own needs, her own desires, her own feelings.

She had taught Josie this so well that Josie hadn't allowed herself to acknowledge her attraction to Judah, who had been Tessa's boyfriend when they'd first met, because to feel something like that for her sister's boyfriend had been unacceptable—a betrayal. A Triune would never betray anyone. If her mom had taught her to deal with her emotions like a normal person, instead of sealing them away in the oubliette—the dark forgetting place in her mind—could all of this had been avoided? Would Judah still be alive?

At some point, the Fire God scooped her up off the ground. Her eyes fluttered. Over his shoulder, she saw ash giants rising into the sky.

"Let's enjoy a bit of this human civilization," he said, "while it lasts."

She struggled out of sleep, losing the fight. "You need to—"

They translocated again.

Wherever they had translocated to, it was dark.

"Where—?" she murmured.

He laid her down on a bed that welcomed her with heavenly arms. In a few seconds, she was asleep.

AUGUST 29TH
THE NEXT DAY

The news was in Japanese. She knew enough to follow what was said. More devastation. More death.

Back in the states, the Eastern seaboard was under fire. Josie watched as four empty eyes of hurricanes, lidded by red and purple on the radar, lined up one after the other along the coast.

The rest of the world fared no better. Floods in Shanghai, Istanbul, and Mumbai had displaced millions and the rains kept coming. Earthquakes in Karachi, Mexico City, Tokyo, Los Angeles. Widespread drought and inexplicable crop failure in the Great Plains, the Canadian Prairies, Ukraine, South Africa, the Murray-Darling Basin in Australia. Rice paddies going dry in Thailand, Vietnam, the Plains of Java.

Plastered across the screen where the words: The End of the World?

Josie sat on the edge of the bed in a cotton kimono, hair wet, skin clean and moist, wafting the soft sweet scent of edelweiss. She'd brushed her teeth that morning, but she couldn't get the bitter scum off her tongue.

The world was dying. Lily was winning. And what was Josie doing? Watching it on the news.

Surging off the bed, she pulled off the kimono and retrieved her dirty clothes. At that moment, the Fire God walked out of the bathroom—one of two in the spacious suite in Hokkaido—naked.

"Get dressed," she said as she tugged on her jeans. "We're going back, now."

The Fire God tossed his towel on the couch that faced the balcony. Early, the light was wavering and dew-edged. Green treetops gave way to the snow-streaked mountains in the distance.

"You're no fun," he said. "That barren hovel of an island is unworthy of a god. The Triune should demand the Other provide more suitable accommodations."

"Thanks for the review, but we've been gone too long. Someone might notice."

The Fire God lifted Judah's brow, but she didn't want to read it, the way she'd read it when Judah had been alive. With Judah, every slant and arch of his brow had spoken to her, but this wasn't Judah. She had to keep reminding herself of that, especially as he moved towards her.

"And what do you think they'll say? Judah has stolen Josie away? I wonder where they've gone. What they're doing?"

"We're not doing anything," she said, putting on her bra.

His finger traced the air, skimming her stomach, hovering over the quartz. She flattened her hand over the pendant. She'd ordered him not to touch it, but she was no less paranoid he might try.

"Only because of your tedious rules." He opened his arms, the face of innocence. "Look at me. I know you desire this body."

Her gaze slid over him, in spite of herself. Her body ached, but she fought against the feeling.

"I want Judah," she said. "Not you."

The Fire God started pouting again. "You ought to be careful," he said, picking up his jeans from the elegant padded chair. "One of these days, I might actually believe you."

"And then what?"

Again, his eyes filled with flames. She gripped the back of the couch, trying to maintain her cool façade.

"How are you doing that?" she asked.

The fire died down, and once again his eyes appeared, mostly, human.

"Doing what?" he asked with a small smile.

"Don't play coy," she said. "Answer me. How are you violating my commands?"

The Fire God pulled on his jeans, taking his time. "I hate this . . . denim. It reminds me of the coarse cloth shit-shovelers wore in Urim. That was prior to the Covenant. Then I could walk the earth as I chose, create my own mortal form from the primordial waters, shape it as I willed, enslave whomever I wished."

He leered at her. "How I long for those days again." He slid on his socks and boots. "One year, during the festival of the moon goddess, I impregnated a different mortal every night for twenty-eight days. They were grateful. Their children were grateful. To be a demigod then was glory. Do you know how a demigod properly displays gratitude to their godly parents? Of course not. Death should never have been allowed to copulate with mortals. It's antithetical to his very nature. And see what it produced . . ."

He shook his head as he laced his boots. "Mortals ruling their own realm. I needed no prophetic powers to discern the fallacy in that brilliant scheme. Look what it has wrought." He gestured to the TV behind her.

She glanced back.

Images flashed across the giant screen: multimillion dollar homes sliding off mountainsides, streets inundated with water, skyscrapers pouring out black smoke. And the faces, always the faces, of the survivors, dirt-smeared and tear-streaked and pleading for help from someone—anyone.

How could someone who was dead inside ache so much? And the worst of it was the helplessness. She couldn't even summon a god and fight like the others, for whatever it was worth.

Against the ancient powers at Lily's disposal, the Core could only do so much—those that were willing to do anything. Not all of them were. Many had retreated to secluded sanctuaries—mountaintops, desert oases, remote jungles, seemingly barren islands—taking their children, their masks, and their gods with them.

One of Tessa and Daisuke's primary missions these last weeks, besides trying to head off the worse of the devastation, was to find those factions of the Core who were sitting on their hands and plead with them to take action. For as bad as it was, it could've been much worse. Thousands of summoners had their masks on and were wielding their powers against Lily and her followers, turning back tidal waves, stilling the shaking earth, urging the crops to grow. But it was much harder to stop a disaster than to start one.

Not long ago, Tessa had brought up repairing the primordial masks, the ones in the Triune's vaults—an idea Josie had quickly quashed. None of this would've been happening, not on this scale anyway, if Josie hadn't already repaired dozens of ancient masks, which Lily had stolen and was now using. With deadly efficacy.

On the TV, hordes of people were shown evacuating New York City ahead of the hurricanes. A father clutched his daughter to his chest; the pink bow on her headband fell away as he stuffed her into the car. An elderly woman was carried out of her burning building by a firefighter. The mayor stepped up to the microphones at a press conference against the backdrop of an entourage, some of whom openly wept, unable to conceal their pain and grief. The crawler read: Abandoning NYC. Mandatory Evacuations Underway.

How could Josie justify keeping back anything if it might help stop Lily? Of course, that's what she'd thought when she'd repaired the first round of masks and brought back the gods that were currently causing this devastation.

Not knowing what to do was tearing her apart. If she repaired the masks of the primordial gods, would she enable the Core to save the world, or would she only speed it towards its ultimate destruction?

"Are you unhappy?" the Fire God asked, bemused.

"No," she said as she pulled on her shirt. "I don't feel anything."

"Yes, you do," the Fire God said. "Even the most deranged of your kind feels something. I recall the high priest of a tribe who once worshipped me in the Ionian Sea. Horrible breath, that man, like rotted swine entrails. He sacrificed every virgin he had on his pinprick of an island. Then he had to import them. The slave traders made a fortune. He would slit a tender boy from groin to gullet without tasting the slightest crumb of remorse, but when his mother passed away, he sobbed uncontrollably for days and begged me to bring her back. When I informed him that was Death's domain, he promptly began sending Death weepy messages carved on the bodies of babies stolen from their mother's arms. The irony was completely lost on him. In the end, I destroyed the island and buried him under a pile of ash ten feet deep."

The Fire God frowned, thoughtfully. "He should've continued sacrificing to me. I'm reasonable. Death has no need for blood. He bathes in it. Did he tell you that when you were cavorting with him in the pathways?"

"I wasn't cavorting with him, and stop trying to change the subject. You still haven't answered my question. How are you able to defy me?"

He stood up, moving closer. But she didn't back up. Giving ground to him was like taking her clothes off and inviting him into bed. She covered the quartz with her hand again.

"You don't really mean it," he said. "You say you want me contained, but you don't. You say you don't want me to touch you"—his fingers hovered by her temple and then caught her hair and moved it back behind her ear—"but you don't mean that either. You wish to control me, young goddess? Then you must be doubly as fierce in your conviction as I am in my desires. I know what I want. I suffer no doubts. You, on the other hand, feel nothing but doubt. You doubt your words, you doubt your will, you doubt even your need to breathe. That is why the Chain's powers are weak. Because you are weak."

"Doubt is not weakness." Her mother had told her that.

His hand slid down the back of her arm. In spite of herself, her skin prickled. His hand slipped to the small of her back, drawing her closer. His lips skimmed her neck. "Perhaps not in humans."

"I am a human."

His laughter whispered hot across her throat. "If you say so."

She grabbed his shoulder and gave him a firm push, though his arms remained locked around her, his thumbs snagged in her waistband. "What does that mean?"

He pulled her against him again. "Be a bit nicer and ... I may tell you."

"You're trying to trick me," she said, tearing away from him. "It won't work."

Boom!

The panoramic windows rattled. The floor shook. She grabbed hold of him to keep her balance. The delicate porcelain tea cups on the table clinked against each other, huddled on their tray like trembling children. Another boom followed the first, the shaking grew more violent.

The TV signal cut out. Flashing for a few moments, the lights finally gave way too. The Fire God held her close against his overheated skin as the chandelier swung and the table pitched, throwing the tea tray to the marble floor, shattering the porcelain cups.

"Are you doing this?" she shouted over the noise of the building groaning and the furniture toppling.

"I?" he asked, indignant. "Do you see smoke on the horizon? Are you swimming in a molten lake of fire? Don't you know the difference between a volcanic eruption and a trifling little tremor?"

She wanted to roll her eyes, but they were bouncing in their sockets as the earth shook. To a god it might've seemed trifling, but the quaking was cracking the ceiling. One of the windows shattered. She couldn't imagine why Lily would've wanted to attack Hokkaido. Were her followers tired of destroying bustling cities like Osaka and Tokyo? Had they decided they needed a break some place more pastoral? Either way, it was a reminder to Josie that soon, no place on earth would be safe from destruction.

"We need to leave!"

"As you wish, master." He pulled her to him and kissed her, translocating away.

CHAPTER 3

AUGUST 29TH

"I TOLD YOU NOT TO DO THAT," she said breathlessly.

The stone walls of her room had reappeared, along with the thin, sulfurish air of the island and the groans of the primordial gods.

"And I told you that you have to really mean it," he said, tumbling her back onto her bed.

Her hand was crushed between them, protecting the quartz, but his hands didn't seem to be interested in the pendant that gave her—some—control over him. They were elsewise occupied.

For a moment, her eyes slid shut and she could almost imagine it was Judah pressing down on her, biting at her ear, lifting up her shirt. Her skin was giving in to his mouth, warming and perspiring. Her breath was submitting to the strokes of his fingers, shortening, quickening. Her lips were even betraying her, parting for him, letting him in. He'd been right. She was weak. She knew he wasn't Judah, but her body didn't seem to care. All it seemed to know was that this was Judah's body, his hands, his lips.

Tears gathered in her eyes. If Death had appeared to her at that moment, she would've given him anything, everything, the entire world, for Judah's soul.

She wasn't impassioned by the Fire God; she was consumed, a body on a pyre. Another virgin for the volcano. Her body gave in, but her soul was elsewhere, lost in the pathways, searching for Judah.

Her sister's voice pulled her back.

"Josie, I—"

Josie pushed the Fire God away—too late. Much too late.

Tessa stood in the doorway, holding open the curtain, her eyes unblinking, her mouth hanging open. Behind her, Allison's icy eyes flashed.

The Fire God's voice was full of hissing mirth. "Oops."

Josie tried to wriggle out from under him, but he had her pinned.

"Tessa—"

Tessa's eyes slammed shut. She held up her hands like she could shove away the image of Josie and Judah on the bed together. "Don't . . ."

Allison placed her hand on Tessa's shoulder. "Should I—?"

A faint glow began to radiate from Tessa's pale skin. Either she was about to go into possession of the Tripartite, or one of its Three Gods—Life, Death, or the Other—was about to take her over. Neither was a good thing.

With a shove, Josie freed herself from the Fire God and jumped off the bed. She grabbed her sweater off the floor, pulling it over her head. The Fire God lounged, shirt off, jeans unzipped, like one of those high-end cologne ads.

"Tessa," she said, "you are in control—"

Tessa's voice was as fragile as spring ice. "Don't . . . talk."

Slowly, as she regained control, the glow diminished. After a moment, her eyes opened again. Hazel with a coppery ring. No trace of black or white or gray.

Josie let out a breath of relief. As she looked at her sister, so thin and pale, she couldn't help but think that if Lily didn't kill Tessa, the power of the Tripartite would.

Tears slipped down Tessa's cheeks. She started to turn like she might leave; but instead, she grabbed Billy the Cat off the dresser. She spun and whipped the carving at the Fire God. He ducked. The wooden kitty boy shattered against the wall and rained splinters over the Fire God's head.

"How could you?" she shouted at him. "You kiss me one day and then my sister the next? You—you—"

"Piece of shit?" Allison offered, holding open the curtain.

"If it makes you feel any better," the Fire God said, sliding off the bed and brushing bits of wood from his hair, "I never wanted to kiss you. But you've been rather pathetic lately, practically begging for it." He shrugged. "Really it's your sister who should be angry. After all, I left you so I could be with her."

Josie almost grabbed Doraemon—another of her whittled cartoon cats, a Japanese robot—to crack against his skull.

What he'd said was true. Judah had broken up with Tessa because of Josie, but this was not the time to be saying it.

"If my little goddess hadn't been so frigid lately, I might not have been so tempted by your desperate advances," the Fire God went on in a bored tone.

"Shut up," Josie said through her teeth.

He lifted his shoulder indifferently.

"It was you," Tessa said to Josie. "You were cheating with my boyfriend—"

"Not . . . exactly."

"Not exactly? Either you were or you weren't. And you were! Admit it! I can't believe you would do this to me. It's like . . . I don't even know you. Gods! I can't even—"

A god in the guise of swirling green water appeared beside Tessa. Daisuke. He was one of the few summoners who had a locator charm that allowed him to find Tessa wherever she was.

"Light of the Divine," he said in that bifurcated voice of a summoner in possession. One half was the god's voice—a deep rolling, rushing rumble—and the other, Daisuke's own voice—warm and soft.

He removed his mask. The guise of churning water disappeared. He glanced around the room, from Tessa and Allison at the door to Josie and Judah near the bed.

"Forgive the interruption," he said, his voice hardening.

"What is it?" Tessa said, wiping at her tears violently.

"Your father has returned. With your Future Eye and . . ."— he glanced at Josie and Judah—"Kai."

"Are they hurt?" Josie asked.

Daisuke nodded.

Tessa rushed out of the room. Allison followed. Josie found her shoes and stuffed her feet into them, but before she could leave, Daisuke caught her arm.

"Perhaps, it would be better if you did not follow," he said.

"My dad's hurt?"

"He will live," Daisuke said. "Your sister will be better able to perform her duties if you and . . ."—his eyes flicked over to the Fire God—"he stayed away from her."

Josie slid her arm from his grip. Daisuke, for all his evasiveness, was incredibly discerning.

"What about Kai?"

"It's not grave," Daisuke said. "If it had been, Caroline would have taken him to a hospital in the mortal realm." His gaze remained fixed on the Fire God.

"Something wrong?" the Fire God asked him.

"Allow me to express my concern," Daisuke said in his oblique fashion. "Times of stress bring about unusual and unexpected reactions from each of us. I don't know you well, Judah, but I have noticed a pronounced alteration in your behavior. If you'll forgive me, you do not seem yourself."

"You mean I'm not a tight ass do-gooder?" the Fire God said.

In Japanese, Daisuke said, "I would say you're an egotistical asshole."

In Japanese, the Fire God responded, "Then you would not be saying much more after that."

"Didn't I tell you to shut up?" Josie said to the Fire God, in English.

"I did not realize you spoke Japanese, Judah," Daisuke said.

The Fire God's eyes narrowed.

Daisuke looked down at Josie. "But Judah does not speak Japanese, does he?"

"Daisuke, please, it's fine, really."

"Josie, is this Judah or not?"

She ground her forefinger against her forehead. "No. It's not."

Daisuke turned his back to the door, blocking it. He held his mask—painted green, tongue lashing, sharp fangs showing—poised to go into possession. "Explain. Quickly."

Josie placed her hand firmly on Daisuke's shoulder. "You don't want to fight him. You won't win. Trust me. And please don't antagonize him either. I'm having enough trouble keeping the reins on him."

The Fire God smirked.

Daisuke looked at Josie from the corner of his eyes, but he didn't stand down or put his mask away. "What has happened to Judah?"

Her words came out in a strained whisper. "He's dead."

Daisuke's posture slackened. "Then who is that?"

"That is Judah's body. Do you remember hearing about the Fire God mask that went missing last winter?" Josie asked. "The first of the ancient masks I repaired? The one that was stolen?"

"The Light of the Divine told me," he confirmed.

"Judah took it."

Daisuke frowned. "Judah stole a mask?"

Josie ran her hand over her head. "I know. I couldn't believe it either, but it wasn't entirely his fault. I didn't know what I was doing. I'd only made two other masks before that. I had no idea what it meant to be a mask-maker, or that I could subconsciously craft a mask to fit the face of a summoner, which is what I did. When I fixed the Fire God's mask, I basically sculpted a new mask. A mask I modeled after Judah. It fit his face exactly. I didn't realize what I was doing. I was repressing feelings I had for him and it just . . . happened. The point is, I made the mask for him. So he took it, but neither of us realized it would allow the Fire God to—"

"Become manifest," Daisuke finished for her. He gave the Fire God a new, wary look. "The god takes possession of his summoner's body."

Josie dragged her hand through her tangled hair. "Judah's body."

"Then Judah's soul?"

Her throat clenched. "Gone."

"And . . . that?" Daisuke gestured to the Fire God.

"He's under control, for the moment," she said, lifting up her shirt and showing him the quartz. "I retrieved the Chain of the Gods."

The faintest hint of surprise registered on Daisuke's face. "You were able to retrieve a divine tool from the Beyond?" His expression hardened. "And you did not tell your sister. You have not told her any of this."

"No," Josie said. "And neither will you." She glanced at the Fire God. "Would you put a shirt on and zip up?"

The Fire God slid back onto the bed, ignoring her.

"You are able to access sacred devices. They may aid us in our battle, Josie," Daisuke said. "The Triune must know this, and she must also know that there is a manifest god walking among us. That you withheld this information . . ." He scrutinized her. "There is more you are not telling me."

"I'm not going to tell you anything more if you're going to report it to Tessa," she said. "Can I trust you or not?"

He flicked his wrist, more violently than necessary. His mask disappeared into his sanctuary. "I am not the one who has been keeping secrets, Josie. My trustworthiness is not in question. That you would allow a god, chained or not, to reside on the Triune's Island without informing the Divine Mother . . ." He bore down on her. "You must tell her. Or I will."

"What good is that going to do? Other than freak everyone out? People are already on edge. This doesn't have anything to do with Lily or the end of the world. Isn't that enough for Tessa to deal with? She already thinks that Judah and I betrayed her—"

Daisuke's face was smooth as marble, which she knew meant he was furious. "Is that not true? The first day I arrived in Portland I could see that Judah was in love with you. And you have admitted that you had feelings for him that led to this—" His hand stabbed in the Fire God's direction.

The Fire God picked up a splinter of Billy the Cat. The sliver of wood ignited, smoked, and turned to ash. He picked up another, repeating the process. Instead of drifting upwards, the tendrils of smoke coiled around his hand and down his arm. Gray wisps slid over his skin like lover's fingers.

Daisuke shifted, almost imperceptibly, back from the god. He was right to be leery. The Fire God was more dangerous than Josie liked to admit.

"In truth, Josie," Daisuke said, savage in his bluntness, "you did betray your sister. And you continue to betray her so long as you keep the truth from her."

Daisuke had been Josie's only friend for a long time. Hearing him speak so plainly felt like a sword to the gut. He'd never cut so straight and sharp before.

"But," he said, rolling back his shoulders, "you may be right in that she has enough to occupy her for the moment. Now that she knows the truth about you and Judah..." His warm eyes were cold as they fixed on the Fire God, who was still burning bits of Billy and playing with smoke. "She failed to understand why Judah left her. She was unable to move forward. Now she may begin to heal." His gaze locked onto Josie again. "I believe it would be best if you and he left, as soon as..." His eyes narrowed, searching her face. "What are you thinking, Josie Day?"

She stepped back, running her fingers along the edge of the dresser. "I don't know what you're—"

"There is more to this," he said, moving towards her.

She moved back again. "Is there?"

"We have known each other too long," he said. "What are you thinking... tell me you are not thinking what I see on your face." He looked over at the Fire God and then back at her. "Judah is dead, you said it yourself."

She tapped her finger on the fake-wood laminate. No real furniture on the island. Nothing that required more than a single person to carry.

"I'm not thinking anything—"

"You have been spending a great deal of time in the archives," Daisuke said.

"And?"

"If you are looking for a way to ... cheat Death—"

"I never said—"

"You did not have to say. I know you, Josephine Day. You think you are ..."

He seized her arms, startling her. It wasn't like Daisuke to get physical unless he had no other choice.

"It is not possible," he said. "What you are thinking ... cannot happen. Judah is dead. His soul is gone."

She held her tongue. She glanced over at the Fire God. He was watching intensely, eyes full of flame. Hadn't she told him not to do that?

"You may be able to touch the faces of the gods, Josie, but leave the dead to their peace."

She glared back up at Daisuke's once warm eyes. Now they were hard and furious.

"Who says he's at peace?"

"He has traveled the paths of Death. He is—"

Josie broke free of Daisuke's grasp. "I heard him. He called to me."

Daisuke stared at her like he didn't believe her or didn't want to believe. But she had heard something when she'd been in the paths of the earth gods, retrieving Lily's mask. A whisper. And she'd seen a glimmer. She didn't know what it was, really. Yet she felt certain it had been Judah.

"It was a mistake," she said. "He never would've given up— he never would've stopped fighting, but when the Fog God kidnapped me, I vanished. Judah thought I was dead. That's why he ..." She shot a fierce look at the Fire God. He gazed back at her, expressionless. "I'm going to find him. I'm going to bring him back—"

Daisuke held up his hands, like he might cover his ears. "No, Josie—"

"He's right, you know," the Fire God drawled, "it can't be done."

"Didn't I tell you to shut up?"

"The god knows," Daisuke said. "You must listen. Josie, you cannot. To thieve from Death—"

"Judah was never his to begin with—"

"We are all his." Daisuke reached for her arms again, but didn't touch her. "Please, Josie. I know..." He pressed his hands together at his chest. "Days pass in which I would give anything, even another's life, yours, to see my mother in this world again, but it cannot happen. I beg you. Banish this thought from your mind. Grieve for Judah. Release him. You do his soul no honor by harboring these delusions. And you damage your own soul by desiring that which you can never, and will never, possess."

"If it were Tessa's soul we were talking about, would you tell me to stop? Would you tell me to give up trying?"

Daisuke's jaw flexed. "I would tell you the truth, Josie. Judah's soul. Tessa's soul. It would make no difference. You cannot undo death. The gods do not even possess this power. You are not a god." He took an abrupt step back. "Please pack and translocate to Outpost One. Gretchen and her son are there. You will be safe. I will inform your sister and your father that you and..."—he glanced over at the Fire God again—"Judah have gone. When your sister is prepared to see you again, she will send for you. At that time, I expect you to tell her the truth, all of it. Or I will. Until then... you may have other work to occupy your mind."

She stiffened. "Other work?"

"The Council of the Eyes will convene tonight," he said, business-like. "Your sister is prepared to make a proposal—"

"Son of . . ." Her fists clenched. "I told Tessa I wasn't going to repair the primordial—"

"She is Triune. Her will is decree," Daisuke said. "The final decision will be the Council's—"

"Like I don't know what they're going to say," she said.

"We are at war—"

"I've heard that argument before," she interjected. "I listened to it, and because of that, almost two dozen ancient masks were stolen—masks that were used to destroy my hometown and yours—"

A dent of pain scratched the dark surface of his eyes. "I was there, Josie. I saw Osaka drowned. You do not need to remind me of it."

"Maybe I do. Lily would never have been capable of destroying Osaka or Portland, not like she did, not as easily, if I hadn't repaired those masks. And now you want me to repair the masks of the primordial gods? Do you even realize—?"

"This is a discussion for the Council, not for us."

"Don't tell me—"

"Know your place, Josie Day," he said brutally. "You are not a summoner. You are not the Triune. You are not a god. You are a mask-maker. You will cease acting as if you are apart and above the rest of us. You will forget this lunacy—bringing back Judah. He is dead. You will accept this. Now pack your things and leave this place. Report to Outpost One at once. When you are needed, the Triune will send for you. You will enact her command, not only because she is the Triune, but because she is your sister. You have betrayed her. You must earn back her faith." His voice grew cooler and more distant with each word. "If there is anything left of the woman I knew in you, you will do this. You must."

He spared the Fire God one last dark look. Then he left.

The curtain fluttered behind him.

She wasn't angry.

She was glad he was so loyal to Tessa that he would risk destroying a lifelong friendship to stand up for her. That loyalty was one of the reasons she and Daisuke had been friends. They understood each other in that way. Once upon a time, Josie would have agreed with Daisuke completely. Loyalty to the Triune above all things. That was the right way.

But Josie had already failed in her loyalty to Tessa, both as a Core member and as her sister. If Josie's heart ever started beating again, she was sure grappling with her betrayal of Tessa would kill her all over again.

Daisuke had been right. Josie wasn't a summoner. She wasn't the Triune. She couldn't undo what had been done. She couldn't save the world. But she could save Judah's soul. There had to be a way, and she would find it, or the world would end. Whichever came first.

CHAPTER 4

HIDDEN IN THE WOODS beside one of northern Minnesota's thousand lakes was Outpost One.

Once it had been known as Big Moose Lodge and Resort. Anyone who might've been interested in riding out the apocalypse hunting and fishing would have been informed that the resort was closed. In fact, the log cabins, from the Big House—a mansion with a touch of rustic charm—to the hotel-style Bunk House, were packed full. Like the island, the former resort had become part command center, part refugee camp.

Josie only caught a glimpse of the hustle surrounding the main buildings. The moment she and the Fire God arrived at the prearranged translocation site, Gretchen loaded them into a utility cart and drove them away from the resort into the woods.

Josie held onto the roof as they bumped along the rutted road. The Fire God sat in the back with their bags.

"It used to be a hunting cabin. We try to keep it off the radar," Gretchen, the Past Eye of Josie's tribe, said of their destination. "But it has all the amenities. The whole resort is self-sustaining, wind turbines, solar panels, well water. You should see the garden. It's unbelievable. I've been canning tomatoes nonstop. I never thought my hands would be free of paint stains, but apparently, canning tomatoes is the answer." She held up her ringed fingers. The tough-looking skin appeared clean and unblemished, except for the tattoos.

The scent of vinegar and smoke clung to Gretchen's spiky black hair and tank top. On her chest, the long trailing scars left by the Wolf were stark and white against her tan skin, exposed with pride like medals pinned to her breast. The deep green of her eyes was pale next to the pines towering over them. In the shadows of the forest, the late summer air was chilly.

"I'm surprised your sister let you leave the island," Gretchen said.

"She didn't exactly," Josie replied.

Gretchen glanced back at the Fire God. "She walked in on the two of you, didn't she?"

"How did you know?"

"Bound to happen, kiddo," Gretchen said, lifting a pierced brow at her. "You should've been up front with her as soon as you realized it." She leaned towards Josie, lowering her voice so it was barely audible over the soft hum of the electric motor. "Took you long enough. Caroline was ready to slap a couple of anti-pregnancy charms on the two of you and lock you in a room together until you figured it out. Judah was driving her crazy."

Josie glanced at the charm bracelets on her wrist. She wasn't wearing that many. She hadn't felt like she'd need them on the island. Her eye caught on the purple beads of a sleep-inducing charm. Simone had given it to Josie to use on Tessa, in case Tessa lost control of the Tripartite.

Gretchen's forearms were coiled with charms from wrist to elbow. Plastic beads, metal beads, stone, and crystal, all of them etched with Core symbols for protection of one kind or another. Most summoners were heavily protected these days.

They pulled up in front of a log cabin. It was larger and more modern-looking than Josie had imagined when Gretchen had referred to it as a hunting cabin. The elevated deck out front seemed to be waiting for a barbeque to commence. Josie doubted it would see anything like that for a long time. Never again, if Lily had her way.

"Door's open," Gretchen said to the Fire God. "Take the bags in, will you?"

The Fire God hefted the two stuffed duffels out of the cart and tromped down the overgrown sidewalk.

When the Fire God had disappeared inside, Gretchen stretched her lean, tattooed arm behind Josie. "What's up, *ma belle*?"

"You mean besides the world ending?"

Gretchen spun the wooden spacer in her ear. "Even still. I didn't expect you and Judah to look so gloomy. True love not all it's cracked up to be?"

A spasm of pain shuddered through Josie's chest.

Gretchen touched the back of Josie's head lightly. "Gods, kiddo, what's wrong? Is it Tessa? She'll get over it. I promise you. It'll take some time and some serious apology-making on your part, but she'll see it eventually, the way all of us saw it. You and Judah . . . you know how I feel about monogamy and traditional roles, but even from my point of view, the two of you were pretty much inevitable."

Strange birds twittered in the branches around them, whistling calls that Josie didn't recognize. Though the trees were not so different from the ones in Oregon and the sky was supposedly the same sky and the sun and moon remained, the world felt alien to Josie. The trees weren't her trees. The sky wasn't her sky. The sun and the moon were actors in a play she was no longer a part of.

She didn't know what she hated more, Lily destroying the world or Judah's soul being gone or the fact she didn't know what to do in either instance. Or maybe this feeling. This dangerous, stupid, selfish feeling, like if Judah weren't in the world, she didn't care whether Lily destroyed it or not.

"Tell me what's going on," Gretchen said. "Something's not right with you."

Josie hesitated. She wanted to confide in Gretchen, she just wasn't sure how to do it.

"You mean it?" Josie asked.

"Mean what?"

"You thought Judah and I were inevitable?"

"Is something wrong with you and Judah?"

"Yes."

"What?"

"I love him."

Gretchen smiled. "What's wrong with that?"

"I really love him."

Gretchen's face straightened. "You're afraid, is that it? I know things are batshit right now. You think something's going to happen to him? You're scared he might be hurt or killed?"

"I'm afraid of what I'll do," Josie said.

"If he's gone?"

"What would you do?" Josie asked softly. "If you lost Roxy?"

"You mean before or after I committed hara-kiri?" Gretchen slouched back in her seat and pulled a silver cigarette case from the ankle of her boot. "That's probably not the sort of thing I'm supposed to say to an eighteen-year-old . . . are you eighteen yet?"

"Three weeks," Josie said.

Gretchen took out a cigarette and tapped it against the case. "Don't tell Roxy I was smoking in front of you, she'd kill me. It's disgusting, honestly." She sneered down at the unlit cigarette and then stuck it back in the case. "Listen. Don't think about what might happen. There's nothing useful to be gained from that. Right now you have Judah. That's all that matters. Don't think about tomorrow, especially when there might not be one. And I'm not just talking for you and Judah, I'm talking about for all of us. I ain't got no spoonful of sugar for you, Josie dear. I ain't no Mary freakin' flying umbrella. I won't lie. Lily's got us by the throat and she is squeezing. Folks are going to die. Folks are dying. What would I do if one of them were Roxy? I don't know. I honestly don't. I'm not thinking about it and I don't want to. Neither should you. Now. Josie. Here. Love it. Be in it. Forget about tomorrow."

No problem. Josie didn't think about tomorrow anyway. She only thought about this moment. This moment without Judah. She couldn't pull herself out of this moment.

"I'm not even making a crack in this coconut, am I?" Gretchen said.

Josie closed her eyes, drowning in the tears she hadn't shed. She wanted to tell Gretchen she couldn't breathe, but how could she? How could someone without breath cry for help? All that was sustaining her was the thought she might be able to find Judah's soul and bring him back. But she felt certain if she told Gretchen the truth, Gretchen would ultimately end up saying the same thing Daisuke had said— it's impossible.

"Why do you think my mother chose me to be the mask-maker?"

Gretchen took out her cigarette case again. This time, she lit up. "Shit, kiddo, why are any of us chosen for anything? Why am I the Past Eye of our tribe? I don't exactly exude authority, do I? But here I am. In charge." She took the cigarette from her lips. "But you're not asking why you were chosen to be a mask-maker. You're asking why you're not the Triune."

"I don't want to be Triune," Josie said.

"Who would? What a crap job that is. Talk about managing difficult personalities. Life, Death, and the Other? Not to mention every Eye in the world"—Gretchen smirked—"and Nancy."

Josie almost smiled. Her tribe's Future Eye, Nancy, had always gone out of her way to be a thorn in Josie's side. Last Josie had heard, Nancy was consulting with tribes in Europe.

"Maybe it's because I'm too selfish," Josie said softly.

"How are you selfish?"

"Because . . . all I care about is Judah. All the rest of this . . ." She shrugged. "Is that horrible?"

Gretchen took a deep drag, watching Josie closely as the smoke curled out of her nostrils. "You want me to reprimand you for loving someone too much? You want me to tell you that the impending apocalypse is more important than he is?"

Josie shrugged again.

"I can't," Gretchen said. "What's Lily really trying to destroy? She already wiped out our city. My city. I loved Portland. It was my home. Don't think I'm not pissed about it, but so what? Take it. Take my city. Take my house. Take my clothes and my money. You can even take my art. But don't touch my woman. Don't lay a finger on my son. That's what she's really after, you know? I can make new art. I can make a new home, but without Roxy or Beech . . ."

Gretchen shook her head, snuffing the half-smoked cigarette out on the dented green hood of the cart. "What are you asking, Josie? Are you asking permission to love Judah as much as you do? Are you asking if it's okay to be more concerned about his life than all the billions of others? Rationally, morally, philosophically? You know the answer, but I see where we're going here. The Triune is the great soul, right? The Mahatma. I've got news for you; there's no such thing. Every great soul, every prophet, every Triune was human. They were flawed. They messed up. They had bad breath and forgot to write thank you notes and cheated on their husbands. Don't be so hard on yourself. Be grateful. You love Judah? You don't want to do anything else? Then don't.

And don't apologize for it. Not even to Tessa. You hurt her. You lied to her. You messed up. Apologize for that and mean it, but don't apologize for loving someone, not unless you actually think it's a mistake. And let me tell you something, kiddo . . . it's not a mistake."

Before Josie could respond, she heard the crunch of rock behind them. She and Gretchen turned.

A square-jawed young man, who shared Gretchen's green eyes, including the mischievous glint, biked up the road towards them.

Beech stuck out his pierced tongue when he saw Josie. He rode up next to the cart and dropped the bike into the overgrown grass.

She gazed at him, feeling like a ghost. Beech was so alive. His grin was bright, wide, and lopsided. Beads of sweat glistened on his forehead. The vivid white and red dragons on his tattooed arms looked like they might peel off and fly away.

"Miss me?" He snapped his fingers as his fist hit his palm. "What am I saying? Of course you did."

The second she slid out of the cart, he wrapped her up in a fierce hug. He even smelled alive, like sweat and boy-musk and faintly of fruit-flavored gum. Judah had smelled alive once too. Since the Fire God had taken him over, there was nothing but the acrid stink of smoke.

"Geez, Josie-pie, you're like a dead fish here," he said, taking her hands and flopping her arms.

Gretchen circled around the back of the cart. "How did you know Josie was here? I don't recall sharing that information. I hope you didn't tell anyone else."

"I didn't know Josie was here, but I knew something was up because when I asked Roxy where you were, she got all flustered and her skin did that weird splotchy thing it does, like when she drinks tequila. So I knew whatever you were doing was something good. I used my spidey-senses to track you down . . . or John told me he saw you take the cart this a-way. Whatever."

"Josie's presence is serious need-to-know info, Baby Bear, got it?"

Beech draped his arm around Josie's shoulders. "Would I put my Josie-slice in danger?"

The door to the cabin opened again and the Fire God strode onto the deck. His gaze swept the forest, like he was calculating how long it would take to incinerate it. He came to the railing and looked down at them.

"Prince Chode—I mean, Judah," Beech called, giving Josie a playful side-squeeze. "Good to see you."

"Let's move troops," Gretchen said, lifting a small cooler out of the back. "I brought dinner."

Gretchen walked ahead.

Beech, arm still around Josie, bowed his head towards her confidentially. "Say it ain't so, Jo."

"What?"

"Judah? Really?"

"Are you surprised? No one else seems to be."

Beech pulled the chain of his necklace into his mouth and ran the medallion back and forth. Finally, he let it drop. He plucked at her chin. "I was hoping you'd find someone who'd help you lighten up. Judah? Sort of the downer king, isn't he?

Too much gravity." Beech drew her closer. "You don't look happy."

"What's there to be happy about?"

Beech gazed at her for a moment and then dropped his forehead against hers. "I never should've left."

CHAPTER 5

August 29th
Later

IT LOOKED LIKE HER DAD HAD BEEN HIT in the face with a baseball bat. A purplish welt swelled his cheek from his temple to his jaw. He limped as he walked across the cabin late that evening.

Josie walked beside him, not offering to help, even though she wanted to. "Are you all right?"

"Fine," he said, grimacing as he dropped stiffly into the chair.

Caroline stood inside the door, arms folded. "Where's Judah?"

Josie had done everything she could over the last five weeks to keep the Fire God as far away from Judah's mom as possible. But the hard look on Caroline's face made it clear that she wasn't about to be put off with stories about how Judah had gone running or was in the shower.

The Fire God emerged from the shadows of the hall and leaned against the wall. Though his eyes weren't flame filled, there was still something too bright about them, too fierce, too...inhuman.

Caroline's sharp face grew sharper when she saw him. Once, she had been all golden glow, like Judah; now, she was gray ash, like Josie. "I don't suppose you two could've chosen a worse possible time to tell Tessa about your relationship."

"We didn't exactly tell her," Josie said.

She closed the books she'd left open on the coffee table. Most of them she'd taken from the archives—myths and legends about the pathways and Death and the Beyond. She had stuffed her duffle with as many books as she could carry. She also had a supply ledger Gretchen had given her after dinner.

Josie had been alternating between reading about Death's realm and checking the supply inventory, comparing it against the last one, determining what was being used and how fast, and what was needed. Mind-numbing, but Josie liked having her mind numbed. She needed it.

Caroline glared at the Fire God, who was fresh out of the shower after spending the evening chopping wood.

A cast iron stove in the corner crackled and radiated warmth from the living room to the adjoining kitchen. A moose head hung over the front door, a sad-eyed sentry. The furniture looked like it had come out of a hotel warehouse, brown, firm, uninteresting. A few plaid throw pillows were tossed here and there. Her dad took the one wedged behind him and dropped it onto the wood floor. His bald head fell back and his eyes closed. As his chest rose and fell, the contours of his ribs bulged through his gray T-shirt. A T-shirt. She couldn't remember the last time she'd seen her dad in anything but a button-down or cycling gear. One more sign the world was ending.

"Oh, so Tessa caught you together," Caroline said. She turned her furious look on Josie. "Even better. I don't suppose either of you have any idea of how much Tessa is struggling right now." Caroline ran a hand through her shaggy, blond hair. "Damn it."

"I'm surprised at you, Josie," her dad said without any of Caroline's anger. He didn't even lift his head. "At both of you. How long has this been going on exactly?"

Josie hung in the empty space between her dad, Caroline, and the Fire God—unable to answer.

"I can't believe you two would be so selfish." Caroline stalked away from the door and into the middle of the living room. She turned, so she was facing off with the Fire God. "Tessa couldn't even keep herself together during the Council."

"She went into possession?" Josie asked.

"Worse," Caroline said. "Death took her over."

Josie stood up again. "What?"

"Right in the middle of the vote. Tessa's eyes blacked out, and Death started spouting off about the end of the Covenant—"

"Is she okay?"

Caroline's gaze smacked against Josie like an open palm slap. "What do you think?"

"Caroline,"—Josie's dad finally lifted his head—"weren't you the one who told me not to be too rough on them?"

Caroline threw her hands into the air. "I know. I'm just—" She turned away towards the curtained window.

"How is Tessa?" Josie asked her dad.

"She's alive," he said. "Fortunately, Daisuke had one of Simone's sleep charms. But it shook up the Council. People are already dispirited. The last thing they needed to see was the Triune losing control of the Tripartite." Her dad bowed over, rubbing his hands slowly together, a deep crease in his brow.

"When I heard Tessa muttering about Judah and Josie as Daisuke carried her out of the building, I felt like I had a pretty good idea of what had happened to precipitate this ... event," Caroline said, turning back to them. Finally, her flinty exterior faltered. "Seriously, you two? I thought you were smarter than that." She took a step towards Judah, the couch between them. "I agreed to let you sit on the sidelines with Josie because I trusted you wouldn't do anything to jeopardize our position, considering how tenuous it is."

Caroline gazed at the Fire God for a long moment, waiting for a response, but he only stared back at her. He had strict instructions not to engage Caroline unless he had no other choice. Thankfully, he was following that order. Josie guessed it was one she actually meant. Unlike the don't-kiss-me rule.

"It's like I don't even know you anymore," Caroline said to the Fire God.

Pain. Chest.

Josie fought it off—dead people don't feel pain—and stepped forward. "It was a mistake not telling Tessa the truth sooner," she admitted. "My mistake," she said to her dad.

He slipped his glasses off. "So this has been going on for some time."

Josie didn't know how to answer that question.

Yes, she and Judah had been together months ago, but it was more complicated than that.

From their first encounter, when Judah had told her he was dating Tessa, Josie had banished any attraction she'd had for him—into the oubliette. That was the right thing to do.

Then Caroline had asked Josie to repair a mask—an ancient fire god mask. Josie had made the mask look like Judah. But she'd lied so well to herself about her feelings for Judah that she hadn't seen what she'd done. Judah had stolen the mask, because she'd made it for him.

When Judah had come to her in the guise of the Fire God, when he'd kissed her, she'd never asked him to take off the mask. She hadn't wanted to see the face behind it.

When he'd worn the mask, he'd been hers. When he'd taken it off, he'd belonged to Tessa. Except all Josie had really done was given Judah to the Fire God.

She'd become so good at lying to herself, at believing that she'd hated him, that he'd believed it too. He'd told himself he didn't really care for her either.

The same morning they'd realized they were lying to themselves and to each other was the day that Josie had been kidnapped and Judah had lost his soul. The same day that Josie had repaired Lily's mask and the same day the first earthquake had hit Portland.

The best, and the worst, day of Josie's life.

"I never wanted to hurt Tessa," she said. And she meant it.

"Well, you did," her dad said. "Both of you."

Some feelings couldn't be avoided, not even by a Triune.

Her dad sighed and slumped back again, resting his glasses on his knee. "Bad enough that all of this is threatening my daughter's life, but that a broken heart might cost us . . ." He seemed to lose weight before her eyes.

Just when Josie didn't think she could feel any worse . . .

"All right," Caroline said, resuming her authoritative tone, like a Present Eye should. "What's done is done. We can't shield Tessa from every wound, no more than we can shield ourselves." She cast Josie's dad a concerned look. "We have to keep faith in her. She's a strong young woman, Marc. She'll pull through this. We all will. We . . . have to believe that."

Once Josie had believed she hated Judah. But in spite of what she'd believed, she'd loved Judah. Belief and truth are separate. Like the realm of the gods and the realm of death. Believe what you want, it doesn't change the truth.

Josie's dad continued to gaze at the fake bearskin rug, his eyes glazed and distant, the welt on his cheek red and swollen.

"In the meantime," Caroline said, "we have other matters to deal with. Number one, being you, young man." She pointed at Judah. "You're done being a benchwarmer. I hate to admit it, but I was selfish. I was content to let you guard Josie and Simone. To keep you safe. But I can't justify it any longer. Frankly, I'm surprised you allowed it to go on this long." She gave Judah another scrutinizing look.

The Fire God remained stone-faced.

Caroline let out a terse huff. "I'm meeting with Nancy in the morning. Daisuke got an anonymous tip that might lead us to the island Lily's followers are using as their base to spin out these monster hurricanes. Russell is due to return with reconnaissance soon. If the intel was correct, then we'll attack. And you're coming with us."

"But—" Josie started. The idea of letting the Fire God out of her sight was terrifying for a host of reasons. She could barely control him when he was in her presence. Who knew how many ways he'd find to misbehave if he were unleashed in a battle between summoners?

Caroline held up her finger. "You don't have anything to say about this, Josie."

No, she didn't. Because everything she wanted to say would've required her to tell Caroline that her son's body was inhabited by an ancient volcanic god. Josie had hoped to have Judah's soul back in his body before it came to telling Caroline the truth, but she wasn't sure she could send Caroline into a fight with the Fire God unaware. Judah had been cool, controlled, reasonable. The Fire God was none of those things. If Josie let him go, she put everyone's lives in deeper jeopardy.

In the caverns of her memory, her mother's smoky voice whispered,

The right way is the only way for the Triune.

The right way. What was the right way? Josie didn't know anymore.

She'd thought she'd been right when she'd exiled her feelings for Judah, but now she was certain that had been wrong. It had cost Judah his soul. What else had her mother told her that had been wrong?

All she had were the echoes of her mother's voice and even those were sinking beneath this weight, this precarious, dangerous feeling. Without Judah . . .

"Caroline, I need to tell—"

"Josie, I think it might be better if we didn't hear from you right now," her dad said, putting his glasses back on with care, grimacing as his fingers brushed the welt on his face.

"Dad, this is—"

"We have other news for you, Josie," Caroline said. "You will be repairing the masks of the primordial gods."

What's the right way, Mom? Mistress Divine. Light of the World. Voice of the Three. Answer me.

Silence.

All Josie heard was her own feeble voice, "I don't think—"

Caroline's face was steel-sheeted. "I don't think you realize how bad things are, Josie. Power's out everywhere. Water and food supplies are being methodically cut off. Every major city in the world is being evacuated, and there is nowhere for all those people to go. People are dying and Lily's nowhere to be found and even if we could find her . . . I don't know that we'd be able to stop her without the Triune . . ." She pursed her lips. "Too many factions of the Core are turning their backs on us. Only about a third of the Eyes showed up for the Council. They think their only hope of survival is to throw in with Lily. And . . . they might be right."

She wiped a tear off her face. Josie's dad started to stand, but she waved him off.

"No one blames you for repairing Lily's mask," Caroline said to Josie. "Saving Russell's life was the right thing to do. And the fact that Lily was able to get her hands on those repaired masks was our fault. We were naïve. You tried to warn us. We didn't listen. But at this point, there is no worse for us. This is it. Either you bring back the primordial gods and give us a shot at saving ourselves or … either way, we fight until there's none of us left to fight."

"And we will," her dad said, voice and gaze level and flat, like an old grave.

Josie looked from her dad to Caroline, both flint-eyed and rail-thin, rigid from their jaws to their spines.

"You know I'll do whatever needs to be done," Josie said.

Caroline's shoulders fell slightly and she nodded. "We know you will, Josie." She beckoned to Josie's dad. He pushed out of the chair, slowly.

"We have to meet with Gretchen," she said, "and then try to get some sleep before we hear from Nancy and Russell. If plans go as I anticipate, then we'll be back early, day after tomorrow." She looked again at Judah, searchingly. "Be ready."

The Fire God held his tongue.

Pain cut deep lines into Caroline's face. She left without another word.

Her dad came to her and hugged her in a careful way, suggesting he had more injuries than just the nasty one on his face. "Expect Daisuke to come for you day after tomorrow too." He glanced at the Fire God. "Caroline convinced him to let you and Judah have one more day before you have to return to the island and begin work."

Josie nodded. He kissed her forehead and followed Caroline out the door into the dark.

"You humans, so dramatic." The Fire God shook his head in apparent bafflement. "This body is tired again. Care to join me in bed?"

"No."

"You heard what your father said. You only have one more day until they force us two wayward lovers apart." He sidled up to her, grazing her cheek with the backs of his burning fingers. "Don't worry though. When they're all dead, I'll come find you."

She drew back from him.

"Have it your way," he said, "while you can."

He disappeared down the hall.

One more day. If only that were true. What she would've given for one more day with Judah.

What would she give? That was the question . . .

But she knew the answer.

Anything.

Everything.

CHAPTER 6

AUGUST 30TH
EARLY

MINNESOTA'S FORESTS WERE deeply dark. Clouds smothered the stars and the moon, leaving the sky black.

Josie sat in one of the deck chairs, wrapped in a sweater and a fleece, shivering. She wasn't sure what time it was. An hour so late that the insects had given up their nocturnal serenades. Or maybe it was too cold for them. The cabin was dark too. The fire in the stove had still been burning when she'd stepped outside, though she hadn't fed it since the Fire God had gone to sleep. He seemed to be able to keep a fire going on nothing but ash and air, even when he was unconscious.

A cool beam of light bobbed up the road towards her. A late night visitor wasn't usually good news. But she doubted she could get any worse news than what her dad and Caroline had brought earlier. Against the surrounding darkness, the approaching light was faint and ghostly.

She waited.

Finally, Beech appeared. He leaned his bike against the bottom step of the deck, detaching the bike light. He bounded up the steps two at a time.

When the light flashed across Josie's face, he flinched, reeling at the edge of the steps. He caught himself on the rail.

"Gods, I didn't expect you to be out here," he said.

"But you did expect me to be awake," she said.

"I know you better than you think," he said, taking off his backpack and plunking it down on the deck. He hopped onto the broad railing across from her and perched, swinging his legs. He set the light next to him, angling it askew. The pale light pushed weakly against the deep dark surrounding them. "Prince Chode getting his beauty sleep?"

Beech and Judah had never been friends. They were about as different as two people born in the same year, in the same place, to the same tribe, could be.

But Josie wasn't offended. With that laidback grin of his, it was hard to take anything he said too seriously.

"Caroline and my dad stopped by earlier," she said.

"I saw them up at the Big House. Not so secret meeting with Mama Bear."

"They want me to fix the masks of the primordial gods," she said.

Beech pushed himself up off the railing, hovering for a second like a gymnast over a balance beam and then plopped down again. "So are you?"

"I have to."

"Because they say so?" he asked with a peaked pierced brow.

"Because we're all going to die if I don't."

"Oh, so they dropped that in your lap. No pressure."

"You've been out there, haven't you?"

Beech slid his butt off the railing and let it hang over the edge, his knees up by his chin. It seemed he couldn't sit still for longer than a second. "I've lived all over this town."

"And are we all going to die if I don't repair these masks?"

He sprung off the railing and onto his feet. "You don't believe your dad and Caroline?"

"I don't believe a nuclear bomb is the answer to gun violence."

"Fair enough. But we're not talking neighborhood drive-bys, Josie." He swung his arms, fist smacking against his palm rhythmically. "You know how I usually think people take everything too seriously, but in this case..." He shoved his tattooed hands deep into the pockets of his dark hoodie. "We're at DEFCON 2, Josie. Cocked Pistol ain't far off, no matter what we do." He brought his fingers to his temple like a gun and fired an imaginary shot. "Bang."

She turned her gaze towards the forest. Though it was the end of summer, the woods were as silent as midwinter. Not even a breeze whispered through the pines.

"Don't let it eat you up," Beech said, pulling out the chair next to hers and dropping into it. He tapped either side of her knee lightly. "Betty hasn't juiced her tricktionary. Let's see how well Lily's mob stands up to some real old school deities."

Josie lost herself in the darkness. It seeped into her mind, extinguishing her thoughts one by one, like a slow flood.

"Hey," he said, grasping her wrist, drawing her attention back to him. "Don't bail on us yet." He dropped back into his chair, frowning. "What the hell's happened to you? The Josie I knew was one freakin' freight train *la femme*. Get out of her way or get your ass run over. Are you really going to let that barrel of a wannabe earth mama stop you? Or is this what happens to a girl when she falls for *das uber*-male? Check your guns at the bedroom door, Annie?"

Even in the dark, under the heavy slashes of his brows, his eyes were vivid. So green they could've been photosynthesizing.

"I'll bring back the primordial gods," she said.

He continued to frown. "But?"

"But I don't think it's going to work."

He leaned forward, hands squeezing her knees. "Then what will?"

She shook her head, eyes burning for lack of tears. "I don't know. I wish I—"

A flicker of movement on the lawn interrupted her words. She stiffened, squinting at the darkness.

"What is it?" Beech asked, standing up.

"Beech?" a meek voice said from the shadows.

Josie stood too, joining Beech at the railing. He grabbed the bike light and swept it across the yard. Simone squinted and staggered back when the light hit her face.

"Simone," Beech said, lowering the light. Another shadow moved in behind Simone. Beech turned the light towards it, almost blinding Kai as well. "Kai-bro. Late night mortal-plane munchies? What are you two doing here? I thought you were island-side."

Simone was spinning her bracelets around her wrists at Tour De France speed. "Beech, what you are doing here?"

"Uh, didn't I just ask that?" Beech said.

"What's wrong?" Josie asked.

"Um . . ." Simone glanced over at Kai, but his gaze seemed to be burrowing into the shadows under the deck. "We thought you'd be alone," she said finally to Josie.

"Hey, I can exit," Beech said, holding up his hands and backing away from the railing. "No problemo."

Josie caught his arm and took the flashlight from his hand, turning it back to Simone and Kai. The look on Simone's face was putting knots in her guts. It reminded her of when Judah had been missing during the wild fires at Crater Lake. "Did something happen to Tessa?"

"No," Simone said. "Nothing like that . . ." She glanced at Kai again, wringing her hands.

"Kai," Josie said. "What's wrong?"

His eyes slid from the ground to the distant trees.

"Maybe you should let Beech leave," Simone said in a trembling voice. "I don't think we can stay long and we . . ." Tears rolled down her cheeks. "We really need to talk to you."

"Come up here," Josie said, beckoning them. Simone hurried. Kai followed, slowly.

"I can leave," Beech said to Josie softly as Simone came up the steps.

The door opened. The porch light flipped on, casting a dull yellow glow over them. The Fire God appeared, wearing nothing but boxers.

"A party?" he asked, stepping out onto the deck.

Simone gave the Fire God a pained look and then turned to Kai, who had stopped halfway up the stairs. "Kai—"

"I should go," Beech said.

"No," Kai said, his voice darker than normal. "Stay." His black eyes touched Josie briefly, then flicked back out towards the forest. "Why not?"

Simone inhaled raggedly, tears falling faster.

Josie passed the bike light to Beech and put her hands on Simone's shoulders. "What is going on?"

Simone collapsed against Josie, sobbing. Josie held her. Josie stared at Kai until he met her gaze. "What the—?"

Simone backed up, chest heaving. "We're in trouble, Josie."

"In trouble?"

"You're not in trouble. I'm in trouble," Kai said.

Simone seized Josie's arms. "You have to understand."

"Understand what?"

"You're not preggo, are you?" Beech asked.

"No," Simone said. "Josie, please. You have to understand. You have to help us."

"There's nothing she can do," Kai said.

"You don't know that!" Simone insisted. "She knows the laws better than anyone. She'll know a way—"

"There is no way!"

"Wait!" Josie detached Simone's hands from her arms. "Explain."

Simone started to cry again, covering her face. Kai bowed his head, taking a step back down.

"Simone didn't know anything about it. Don't let them punish her." Kai's eyes fixed onto Josie's. Tears rippled on their surface.

Kai? Crying?

Josie moved to the top of the steps. "Punish her for what? What did you do?"

Kai gazed at her for a long moment and then looked away. "When she told me it was my life or Simone's. I chose Simone. I don't care about many people. Very few, actually, which I know won't come as a surprise to you."

When Josie took a step down, he stepped down too, not letting her get any closer. "What are you talking about? Someone threatened Simone? Who—?"

"Everything I've done this last month has been real," he went on, like he was talking to himself. "All those anonymous tips Daisuke received, that was me. A lot of good it did." He snorted, shaking his head. "She stopped trusting me a long time ago. Maybe she never really trusted me at all." His hands fisted on the railings. "She was right not to." His eyes flicked up to Josie again, black half-moons. "I'm going to find her. I'm going to kill her myself. It's her or me."

"Who are you talking about—?"

"My mom."

"Your mom?"

Kai's sideswiped smile returned, more bitter and melancholy than ever before. "You still don't see it." He shook his head. "You know, Josie Day . . . you have the craziest effect on people. When you told me you trusted me . . ." His voice sounded choked. "I actually wanted to be the person you thought I was. For the last month, I tricked myself into thinking I could be, because somehow . . . if Josie Day believes it, then it might actually be true."

The darkness was closing in around her, squeezing like a fist. "I don't understand what you're saying."

"Yes, you do." Kai's smile withered. "Come on, Lady Day."

Her breath stopped.

Only one person had ever called her Lady Day.

The Fog God. Lily's son.

Simone continued sobbing behind her.

"I don't believe it," Josie whispered.

Kai's gaze skimmed the starless sky. "I know. It's funny. Back in that alley, when I almost had you, Judah was the one who saved you. You didn't know it was him behind that mask of fire, and you didn't know it was me"—he twisted his wrist, reaching into his stash, and brought a mask to his face—"behind this mask."

Fog unfurled, encasing him. A guise of blue-white clouds stood at the bottom of the stairs, one she knew too well. The hollow eyes gazed up at her.

"Son of a bitch." Beech vaulted over the railing and landed with a thump, five feet below, next to Kai.

Kai. The Fog God.

The Fog God who had held her back while her mother was murdered. He'd attacked her at the beach, which had led to her drowning. He'd cut off her protective charms, leaving scars on her arms. He'd nearly killed Beech, forcing Josie to give herself up to Lily. And he'd kidnapped Josie in the Fire God pathways, causing Judah to think she was dead, which was why he'd given up fighting the Fire God and why his soul was lost.

Kai was Lily's son. Kai was the traitor.

Beech lunged at Kai.

The fog swirled away and reappeared on the deck behind them.

"Would you like me to kill him now?" the Fire God asked as if he didn't care either way.

"No!" Simone threw herself between Kai and the rest of them. Beech stomped up the steps behind Josie, plowing by her. "Stop!" Simone collided with him. "Please!"

He pushed her aside.

Josie snagged Beech's arm, stalling him. He bore down on her.

"Don't, Josie," he said through his teeth. "Mofo almost ended me. He almost—"

"He saved you, Josie," Simone said, crowding close too. "Lily was going to kill you. He saved you, remember?"

Josie's head throbbed. First Judah, now Kai. How could she have been so blind? A phantom of anger passed through her, but it was gone as quickly as it came.

Josie placed a staying hand on Beech's chest, edging past Simone.

Josie faced him. His guise was a tangle of mist. The Fog God.

Then he took off his mask. The fog vanished. And there was Kai.

Anger wouldn't take hold, but pain ... there was pain. Looking at him, all her half-healed invisible wounds felt as if they were being sliced open again.

She didn't trust many people. She didn't have many friends, but Kai ... she'd trusted him. Kai had been her friend.

"Someone found out," Simone said. "I was taking Daisuke another access charm and I overheard him talking to Allison.

He said an anonymous source claimed Kai was Lily's son. He said if it's true then Tessa will have to execute him." Simone gripped Josie's arm. "You can't let them."

"Hell yes, she can," Beech said. "Dude played us. He is going down—"

"He's on our side now!" Simone cried.

"He murdered the Triune!" Beech shouted.

"No! Lily murdered your mom, Josie. Not him."

"He was there—" Beech continued

"He didn't do it—"

"He helped plan it—"

"But he's sorry—"

"Are you?" Josie interjected, never taking her eyes off Kai's.

Her hushed question silenced Simone and Beech.

"Does it make a difference?" he asked.

"I don't know."

His dark eyes glimmered. Was there regret in those unshed tears? She didn't know. She didn't trust her eyes anymore. They'd lied to her too often. They saw only what they wanted to see. They hadn't wanted to see Kai behind the guise of fog, but he'd been there anyway.

Kai gripped the fog god's mask in his hands, like he was going to snap it in two. His voice was husky with pain. Or it sounded that way. Her ears might've been liars too.

"Want to climb in the Wayback machine with me, Lady Day?" he asked her.

Heart. Breaking.

"Where are we going today?" she asked.

"Brunei. Seven months ago."

"Why would I want to go back there?"

Tears broke the dark edges of his eyes. And fell. "Because we're going to stop a murder."

Pain. Everywhere.

"I wish we could," he said.

Josie wished they could too.

"The Covenant is clear," the Fire God said in a bored tone. "He participated in the murder of a Triune. He must be executed and his soul consigned to Oblivion."

Beech was close at Josie's ear. "He deserves it."

"No," Simone whimpered. "There has to be a way—"

"You cannot hide him," the Fire God said. "If you do, you will be considered a conspirator and handed the same sentence."

Simone clung to Josie's arm, pleading, "Josie . . ."

Josie didn't know if the tears on Kai's cheeks were real, but she knew that the ones on hers were.

Her voice was choked, tear-strained, little more than a whisper.

"Run away."

The door banged open.

Simone flinched and then burrowed deeper into the chair, hugging a throw pillow to her chest. Beech dropped down from the threshold of the hall, where he'd been climbing, hanging, dropping, climbing, hanging, dropping, for the last twenty minutes. The Fire God's eyes cracked open.

Josie stood in the middle of the living room, waiting.

Daisuke's gaze swept the cabin, blipping on Simone. Finally, he fixed on Josie.

"Where he is?" Daisuke asked.

"We don't know," Josie said.

Daisuke took a few steps into the cabin. "You did not stop him?"

"How do you stop fog?"

His eyes narrowed.

"You let him go," another voice, softer, said from outside. Tessa.

She hovered in the doorway, so thin, so pale. The hollows around her eyes were too deep, too dark. She was turning into a ghost right before their eyes. Josie ached. Her sister was dying. What could Josie do? Nothing.

"You know who Kai is," Tessa said to Josie. "You know what he did."

"I do," Josie said.

"And you still let him—" Tessa leaned against the door, closing her eyes. Allison, who had been prowling behind her, grasped her arm. Tessa shook her head at Allison, gathering herself again. "Simone, you have to come with us. The rest of you meet us at the Big House at dawn. You'll all be questioned. If any of you knew anything—"

"We didn't," Josie said.

Tessa's faded hazel eyes flashed black. Death was there, lurking. Josie's heart leapt. Death was so close. If only she could get a minute alone with Tessa, maybe he would come through, like he had at the Council of the Eyes . . . except, Josie wasn't sure Tessa could handle Death assuming control of her body again. He wasn't supposed to be able to do so. It was a bad sign. A sign that Tessa was losing.

"Don't interrupt me," she said.

Josie inclined her head. "Forgive me, Divine Mother. I forget myself . . . too often."

"You're right, you do." She turned obliquely. "At dawn."

"Yes, Mistress of the Will."

Daisuke grasped Simone's arm and propelled her up to her feet. She stumbled as he hauled her out the door. Tessa stepped aside as they passed. She glanced back at them—at the Fire God, who remained on the couch, feigning sleep.

Allison grasped the doorknob. Her lips puckered, her cheekbones looked sharp enough to cut through her own skin. "No mercy for traitors."

She shut the door.

"That one smells of wet dog," the Fire God commented, eyes still closed.

Beech leaned on the back of the couch. "Let's talk fire god masks."

The Fire God opened his eyes, smiling. "One revelation after another."

"You stole that mask," Beech said, shaking his head. "That almost makes me like you." He pulled the chain of his necklace into his mouth, bobbing his head for a moment. Then he turned and headed for the door.

"Beech—" Josie started, though she wasn't exactly sure what she was going to say to him. Other than to ask him not to tell anyone about Judah.

"I guess nobody's who they seem to be," Beech said to her as he opened the door. "Except me. I'm still Beech." He gazed at her. "What about you, Jos? Did I get you wrong too?"

"There's more to it—"

Beech held up his hand. "Better not."

"Beech—"

"It's interesting to me," Beech said, leaning against the door, "that Kai came to you. And Simone. They really thought you could help him ... Once upon a time, I said you weren't the sheriff anymore, that you were turning outlaw, remember?"

"I remember."

He grinned. "I didn't think you'd take me seriously." He started to close the door, but then stopped. "By the way, I didn't have anything to do with this shit, right?"

"I won't let Tessa or the Eye punish you—"

Beech cocked his head at her. "What are you going to do if the Divine Will decides to bring down the hammer? You told Kai to skate. You covered up Judah's thieving. I don't know the laws as well as you do, but ... seems to me you in a whole heap of trouble, Hoss."

Josie scrubbed her face with her hands, raking her fingers back into her hair. "I'm trying to make things right again."

"Right according to who? Not the Covenant. Not your sister. She's the Triune. I don't think you got that straight yet. She's the law. You done broke the law. You on the run, rebel-girl, and you don't even know it. But it won't take them long, once they start pulling out the truth-charms tomorrow, to figure who you really are."

"And who's that?"

"Outlaw Josie Day. Looking for revenge."

"I'm not looking for revenge."

"Then what are you looking for?"

Judah's soul? But she knew that's not what he was asking. Not really.

"You know what I liked about you, Josie-pie?" Beech asked with that Puckish glint in his vibrant eyes. "Cranked to eleven," he said, spinning an invisible dial. "Intense. You started down this path, outlaw, don't back down now. What have you got to lose? Own it. Take it all the way."

"You could've stopped Kai," she said. "You didn't have to listen to me."

"You know the thing about you, Outlaw Josie Day?" Beech grinned, that off-kilter grin that was like a magic elixir, silencing fear, making irrational thoughts seem reasonable. But Josie didn't need anyone to encourage her wild thoughts. They seemed to be flourishing all on their own. "You have the craziest effect on people," he said with a wink. "Go down shootin', Annie. Go down shootin'."

CHAPTER 7

AUGUST 30TH

"YOU SHOULDN'T BE HERE," she said to Kai.

Fog curled over the lake. The sky faded from black to purple, like a bruise.

Josie stood at the end of the dock. She'd been on her way to the Big House, the lodge that had been set up as a command center, to face the inquiry. But, along the way, she'd wandered off the path and out onto a weathered jut of creaking wooden planks.

The mica-silvered water lapped against the wood. The air was chill, damp, and sweet with pine. How could this place be so peaceful, so calm, while the rest of the world writhed and shuddered in its death throes?

She'd felt the whoosh of air behind her as Kai had translocated onto the dock, but she didn't turn. She'd known it was him without looking.

"How's Simone?" Kai asked.

"I don't know," she said.

"I'll take her away," Kai said. "Just give me the chance."

"Do you think that's what she wants?"

"Better than being executed."

"Tessa won't execute her."

"No," he said. "She won't."

"Don't make threats." She looked back at him. "Not now."

His hair was shoved back from his face, exposing his dark eyes and the heavy shadows pooling around them.

More than once this last month she'd heard how invaluable Kai's efforts had been against Lily's forces. No one would care what he'd done now that they knew who he actually was—or had been. Even if he'd changed sides like Simone had claimed, the law demanded his blood.

But like Beech had said, Josie wasn't the law anymore.

"How do think Daisuke found out about you?" she asked.

"The Wolf? My mother? She told me that if I didn't bring Simone to her, she'd make sure I paid."

The Wolf.

Josie rubbed the scars on her upper arm. Four long thin trails. A summoner in possession of a tree god, who took the form of a wolf, had left her with the scars and more on her thigh. The Wolf had almost killed Gretchen and had stolen the ancient masks that were now destroying the world. They suspected she was part of their tribe—a traitor, like Kai. But between fleeing Portland and trying to stop the end of the world, they hadn't been given much time to discover her identity.

"Do you know who the Wolf is?" she asked.

"I wish."

"Simone forgave you, right away, didn't she?" Josie asked.

"I love her. That was always true."

"And all those things you said to me, all of your mother's propaganda, rape of the earth and plague of humanity, is that still true?"

"I don't care," he said. "Do you believe me?"

"Does it matter?"

"It matters to me."

"How did you find me? Now. And in the pathways? You're an air god. You shouldn't be able to cross into the paths of fire."

He plucked at a bracelet of polished black stones on his wrist. "Locator charm." He gestured to a matching bracelet on her arm. "I can find you anywhere. I can translocate to wherever you are."

She touched the bracelet. A month ago he'd given her a whole bag of charms from Simone. He must've slipped the locator charm in then.

"You know I'll have to tell them about this," she said. "I'll have to tell them I saw you. I'll have to tell them everything."

"You going to tell them about Judah?"

"If they use a truth-charm on me, I won't have a choice."

"It's futile, Josie, you know that, don't you?"

"You think we're going to lose too."

"Have you looked at your sister lately?"

"Tessa is the Triune. She's stronger than she looks."

"Come on, Josie . . ."

"If you want me to say my sister is going to die, that's never going to happen."

"We're all going to die someday."

"Yeah, but not all of us are going to be consigned to Oblivion."

He still held the fog god mask. He moved it to his other hand and then, with a flick of his wrist, a sword appeared. She stepped back from the gleaming edge, the blade of rippling metal. The Sword of Eternity. The sword that had killed her mother.

"If I'd wanted to hurt you, I would've let my mother do it," he said. "She's much better at hurting people than I am anyway." He swung the blade under and back towards his own body, holding the hilt towards her.

He was giving it to her.

"How did you find—?"

"I told you my mom was right not to trust me," he said, a hint of his half-smile returning. "I know where most of her stashes are, or were, even though she didn't know I knew. It took some digging, but a little earth moving is a lot easier when you have the powers of an ancient ocean god."

Josie was tempted to ask for the ocean god mask back too. After all, it belonged to the tribe. And he'd betrayed the tribe. She still couldn't believe he was the Fog God, even though he was holding the mask and the Sword of Eternity—more than enough proof. Yet, somehow, when she looked at him, she still just saw Kai.

He held out the sword and the mask.

"Take them, Josie," he said. "Destroy the mask. Give the sword to your sister. Or take it back to the pathways and pitch it into the Beyond. If you run into Death again, maybe you can use it to convince him to give you Judah back. They say it's capable of killing a god, you know."

Her fingers moved from the scars, left by the Wolf God, on her upper arm to the long thin one on her forearm. She had a matching one on the other arm—from where he'd cut off her charm bracelets when he'd been trying to kidnap her.

"This whole end of the world thing sounded pretty good to me for a long time," he said. "Maybe it was just Mom's negative influence, but I bought in, you know." He smirked. "Except . . . these last couple years, things started to change."

"Because of Simone?"

"Her, and the band. Russell moved out, so the daily torture stopped. And Mom ratcheted up the human sacrifices. Believe it or not, I never liked that part."

She held up her arms, showing the scars. "You cut me."

"I told you not to fight," he said.

She scowled.

"I'm sorry," he said.

"I want to believe you."

"Tell me what I can do to prove it."

"I'm not the one whose opinion matters—"

"I politely declare bullshit."

"Kai—"

"I was there, Josie, when the Other said you were the chosen one. Not Tessa. She's the one who got stuck with the Tripartite. You're the one who's supposed to save the world—"

"That's not what it said."

In fact, the Other had told her the fate of the Covenant was tied to her fate. Whatever that meant.

"Isn't it? Maybe my evil ears heard wrong."

"You're not evil, Kai."

He held out the fog god's mask again. "Would you have said that to him?"

She gazed down at the smooth slick surface of the mask.

"Please take it, Josie. I don't want it anymore."

Her hand closed around the edge of the fog god's mask. Cool to the touch and light.

"It's not really the god's fault," he said. "That's the bitch of it for them in this whole Covenant deal, huh? That they bow to our will. That's why my mom's goddess wanted to end the Covenant, you know. One of the reasons, anyway."

"Don't you want your mom to win? Don't you want the Covenant destroyed?"

"So I can save my soul from Oblivion?"

She nodded.

In response, he held out the sword to her again too. She took it from him, gingerly. The weapon was surprisingly light. For some reason she'd imagined the sword that had murdered her mother would be heavy. So heavy it would take a god to lift it.

"Do you know the story behind the Sword of Eternity?" he asked.

"Lu-Ji forged it. A gift from the first Triune to her daughter, who would inherit the mask of the Tripartite."

"Yeah, but do know how she created it?"

Josie searched her memory, but couldn't recall the details of the story.

"When she was dying," he said, "she forged the sword in the flames of the primordial volcano and tempered it in her own blood to give it the power to kill the gods. It wasn't a gift, Josie. It was insurance."

"Insurance?"

"Lu-Ji forced the gods to serve us in the mortal realm. You know better than any of us that the power of the Tripartite is hard to handle. It's killed more than one Triune. Look at your sister."

Josie frowned at him.

"Point is," he said, "Lu-Ji knew Death and Life would try to cut out of the bargain the first chance they got. What would the world be like if the gods walked the earth again? Lu-Ji didn't think it was a good idea, which is why she made that sword, in case the Covenant was broken and some god-killing was required, but apparently, there's a catch."

"Isn't there always?"

"Do you know why my mom spent the last ten years gathering all her power to summon a demon capable of bringing this god-killer back to the mortal plane?" he asked, gesturing to the sword.

"To murder my mother?"

"You think she needed the Sword of Eternity to do that? She had a time bender. She had the element of surprise. All the upper hand. There were a dozen ways she could've killed your mom—subtler, cleaner ways. But no, she had to go in for the big show. That's the goddess, you know. This whole big show. That bitch has been eating away at my mom's brain since the beginning. You know my mom told me that it had been a drunken dare. She had been staying with my dad and his tribe in China. They got wasted one night and snuck into this ancient temple where there was a mask on display. They called it the Profane Mother. No one was allowed to wear it. No one had touched it in . . . thousands of years. My dad dared her to touch it. Just to touch it. She did. She said that the goddess cried out to her, pleading for help. So she went back later and stole it—liberated it, is what she said."

"Did you know your father?"

Kai shook away the question, eyes darkening. "My mom was convinced the goddess was Mother Earth. The reason my mom spent the last ten years bleeding people to get the Sword of Eternity is because the goddess told her it could destroy the mask of the Tripartite, destroy the Covenant. That's the catch apparently. Lu-Ji created the sword to aid mortals in case the Covenant was broken, but at the same time, she created the weapon that could destroy the Covenant. So that was our original plan. Kill your mom. Then you'd inherit the mask. My mother knew that yours wasn't about to give up the mask of the Tripartite, but she thought maybe you would. You know, being young and naïve . . ."

Josie snorted. Kai's smirk grew.

"She didn't know you," he said. "No one did. And even if you'd refused to give up the mask, we would've just killed you and moved on to the next Triune."

"But you didn't. You and Lily were both in the tribe. Why didn't you kidnap Tessa as soon as you realized she was the new Triune?"

"Know a guy named Judah?"

"Lily was afraid of Judah?"

"No. I was afraid of Judah. I knew he was a badass summoner. He was always with Tessa. And if he wasn't, it was your dad. We couldn't use the time bender again. It juiced my mom to use it just once in Brunei. She could barely walk the next day. If we had attacked Tessa . . . we risked revealing ourselves. We decided to lay low for a while, regroup. Wait for a better opportunity. Mom didn't like it, but she went along because she still had some semblance of reason at that point..."

He must've read the skepticism on Josie's face because he added, "Like I said, the Earth Goddess has been rotting my mom's brain for a long time. I admit it. But the thing is, when I tried to get my mom to explain to me how the Sword could be used to destroy the mask, she refused to answer. She said it would all be revealed. One step at a time. I don't think she knew. So I wasn't surprised when she jumped on the chance to use you, instead of going after the mask of the Tripartite, to get Mother Earth's revenge. I think that decision was my mom's, not the goddess's. I think the goddess would've rather been freed."

"All the gods would," Josie said. "Honestly, at this point, I can't imagine that the gods walking the earth would be any worse than what's happening now. At least if the Covenant were dissolved . . . your soul would be saved."

Far across the lake, behind the black wall of trees, the sun rose—burning away the night and lighting up the clouds, pink and indigo.

"Don't feel bad for me, Josie."

"Isn't that what you want?"

"Is that why you think I'm doing this, spilling my evil secrets, turning my back on my mom, giving up her most powerful weapon? For sympathy?" His half-smile returned. "Nah. I'm doing this for a girl."

He brought the ocean god mask to his face and was swallowed by a guise of water, clear and black, still and silent, close-fitted to his body, like a second skin. When he'd been in possession of the fog god, his voice had sounded hollow, just like the god's. In the ocean god's form, it was a distant murmur, made deeper by the god's low resonant voice.

"When my mom thought I betrayed her, she threatened to kill me. When Simone found out I betrayed her, she helped me escape. I won't let anyone hurt her. She's the only thing I have left to lose and I won't let that happen."

"Where are you going?"

"Hunting."

"Don't be a vigilante," she said. "If you find your mother, send word back to us."

"And Simone?"

"They won't hurt her," Josie said, "so long as she tells the truth."

"'Speak the truth, do not yield to anger; give, if thou art asked for little; by these three steps thou wilt go near the gods,'" he said. "Maybe that's why Simone can't summon any gods. If Confucius was right, then my Simone isn't near the gods. She's already a god."

"Ooo, quotey."

"I'm trusting you, Josie."

"Why?"

"Because I have to trust someone and I choose you."

"You must be pretty desperate."

"No doubt about it."

Josie's grip tightened around the sword. "I won't let anything happen to Simone."

"Think you can stop it?"

"I am holding the Sword of Eternity."
"I am sorry, Josie. Really."
"Me too."

CHAPTER 8

AUGUST 30TH

"IT NEVER ENDS WITH YOU, does it?" Nancy said archly. Even during an apocalypse, she wore pearls and silk. Not a single strand of silver hair was out of place.

Josie kept her gaze fixed above Tessa's head, at the stone fireplace which rose between two columns of windows overlooking the misty lake. Her dad, Caroline, and Gretchen all sat on the edges of the overstuffed leather furniture wearing strained expressions like they were fighting the couches' attempts to make them comfortable. Simone, Beech, and the Fire God were there too, hovering in the back corner near the doors. Tessa stood before Josie, looking as if it was taking all her strength to stay on her feet. Allison and Daisuke flanked her.

Nancy stood off to the side, in front of the desk and built-in bookshelves. Russell was with her. He watched Josie from the corner of his darkly clouded eyes. After Lily had kidnapped him and used his life as leverage, forcing Josie to repair Lily's mask, the Wolf had dumped him back in Portland. Since then, all his interest in Josie seemed to have evaporated. Even when she had approached him at the Core center soon after the kidnapping, before Portland had been reduced to a smoking crater, to ask if he was okay, he had backed away, muttering a reply and then had fled.

Nancy, the Future Eye, seemed to have the same opinion of Josie as she'd always had. If anything, she seemed even more convinced that Josie was, if not the primary cause, then a major contributing factor in the world's downfall. And she wasn't entirely wrong. Without Josie, Lily wouldn't have had half the strength that she did.

"An imbecile would know better than to walk in here with a sacred tool," Nancy was saying. "Every protective charm was triggered. Summoners from all over the world were alerted and forced to return. Melbourne and Calcutta are surely lost now..."

Nancy continued listing all the disasters that had been worsened thanks to Josie.

The sword had set off the perimeter alerts. They should've prevented her from crossing altogether, but they hadn't. Since they were silent, Josie didn't have any idea what was happening until two dozen summoners had appeared and surrounded her. Nancy was right, again. Josie should've realized what would happen if she came too close to the resort with the Sword. It had been a stupid mistake.

"...Rio under water, tens of thousands of people, dead—"

"Enough, huh, Nancy?" Gretchen said. "She gets it."

"Oh, I agree. Not even an idiot would have crossed the inner circles with a divine tool of that magnitude. She got it, all right. It was deliberately provocative and disruptive."

Every eye turned back to Josie.

"I won't make excuses," Josie said, still holding the sword and the fog god mask. "I should've realized... I wasn't thinking."

Actually, she had been thinking. Too much, that was why she'd forgotten about the perimeter circles. She had been preoccupied, her head, her heart, her entire body weighted down by thoughts of Judah and Death, Kai and Simone, the Earth Goddess and the end of the world, and Tessa.

Josie dropped her gaze to the rug decorated with moose and bears, deer and wolves. She couldn't look at Tessa. If she did... she was afraid of the thoughts that might start to preoccupy her mind, the things she might start to forget if she looked up and saw her little sister dying. Her head was already filled with crazy thoughts because of Judah.

"An honest mistake?" Nancy said with a curt laugh. "You expect us to believe that? Why should we believe anything you say? Now that we know you've colluded with a traitor."

Gretchen spoke up. "She didn't—"

"She's holding his mask. She's carrying the sword that killed her mother. What more proof do you require, Eye of the Past?"

Gretchen slumped, her cheeks flushed. She seemed to have run out of steam. No one else attempted to defend Josie. Not even her father. He stared at the floor too, kneading his hands together. The long welt on his face was purple and swollen, so much so that he wasn't wearing his glasses.

"I would suggest that you drop the sword," Nancy said in a triumphant tone.

"Then you would be the imbecile," Josie said.

Her dad's eyes closed. Caroline winced.

Nancy brandished a rigid finger in Josie's direction. "You will not speak to me in such a—"

"I'm not dropping the Sword of Eternity in a room full of people, any one of whom could also be a traitor."

"You're one to speak of traitors—"

"For all I know, any one of you could be the Wolf."

"Well, why don't you ask your good friend, Kai?" Nancy replied smoothly. "You know, Lilith's son?"

"I did," she said. "He doesn't know who she is—"

"Of course he doesn't—"

"That's enough," Tessa said with a heavy sigh. "Daisuke take the sword."

"No," Josie said.

Tessa's pale eyes hardened.

"Forgive me, Divine Mother," Josie said to her sister, "but this may be the most powerful sacred tool ever created. And I won't hand it over to anyone but the Triune." She glanced at Daisuke. All the warmth and openness was gone from his face. "Nothing personal."

Daisuke looked to Tessa, waiting. Tessa's arms wrapped around her waist as if she were trying hold herself up. Her white T-shirt and blue jeans looked pale, washed out, like they were being sapped by the Tripartite too. Josie ached for her sister, hating herself for seeing nothing but the sallow hue of Tessa's skin, the dull glaze over her eyes, the shallow and rapid pace of her breathing . . .

Josie refocused on the oil painting above the desk, a landscape of ducks flying off towards a hazy horizon.

Nancy sighed and checked her watch. "We don't have much time for this. If you want to question them—"

"Just one thing," Josie said, tossing the fog god mask to the floor. She stepped forward and tapped the forehead of the mask, the weak point, with the tip of the sword.

Without ceremony or sound, the mask split down the middle. Destroyed.

Everyone in the room seemed to recoil.

She should've realized that, for a summoner, watching a mask being broken must've been like a violinist watching a Stradivarius smashed against a brick wall. Though Josie had brought forth enough masks to precipitate the end of the world, she felt no pain in shattering this one. Besides, she hadn't killed the god. She'd only prevented him from being summoned.

Tessa held her hand out to Daisuke. "Give me the truth-charm."

He took a thin bracelet of silver beads off his wrist and handed it to her.

She turned it around in her fingers and then pressed one of the beads to her lips.

"Josephine Day," she said, activating the charm.

She tossed the bracelet across the rug at Josie. It fell far short of Josie's reach.

"Put it on," Tessa said.

Josie stepped over the broken mask and picked up the truth-charm. They didn't trust her to tell them the truth on her own. They needed to force it out of her with a charm. With good reason.

She slipped the bracelet over her wrist, along with the other charms, including Kai's locator charm. She hadn't taken it off.

"Did you know that Kai was the Fog God?" Tessa asked.

"Not until last night."

"Do you know where he is?"

"No. He said he's going to find his mother and kill her before she kills him."

Simone let out a meep.

"He gave you the sword. Why didn't you kill him?"

"Administration of justice in the Corpora is the duty of the Triune," she said. "I am not the Triune."

"Do you wish you were?" Tessa asked.

Discomfort swelled in the air, making the spacious room seem small and overcrowded.

"Yes," Josie said. "I would trade places with you right now if I could."

"You think you're better than me," Tessa said.

"No," Josie said.

"Liar."

"I can't lie," Josie said, holding up her wrist bearing the truth-charm.

"But you think you'd be a better Triune than I am?"

"I don't know, but at least it would be me and not you."

Tessa's face twisted—confused, annoyed. "What do you mean?"

Josie tried to hold back the words, but she couldn't. The power of the truth-charm was pushing them into her throat and past her lips. "At least it would be me . . . losing . . . dying."

Tessa's brow furrowed. Her hands fisted.

Daisuke touched her shoulder. She shook him off.

"Leave," Tessa said. "All of you. Get out. I need to talk to my sister alone."

"But what about the traitor?" Nancy said.

"There he is," Tessa said, pointing to the broken mask on the floor. "If you want him, take him. Now leave."

The Fire God opened the door. One by one, the room emptied.

Her dad stopped and touched Josie's cheek, smiling slightly, tears in his eyes, before shuffling out. Daisuke lingered, giving Josie a guarded but no longer entirely cold look as he passed. The Fire God was the last one out. He winked at Josie and then shut the door.

"How long?" Tessa asked.

Josie frowned. "How long what?"

"How long have you been cheating with Judah?"

Josie was tempted to rip the bracelet off, but she didn't. This seemed like such a waste of time, considering. But she guessed she couldn't blame Tessa for wanting the truth. "It depends on what you mean."

Tessa's scowl deepened. "How does it depend?"

"Because I didn't know it was him at first."

"How could you not know?"

"Because he's the Fire God."

Tessa's eyes widened. "He's what?"

"He stole the mask I repaired last winter. The first time I kissed him was while he was in the Fire God's guise, but I didn't know it was Judah behind the mask. And he didn't kiss me back . . . that time."

"That time?"

"Later . . ."

"But you're the reason he broke up with me."

"Yes."

Tessa turned her shoulder to Josie, arms pinched tight over her chest.

"Neither of us wanted to hurt you," Josie said. "That's the reason everything happened the way it did. I refused to let myself have feelings for him—"

"He kissed me the other day."

"That wasn't him."

"Then who was it?"

"The Fire God."

"He wasn't in possession. He wasn't wearing a mask."

"The Fire God is manifest. He's taken over Judah's body. Judah's soul is gone. Judah is . . . dead."

Tessa's hand flew to her mouth. She shook her head, slowly at first and then faster. Tears brimmed and fell.

Josie felt like crying too, but she couldn't. She hadn't cried for months, not really. She clutched the sword tighter.

Tessa dropped down onto the edge of the hearth, burying her face in her hands.

"I wish I could go back, Tessa," Josie said. "I wish I could tell you the truth right from the start. I wish I had been honest with myself—"

"Honest about what?" Tessa cut in. "That you wanted to steal my boyfriend?"

Josie swallowed hard, fighting her answer again. "I didn't want to steal him, Tessa. I fell in love with him. And . . . he fell in love with me."

A flash of light blinded Josie.

Blinking against the radiance, Josie found Tessa on her feet again. Tessa's skin glowed white with reflected godly power, like the full moon on a clear night. Her eyes were black as a starless sky.

Death. Josie's heart leapt and clenched. Finally. But if Death held possession of Tessa for too long, then Tessa would die.

"About time," she said.

"Yes." Death's voice was smooth and dry as snake skin, whispering and seductive.

"I looked for you."

"I was, unfortunately, prevented from meeting you in the pathways."

"Prevented by the Other?"

"Oh no, the Other is quite distracted at the moment. Life too. She's rather put out by all of this destruction . . ." The thin smile on Tessa's face was sickening. "But I only have a few moments, I'm sure, before they attempt to intercede. I have been otherwise occupied myself, entertaining a certain . . . guest."

Josie's breath caught. "Judah."

"Yes, I'm keeping him close for you. We wouldn't want his soul to slip away, would we?"

"Away?"

"Else he'll be lost . . . for good."

"Lost? I thought mortal souls resided in your realm."

"They travel my pathways and through my realm. Once they pass through, they are gone. Think of me as a gatekeeper."

Gatekeeper?

More like a highwayman.

"Gone where?" she asked.

"Beyond."

"But your realm is in the Beyond."

"Multitudinous is the Beyond, and vast, but for it too, there is a Beyond."

Josie's head ached. Obtuse answers were usually the Other's forte, but they were wasting time. Her only concern was here and now, and Judah. And Tessa. She had to get answers and get Tessa back, before her sister was lost to the multitudinous Beyond—whatever that was.

"What do I have to do?" she asked.

The curdling smile spread. "You know."

Josie forced herself to breathe. She wanted to pretend like she didn't know, but she was still wearing the truth-charm. She did know. She's always known what Death would ask for, when the time came.

"I can't destroy the Covenant," she said.

"Do you want him back or not?"

"I don't know how."

"Don't you?" Death asked. "That's unfortunate, because you know I am prevented from divulging to you how the mask of the Tripartite might be destroyed." Death's eyes seemed to lower. "Oh dear, what happened to our friend there?"

Josie glanced down at the fog god mask. "I..." She understood then what Death was telling her. "The mask of the Tripartite has a flaw?"

"If it did, I certainly couldn't tell you so."

"It doesn't matter. Tessa would never give me the mask. And I won't kill her or anyone else to get it."

Death lifted Tessa's hand and showed Josie the ring. "Did you know that only the Triune's sanctuary charm is protected? All the others must be, by decree of the Covenant, accessible by any summoner. Only the blood of the Triune can access the sanctuary containing the Tripartite's mask. Only the blood of the Triune can remove the mask from said sanctuary."

Josie's throat was tight. "You mean I can take the ring and the mask? It will come to me?"

"I never said any such thing."

But he had, he just wasn't supposed to be saying it.

"And if I do, if I take the ring and the mask and destroy it, then you'll be free. And you'll kill us all."

"Name those you would have me spare. I shall not touch them until that time the Fates have allotted. The sisters do become rather annoying when I open the gate for a soul prematurely."

"I don't want you killing anyone."

"I am Death."

Josie dug her finger into her forehead, hating this. She couldn't believe she was actually discussing this, actually considering it, actually... but her lips were moving. "Leave my tribe alone. My dad, Simone, Beech, Gretchen, Caroline, everyone in my tribe. Don't touch any of them before their time."

"As you will it, Mask-Maker. I shall not touch those born to your tribe before the Fates have called them. Now set me free."

"What will you do?"

"When I am free?"

"It won't just be you. It will be all of the gods." Her hands started to shake, her palms sweat. "Without the Covenant, the gods will walk the earth."

"Yes. And they will thank you, my daughter, believe me."

Her breath was ragged and gasping. Her stomach was turning itself inside out. Was she really thinking about destroying the Covenant? She'd spent her entire life training to become the guardian of the Covenant. She'd been taught that it came before all things, even her life, even her family. Duty to the Covenant, duty to the Core.

"I don't think . . . I can't—"

"If you do not, your sister will die. Free me, end the Covenant, and save her life as well. Otherwise, I'm afraid she will be quite dead very soon."

Josie stabbed the sword into the floor. It slid through the rug and into the wood. She ripped it free again. The room seemed to tilt and distort around her.

She couldn't—she couldn't—but Tessa, and Judah . . .

"End the Covenant and you end that silly little woman's rampage," Death continued. "Her army will be rendered useless. Once they are free, the gods will not serve her or her summoners any longer. If you think about it," Death said softly, convincingly, "it is the only way. Save your sister, save the world, save the soul of the one you love. Frankly, I don't know why we're still talking—"

"You want me to think it's simple, but it's not. You're asking me to undo the basis of human civilization. Without the Covenant—"

"Human civilization? What civilization? While you dither, it is disappearing."

"How do I know the gods won't finish it off?"

"You don't," Death said. "Then again, humanity somehow managed to thrive prior to Lu-Ji's betrayal … gods like to be worshipped. That can hardly happen if there are no humans left to worship …"

Tessa grimaced and doubled over.

Josie dropped the sword and rushed to Tessa's side, gripping her shoulders. Tessa's body felt like it was made of tissue paper and toothpicks. "You're killing her."

"Her mortal body fails her. Quickly." Death grasped Josie's hand with Tessa's. "It has been you all along. Only you are capable. You see? You see?"

She slammed her eyes shut, gritting her teeth. She didn't see. She couldn't see—

Her eyes peeled open. "You swear you won't kill my sister, you'll return Judah, you won't hurt my tribe—"

Tessa's teeth were clenched, her face contorted in pain. "All those things, yes—"

Time froze. The black eyes of Death stared up at her. Her sister's frail body hung in her arms. The fate of the Covenant in her hands. Just like the Other had told her it would be. At the time, she hadn't believed the Other's prophecy, not really.

She hadn't understood how it could be possible. She hadn't seen.

But now she saw.

To save Judah, to save her sister, even to save Kai's soul . . . it was the only way.

All her life Josie had been taught to do what was best for the Core, to abide by the laws of the Covenant, to put her duty before herself—the right way. The way of the Triune.

But Josie was not the Triune. And she never would be.

She gripped Tessa's hand and pulled off the ring—the key to her sanctuary, the hidden place where she kept the mask of the Tripartite. The ring came off easily. Tessa's fingers were so thin, little more than bones.

Stealing the Triune's ring was a crime on par with murdering the Triune. Now Josie truly was an outlaw. The only way to save her own soul from Oblivion was to do what Death wanted: destroy the mask of the Tripartite, end the line of the Triune, unleash the gods into the world.

Tessa's eyes rolled back. She collapsed against Josie, seizing. Josie eased her to the floor as quickly as she could.

Josie ripped one of the sleep charms off her wrist and put the initiation stone to her lips.

"Theresa Day." She pushed the charm over Tessa's hand.

Tessa's convulsions slowed and, finally, stilled. Josie put her hand on her sister's chest. Lungs moving, heart beating.

Josie slumped against the hearth, Tessa's ring in her hand. The ring of the Triune. The fate of Covenant. The fate of the world, of humanity, of the gods, clutched in the sweaty fist of the outlaw Josie Day.

Time for doubt? Too late. Far too late.

Time to end the Covenant and save her sister? Time to bring Judah back?

Now.

CHAPTER 9

AUGUST 30TH

IRONICALLY, HER TRIUNE TRAINING kicked in.

Not the part that had been taught to protect the Covenant at all costs. Rather, the part that had been trained to step back from the heat of the moment and take in the big picture.

Summoners were out there, battling storms, pushing back floods, quelling fires, doing everything they could to stop Lily. They had to be called back, told to come out of possession. If they weren't, when Josie ended the Covenant, when their masks stopped channeling the powers of the gods, their mortal bodies would be stranded wherever they were—in the air, in water, in the fire.

The Triune's messaging system worked both ways. Any Core member could send Tessa a message merely by writing it on a piece of paper and committing it to an element—burning it or tossing it into a river. The Triune could send a message to every Core member in a similar manner.

Josie jammed the ring onto her finger.

She hefted Tessa up under her arms and heaved her onto one of the couches. She laid an afghan over her sister, smoothing back her limp blond hair and making sure that her arm bearing the sleep charm was hidden under the blanket.

Asleep, Tessa looked even worse, already like a corpse—waxen, emaciated, lifeless.

Josie found the remote for the blinds on a side table. With the press of a button, wooden slats slid down over the windows on either side of the fire place, darkening the room.

Removing the truth-charm, she found a pad of paper, printed with the resort's banner, Big Moose Lodge, and took her time copying Tessa's loopy handwriting: Take off your masks. Do not go into possession. Seek safe ground. Return to mortal plane immediately. Wait.

Terse and cryptic, but it would have to do.

Picking up the sword, she weighed it for a second. She'd never used a ring to access a summoner's stash—she'd never had a mask that required a sanctuary, but she knew the basics of it.

The ring connected to a sanctuary, an actual physical place somewhere in the world. She needed to focus on her intention, accessing the sanctuary, and the ring would do the rest. She hoped.

Closing her eyes, she concentrated on stashing the sword in Tessa's sanctuary and flicked her wrist a bit . . .

The sword flew from her hand and clattered on the floor.

She cringed, glancing at the door. Allison and Daisuke would be on the other side, waiting. Obviously, Daisuke had kept Allison from eavesdropping; otherwise, they would've busted in as soon as Death had taken over Tessa.

She picked up the sword and tried again. On her second attempt, the tip of the sword disappeared. She could feel it butting against another hard surface—metal? It hadn't occurred to her that Tessa's sanctuary might be too small to hold a sword. That would make things difficult.

Pulling the sword back, she flicked her wrist one more time. It felt strange to be reaching into a place that she couldn't see. Her knuckles brushed slick, cold metal as she positioned the sword, wedging it inside. There!

As she drew her hand back, her fingers grazed the smooth surface of something else... she didn't have to see it to know—the mask of the Tripartite.

She pulled her hand back, rubbing the spot where the mask had touched her palm.

She found a lighter on the fireplace mantle. She stood on the ledge of the hearth for a moment, thinking.

Once she lit the message, she would have to move quickly. The Eye—Caroline, Gretchen, and Nancy—would be close and expect answers.

Daisuke was the one she was most worried about. If he discovered what she'd done, he would kill her without a moment's hesitation.

She closed her eyes and cleared her mind. Her whole life she'd trained; now was the time to see if it had been successful.

She returned to Tessa. Lifting Tessa's hand, Josie placed the ring back on her sister's finger and the message in her limp palm. The lighter clicked a few times, sparking, before it caught. In a flash of flame and a puff of smoke, the paper disappeared. Quickly, Josie took the ring again, pushing it deep into her pocket. She returned the lighter to its place on the mantle. Then she went to the doors and waited.

Not too long. Not too soon.

She watched the clock mounted over the desk. A different bird call would sound every hour. But Josie wasn't going to wait another twenty minutes to hear the Carolina Wren's song.

At a minute, she closed her eyes, breathing deeply, slowing her pulse, composing her face.

At two minutes, she took the truth-charm out from her pocket and put it back on her wrist.

At two minutes and forty-five seconds, she opened the door.

Daisuke stood in the hall, facing her. Allison was behind him, artic-blue eyes narrowed. They both held pieces of paper, each an exact match to the one Josie had burned.

Daisuke stepped forward, but Josie closed the door softly behind her.

"Tessa's exhausted," she said, facing Daisuke. She took care not to show too much confidence, too much force. "You need to take me back to the cabin. Judah needs to go too."

Daisuke's dark eyes searched Josie's. "I do not take commands from you."

Josie stepped aside. Daisuke opened the door. He and Allison went inside. She watched the bottom of the stairs.

afraid that the Eye would charge up before Daisuke was positioned. The fact that they'd waited this long was probably because they expected Tessa to come to them and explain her mysterious message. They were well trained. But Gretchen was a wildcard; she'd get impatient. And Nancy sat too high on her horse. She'd never respected Tessa as the Triune.

"But, but..." Allison was stammering in a low, irritated voice as Daisuke herded her out into the hallway.

Daisuke closed the door again.

Allison scowled, holding up the paper. "What about this?"

They both looked at Josie. Josie struggled against the truth-charm's power. She couldn't lie. If they asked her a direct question, she would have to tell the truth. But she could feign a certain degree of ignorance. "You both look upset."

"The Triune instructed all summoners to stand down," Daisuke said, glancing back at the door, a suspicious tilt to his brow.

"Right in the middle of a war," Allison said through her teeth.

"You don't trust her?" Josie asked.

Allison sneered at her. "She told her army to take a break while the world is being wiped out, and then she takes a nap?"

"She didn't have a choice. She was on the verge of collapsing when all of this started. Will it kill you to let her sleep for a few minutes?"

Allison took a threatening step towards Josie. "All those questions wore her out, is that it?"

"Holding in check the powers of the Supreme Divine wore her out," Josie said, not backing down. "Mastering the will of the Other, holding Life by the throat and Death under her heel—in her place, you would've been dead months ago."

Before Allison could respond, Josie turned to Daisuke.

"Are you going to take me back to my cell?"

He gazed at her for a long moment. "Did you tell your sister the truth?"

Josie lifted her wrist, showing him the charm. "I had no choice."

He gave her a significant look. "About Judah?"

"Yes."

"All of it?"

"Not every detail. But yes, she knows."

"This message is strange," he said. "Did she tell you—?"

"Why would she tell me anything?" Josie interrupted. "Don't you have an idea of why she might send out a message like that?"

Daisuke frowned, searching her face, but she steeled it against him. She wouldn't let him suss out the truth like he had earlier with the Fire God and Judah. Not this time. Sorry, old friend.

Allison crossed her arms. "It makes no sense. Lily will have gotten this message too and all of her followers. Tessa's basically telling them to go ahead and finish us all off because we're not going to be fighting. I'm going to wake her up—" Allison started forward, but Daisuke caught her arm.

"I will wake her. Take Josie to the room with the others—"

Josie swore inwardly.

"Is that a good idea?" Allison hissed.

"Charms are in place. They cannot flee." He raised an eyebrow at her. "Not even the Triune could translocate out of the room."

"But—"

"Lock her inside. Go downstairs and inform the Eye that the Triune will be there shortly to explain the meaning of the message."

Allison looked like she wanted to argue, but Daisuke's expression was adamant.

Allison snagged Josie's arm and propelled her down the hall, away from the stairs. Daisuke opened the door and went back into the room.

Josie picked up her pace until she was almost towing Allison. She wouldn't have much time.

At the end of the hall was another set of double doors. Allison removed the charm, attached to a steel chain, from around the curved iron handles. She pushed Josie inside and slammed the door again.

Simone jumped up from the bed, pixie face tear stained and pale. "Josie, what happened?"

Josie scanned the master bedroom: king-sized bed, vaulted ceilings, attached bath. The Fire God stood by a set of French doors that led out to a balcony and overlooked the forest beyond. He glanced at her over his shoulder, looking bored.

"Where's Beech?" Josie asked.

"Gretchen took him downstairs," Simone said. "Are you okay? You look a little—"

"Do you have another sleep charm?" Josie asked, gesturing to the dozens of bracelets on Simone's twiggy arms.

"Sure," Simone said, pulling at one near the middle of her forearm. She started to take it off.

"No, leave it," Josie said. She took Simone's wrist and lifted her arm. "This one?" Josie asked, picking out the bracelet.

"Yeah, but—"

"Is this the initiation stone?" Josie asked, finding the largest bead on the band—a neon green one.

Simone frowned. "Yeah—"

Josie put her lips to it. "Simone Goodwin."

Simone's mouth fell open and then . . . her eyes slid shut. Josie eased her back onto the bed.

"That's interesting," the Fire God said, turning around fully.

"Stand guard at the door. If someone tries to come in, stop them, but don't kill them. And don't hurt them too much and don't interfere with what I'm about to do."

His brow slanted sharply. "Interfere? With what?"

She dug Tessa's ring out of her pocket and put it on her finger. She focused on the sword. Snapping her wrist, a smooth, breezy sensation passed over her skin, as if she'd stuck her hand out a window. Her fingers closed around the handle. She drew her arm back, the Sword of Eternity in hand.

The Fire God positioned himself in front of the doors, his back to them. He crossed his arms. Such a Judah pose.

"Now that is interesting," the Fire God said as she moved the sword to her other hand and flicked her wrist again.

A mask appeared, blinding her momentarily, filling the whole room with ethereal white light. She turned her face away until the light faded and died. What was left in her hand was a plain brownish mask, like sunbaked clay. It weighed next to nothing. Nearly featureless, it bore no marks or ornament.

The Fire God's eyes widened and pooled with fire. "Very interesting."

She pointed the sword at him. "Do not try to stop me."

"Stop you from what, is the question," he asked.

The mask of the Tripartite. Finally in her hands. She'd waited for it the day her mother had been murdered. She'd been so sure it would appear to her, but it never had.

She inspected it. The longer she looked at it, searching for its flaw, the more its unusual nature became apparent. It was, in fact, three masks in one. Trapped within the seemingly prosaic pitted clay, she glimpsed the white sheen of Life's mask, the black matte of Death's, and the gray mist of the Other's, like layered holograms.

Her stomach was knotting, her hands sweating. She had to act quickly, before Daisuke found the sleep charm and woke Tessa. Before Tessa realized that her ring was missing. But Josie was having trouble pinning down the flaw that would allow her to break the mask.

Her gaze caught first on the lips, which were sealed. But then it skipped up to the nose and then further up to the center of the forehead. Then down to the lips. The flaw seemed to be fleeing from her, which she guessed was possible. She was about to swear in frustration when she became aware of the Fire God's ongoing commentary.

"And who would have guessed it? The mask-maker, thief of the Three Faces—"

"That's it," she said, jolting with realization. The mask of the Tripartite was three masks in one, which meant . . .

Blue flames dripped from the Fire God's eyes like tears. "Oh, wonderful, you've had some sort of revelation. To think I waited all this time ... if only I'd waited a bit longer, I would have been truly free—"

Three masks. Three flaws.

She laid the mask down on the floor and stepped back, grasping the sword with both hands.

"The other gods will walk again, and I will be trapped in this mortal body until it expires—"

"Stop whining," she said, licking her lips.

Her heart went from jackhammering to still and silent, like it had stopped beating altogether. Her whole body, which had been thrumming with anxiety and near panic, quieted.

For Judah, and Tessa, and Kai ...

This was the only way. The right way.

The mask of the Tripartite lay on the floor, hollow eyes watching.

"I'm sorry, Mom," she murmured.

She stepped forward and plunged the sword down onto the sealed lips of the mask.

The sword slipped through the mask and into the wood silently.

The mask splintered and fell apart.

She blinked.

The mask lay there, whole, intact. At the same time, broken pieces—white—fell away and vanished.

The mask of Life—destroyed.

She pulled the sword out of the floor and brought it down again, across the bridge of the nose.

Again, it split apart. The jagged halves—black—toppled to the floor, but before they hit, they disappeared too.

The clay mask remained, seemingly untouched.

She lifted the sword. One more time.

Distantly, she thought she heard the Fire God speaking, the jingle of metal on metal as the chain was removed from the door handles, angered voices on the other side of the door . . .

The sword's tip tapped the center of the mask's forehead, the third eye.

With a sigh and a faint murmur, the mask broke and vanished. Gone.

The Age of the Triune was over.

The gods were free.

CHAPTER 10

AUGUST 30TH

THE FIRE GOD STAGGERED away from the doors and collapsed face-first in the middle of the room.

"Judah." She dropped to her knees next to him.

The doors opened. Tessa and the Eye, Daisuke and Allison, her dad and Beech crowded into the threshold.

Josie rose again. The Sword of Eternity dangled in her hand.

Everyone was staring, but not at her.

She turned.

Judah stood near the French doors.

Josie frowned and glanced back. Judah remained on the floor behind her.

She faced the other Judah again. His hair, eyes, T-shirt, and jeans were black. He was taller and paler than Judah too. Josie's grip tightened on the sword.

Not Judah.

Caroline stepped forward, brow knitted, looking from the golden Judah on the floor to the dark Judah by the doors. "Judah?"

"No," Josie said, lifting the sword slightly. "Death."

"Well done, my dearest daughter," Death said through lips that looked just like Judah's. He pressed his hands together at his chest and bowed. "Very well done."

Daisuke surged forward. He sprung over Judah on the floor and past Josie before she could stop him.

"Daisuke, no!" Tessa called.

"Leave this place, demon." Daisuke's hand twitched, but no mask appeared. He stared down at his hand, snapping his wrist again. Still, no mask.

Josie reached for him, to pull him back. "It's not a demon. Daisuke—"

"No, I'm not," Death said with a smile. "Allow me to clear it up for you, Daisuke-san."

He winked at Josie.

Daisuke's hands dropped to his sides. He swayed. Josie grabbed for his arm. Before she could catch him, Daisuke crashed to the floor.

Josie stared. His eyes stared back. Empty . . . lifeless.

"Daisuke!" Tessa screamed. She rushed forward and dropped to her knees beside him. She shook him, but he didn't move.

Josie whipped around, pointing the sword towards Death's throat. "We had an agreement!"

Death's dark brow rose, but he didn't flinch. "Yes. We did. I would take no one *born to your tribe* before their time." He glanced down at Daisuke and then at Tessa, who was clinging to Daisuke's shoulders. "He was unworthy of you," he said to her.

The French doors blew open, banging, the glass shattered. A whirlwind of frigid air gusted around them. Josie staggered back.

She regained her footing, glaring at him as the wind ripped water from her eyes. "Son of a bitch."

"Son of none," Death said, smile widening.

He opened his hands, stepped back, and disappeared. The wind died.

Tessa's sobs filled the room. Her face was pressed against Daisuke's motionless chest.

Josie spun away, eyes burning again.

She stabbed the sword into the mattress, sinking it all the way to the hilt. She bowed over it, trying to get in a full breath, but the air wouldn't come.

Nancy's sharp voice cut first through the silence. "My mask is gone."

"So is mine," Allison growled. "What the—?"

"Judah?" Caroline murmured. Josie turned back as Caroline knelt beside Judah, touching him tentatively.

Tessa was glaring at Josie through a waterfall of tears. "What did you do?"

Josie's gaze kept returning to Daisuke's slack face. A terrible knot twisted in her chest, growing bigger and more tangled with every heartbeat. Daisuke had been her oldest friend, the first boy she'd ever kissed. He'd been with her when her mother was murdered and had helped her escape back to Portland, and now he was lying on the floor, losing color, not breathing, dead. In her hasty negotiations with Death, she'd forgotten to mention him. Because of that, he was gone.

"What about Simone?" Gretchen asked, pointing to where Simone lay on the bed.

"Sleep charm," Josie murmured, barely aware that she was answering.

Tessa bowed over Daisuke again, sobs redoubling. Their dad went to Tessa and pulled her to him.

"I want answers," Nancy declared. "I want them now!"

"We all want them," Josie's dad said. His eyes locked onto Josie's. "Explain—"

From outside, shrieks and screams sounded, echoing through the French doors.

Beech hopped where he stood. "Sounds like trouble, Mama Bear."

"Big time trouble," Gretchen agreed. She held her hands open to Josie. "What am I looking at here, kiddo?"

More screams joined the first.

"It must be Lily—" Nancy said.

"No," Josie said, seizing the sword again and ripping it free. "It's not Lily."

Nancy stiffened. She pointed a rigid finger at Josie. Russell, who'd been lurking in the shadows behind her, turned and ran.

"You will drop that, now," Nancy said. "As the Future Eye . . ."

"You're not the Eye anymore," Josie said. "You're not even a summoner anymore. None of you are." She hefted the sword and started towards the door. "The masks are gone. The gods are free. The Tripartite and the Covenant have been dissolved."

Nancy backpedalled as Josie approached, bumping into Allison, who was gaping.

The screams issuing from outside multiplied. Screams of horror, screams of panic, screams of pain.

Screams of fear.

Josie swore again. What had she expected? A honeymoon? Lily's army may have been neutralized, but now the gods were back.

She charged forward. She had to go outside and deal with whatever god was out there. This was her fault.

"I always knew you were unstable," Nancy murmured, eyes darting between Josie and the sword. "You don't expect me to believe—"

Gretchen put a hand on Josie's shoulder, stopping her. She turned Josie towards her. "You ain't lying, are you, kiddo?"

Josie shook her head.

Gretchen blinked like she'd had sand thrown in her eyes. Her grip on Josie's shoulders tightened. "Why would you—?"

"Judah," Caroline said, "are you all right?"

Josie turned.

Judah rolled onto his side, groaning. Caroline placed a supportive hand on his back as he sat up.

Josie was trapped in her own personal time disruption. Everything stopped.

Caroline cupped his face.

He ran his hand through his hair. Brow—confused. "Mom?"

The knife that had been buried in Josie's chest for the last month shifted. His voice was warm and deep . . . Judah's voice.

Tears ran down Caroline's cheeks. She wrapped her arms around Judah and hugged him tight.

"It's you," she said in a strangled voice.

Had Caroline known the truth all along? Or least sensed it?

He hugged her back, eyes roving the room, confusion setting in deeper. His gaze snagged on Allison and Nancy. Then his head turned, and—

His eyes locked onto hers. "Josie?"

The knife slid free. Her eyes ached, fighting the tears that formed . . . and slipped down her cheeks.

She inhaled, finally. Breathed again, finally. Alive again, finally.

"Judah—"

The rising shouts and shrieks from outside made him wince and twist towards the broken French doors. His gaze seemed to settle on Tessa and . . . Daisuke. His frown deepened.

Gretchen grasped Josie's chin and forced Josie to look at her. "The things we do for love, huh, kiddo?"

Josie swiped the back of her hand across her cheeks. She stepped back from Gretchen. She glanced at Judah. He was pushing up to his feet. She could see his thoughts, written all over his brow.

WTF?

She almost fell apart then. But if there was a time for an emotional breakdown, she didn't know when that was. She'd never known.

"I invited the gods into the mortal realm." She lifted the sword and looked over at Judah. His expression was shifting from confusion to fury. So much for the honeymoon. "I'd better go welcome them."

And make sure they don't kill anyone.

Summoners were strewn across the sloping lawn. Most appeared to be unconscious rather than dead—thankfully. Others were running away, fleeing towards the cabins.

In the midst of the lawn was a ten-foot giant in a tree costume. At least that's what it looked like. Clothes of black bark, hair a cascade of blue-green needles. But as Josie raced towards it, it turned and showed a human face. A woman's face. Dark and beautiful, eyes of rich black earth. A goddess.

"Emancipator." Her voice was booming.

Josie staggered to a halt short of the goddess's shadow.

The goddess inclined her head at Josie. "What an honor."

Josie cringed. Her eardrums ached. "Want to bring it down a notch for me? Mortal ears here."

The goddess smiled. A brilliant, alluring smile. When she spoke again, her voice was softer, melodic, like bird song. "My pleasure. Whatever I can do for you, Emancipator. Simply name it."

"You can stop attacking these people," Josie said, gesturing around to the Core members strewn across the lawn like twigs after a storm. She caught sight of Gretchen and Beech jogging towards her . . . and Judah.

All traces of the Fire God were gone from his face—that cocky smirk, the ghost flames, the subtle dancing shadows that had played under his skin for the last month. Now, he looked like Judah again—annoyed and frustrated and concerned.

She wanted to throw down the sword and run to him, but she couldn't. Not only because she had a goddess to deal with. She didn't know how to throw herself into someone's arms, not even Judah's. It was such a human gesture. She'd never been very good at being human.

"Are these your people?" the goddess said, like a thief who had been caught stealing apples by a farmer. "I thought they were the ones responsible for razing my forest."

"Yes,"—she forced herself to look away from Judah and back at the goddess—"they are my people, and they haven't razed anything. They are Core. My tribe. They respect Mother Forest and all her children."

"Oh... my mistake." The goddess shrank and shrank again, until she was only slightly taller than Josie, though much better built. The bark of her clothes became softer and flowing, a clinging gown of deep brown silk. Her hair turned from blue-green needles to blue-green locks, falling to her waist. "Of course, I would be honored if your tribe dwelt within my bosom, Emancipator."

Her black eyes flicked over Josie's shoulder. Josie glanced back. Beech and Gretchen stood a few feet behind her. Judah approached more slowly. Behind him, Nancy and Allison had emerged from the Big House's door, but weren't moving any closer.

"Oh, yes," the Forest Goddess said, her gaze seeming to linger on Beech. She smiled at him. "Children of my own heart, I see." She lifted the hem of her skirt with one hand and moved closer. "You are more than welcome." Her voice was as warm as an embrace. "More than welcome."

Beech raised his eyebrow, grinning.

Josie set her teeth and held tight to her sword. "Thank you, Mother Forest. We do not mean you harm. If any of my people should cause you offense, you will bring them to me, of course, so that I may punish them in my own way."

The Forest Goddess continued to smile at Beech. She lifted her bare shoulder in an indifferent gesture. "Yes, of course."

Her gaze flicked from Beech to the sword. Her voice shifted from alluring to vaguely menacing. "The Sword of Eternity. God-slayer." She sneered. "You have no need of such an ugly weapon."

She held her hand up and a bow and quiver of arrows appeared. She held them out to Josie. "Please, take this instead." She lifted the long black bow. "I call her True, as is her aim." She lifted the black leather quiver. "And this is Decree. Any arrow pulled from her womb will strike its target only where it is just." She inclined her head again. "My gift to the daughter of Death."

Josie could feel Judah close behind her. She peeked back at him. Just for a second. If she looked much longer, she wouldn't be able to stop. And taking her eyes off the goddess seemed like a mistake.

"I'm not the daughter of Death," she said.

The Forest Goddess smiled an unsettling smile. "As you say. But you would not refuse my gift . . ."

The tone of her voice made it clear that if Josie did refuse, the goddess would be very unhappy. The dozen or so Core members around her were beginning to pick themselves up off the ground.

"Of course, I wouldn't," Josie said. "I am most grateful and deeply honored." The sword remained firm in her hand. The grip seemed to be glued to her palm. But the idea of approaching the goddess with the Sword of Eternity seemed a bad one, almost as bad as refusing her gift.

Josie was bone-weary. And Judah was so close; the skin on her back ached, as if it were full of iron filings and he was a magnet.

"You will be so gracious as to allow my..." Judah hovered in the periphery of her vision. What should she call him?

"Is he your consort?" The goddess eyed Judah warily. "He appears to be holding a fire god prisoner." She shifted back, frowning. "Fire has a seductive dance, but heed my word, Emancipator, once he has ravaged you, you will never be the same again. This I know, too well." The distant trees seemed to moan and whisper in agreement.

Josie regained her composure. "Then you'll understand why I don't put down my sword."

The goddess arched her brow. "Indeed."

The goddess was still holding the bow and quiver. Josie didn't want to insult her by making her hold it much longer or by sending a mortal who was holding a fire god within him too close.

"This is Beech," Josie said. "A member of my tribe." She lifted her eyebrow at Beech who was running the chain of his necklace between his lips rapidly. "Please allow him to accept your most generous gift on my behalf."

The goddess's gaze shifted from Judah to Beech. The hard wariness in their black depths was replaced by a warm gleam.

Beech's cheeks flushed.

Josie narrowed her eyes at him. Gretchen bumped him with her shoulder.

"Oh, yeah, sure," he said, stumbling forward. "Whatever you want," he said to Josie as he passed her.

The goddess smiled at Beech as he took the bow and quiver from her hands. The tips of his ears reddened as he backed away, tripping and almost falling.

The goddess's smile broadened and the entire forest seemed to lighten. The birds began to chirp and twitter, the chill left the air, even the sky seemed bluer.

The goddess flourished her hands. "I think I shall be quite content to sustain your tribe. It has been too long since I have fostered mortals. I think I will keep you—"

A chilled voice interrupted, "Are you still talking?"

CHAPTER 11

AUGUST 30TH

A FIGURE OF WATER APPEARED next to the Forest Goddess.

Beech stumbled back from the goddess. He gave Josie a sheepish look, still grinning. Gretchen seized his shoulder and yanked him to her side.

"Oh, you're awake, how nice," the goddess said to the water god with a roll of her eyes.

"I was woken by this—" The Lake God was broad, the color of steel, but translucent, like a mold of a man filled with water. His belly bulged and from it burst a figure clad in black, who sprawled on the ground.

Kai sputtered, spewing water. He gasped.

The Lake God transformed into a lean, gaunt man with steel blue eyes and pale gray skin. "When he appeared he brought some foreign salt water god with him. I still have the foul taste of it in my mouth."

"Must you complain about everything?" the Forest Goddess said with a huff. "Why don't you go back to sleep? Can't you see I'm in conference with the daughter of Death."

"I'm not the—"

"Death?" the Lake God said, looking around. "Is he here? He owes me the blood of an ox—"

"Oh, here we go again," the Forest Goddess said, shaking her head. "Death owes me the blood of an ox and the hide of a buffalo and the tears of a crow—"

"He does," the Lake God said.

"We've just returned to the mortal realm. Don't you know how to show proper gratitude?" The Forest Goddess gestured to Josie.

The Lake God's cool eyes slid up and down Josie. In his hand a silvery bundle appeared. He tossed it at her. She caught it.

"Thanks a lot," he said dully. "You look more like the bastard of Life to me."

"I'm not—"

The Lake God turned to the Forest Goddess, ignoring Josie. "Let's talk about all the beavers—"

"Ugh, not the beavers again!" The goddess turned and stalked away towards the trees, skirts in hand.

The Lake God followed at her heels. "You favor them too much. They clog up every corner—"

"Me? What about you? Don't think I didn't notice that flood last summer. You swallowed up my favorite mushroom grounds."

"That's not my fault," the Lake God continued as they strode into the trees. "If a storm comes—"

"Oh, yes, just another passing storm, dear. She meant nothing, really. How many times have I heard—?"

The gods disappeared between the trees.

Kai pushed up to his knees, dripping wet, chest heaving. "Hey," he said to Josie.

Josie lifted her eyebrow at him and then looked down at the bundle the Lake God had given her. Silvery and light, the material was cool to the touch, patterned like fish scales, but hard as metal. She let it uncoil and dangle from her hand. Two belts joined together and a scabbard.

"What should I do with this?" Beech asked, holding out the bow and quiver.

Josie turned toward him. "Keep it."

"Sweet." Beech grinned, slinging the quiver over his head.

"You!" Nancy strode down the hill. A number of other summoners were clustering behind her and following, including Allison.

For a moment, Josie thought she was the one Nancy's eyes were fixed on, but then she realized that it was, in fact, Kai.

"Take him," Nancy said to a couple of the closer summoners, who weren't actually summoners anymore and had only begun to pick themselves up off the ground after being tossed around by the Forest Goddess. "He's Lily's son and a traitor."

Four of the Core members rushed at Kai, grabbed him, and pulled him to his feet.

"You don't have to do that," Josie said. "He's not a threat anymore. Lily's not a threat any—"

"I wouldn't say that," Kai said.

"Inside," Nancy said, pointing towards the Big House. "He'll be interrogated."

"What do you mean?" Josie said to Kai as he was dragged past her.

"Funny story," Kai called over his shoulder. "She was ready, Josie. She knew—"

One of the women hauling him away punched him in the gut. "Shut up, traitor."

"What do you mean—?" Josie started after them, but stopped short when she came face-to-face with Nancy.

"And you." Nancy's gray eyes were sharp as the edges of a shattered mirror. "I am arresting you."

"Arresting me?" Josie repeated.

Around them, the crowd grew as people emerged from the cabins where they'd hidden during the Forest Goddess's rampage. Dozens circled around. The more eyes on them, the straighter Nancy's back and the thinner her mouth became, until she was as stiff as a steel girder and just as lipless.

Josie was taken back to that day when she'd first arrived in Portland. Nancy had stood at the door of the sanctum, the same disapproving gleam in her eyes.

"For crimes against the Core, the Triune, and the gods," Nancy declared.

Josie sagged, letting the point of the sword fall to the grass. "Oh. That."

"Yes. That." Nancy gave the words poisonous barbs.

Josie wanted to look at Judah. She wanted it so badly her eyes watered.

"You can hardly arrest me for something that doesn't exist anymore," Josie said.

Before Nancy could respond, the crowd began to close in.

"Where are our masks?" a horse-faced woman asked.

"Wonderful question," Nancy said, glaring at Josie.

"Those were gods. In the mortal plane?" a red-cheeked man with a mop of frizzy brown curls asked.

"It's not possible," a tiny woman with fierce eyes replied.

"It is possible," a dreadlocked woman said, grimacing as her fingers poked lightly at a growing knot on her forehead. "That wasn't Vanna White who chucked me fifty feet."

"It was a goddess," someone else said, a high pitch of fear in his voice. "The gods have returned."

People began to mutter and scowl.

"Okay!" Gretchen held up her hands. "Everyone, please, chill. Give us a chance, huh? And back off a bit." She waved her hands, like she was dispersing a flock of geese.

A strangled scream echoed from somewhere... people stopped, they cowered, they yelped.

Another scream, from behind the cabins near the forest's edge, and a low growling sound that made Josie's blood curdle.

"*Kuso*," Josie muttered. She started forward, the crowd parted for her, in spite of Nancy's commands for them to stop her. The sword probably had something to do with it.

She dashed up the lawn and into the shadows behind Sunset Cabin. She could hear others following, but didn't turn to see who.

She rounded the corner of the cabin and staggered to a halt.

Gold eyes the size of dinner plates gazed at her from the shadows.

A god in the form of a wolf. Silver fur. Tall as Josie. All sleek prowling muscle. *The* Wolf. She knew without knowing how she knew.

And Russell.

He hung limply from the Wolf's massive jaws. Its fangs were buried deep in his torso. Blood dripped from . . . everywhere, pooling in the grass.

Josie put her arm to her mouth, sucking back the desire to vomit.

Russell's satiny black eyes were open and alive. A sickening gurgle issued from between his lips, blood running out of his mouth and running and running . . .

"Fuck," Beech breathed from behind her.

Judah grasped Josie's shoulders, urging her back, but she couldn't move. She had done this. She had unleashed the gods back into the world. She had traded Judah and Tessa's lives for Daisuke's and now . . .

She lifted the sword. The warm gold sunlight slipping over the roof's peak reflected on the blade's length, turning to quicksilver.

In the Wolf's amber eyes the sword's reflection was a wavering sliver of light.

"Get them back," Josie said in a low voice to Gretchen, who she could see from the corner of her eye. "Don't let anyone else come any closer."

Too late.

She heard more gasps. A scream.

"Oh my gods, Russell," Allison's voice was strangled. "Oh my gods—"

The Wolf growled. The sound shook Josie like a tremor. More blood gushed from Russell's mouth. His eyes rolled.

"Gretchen," Josie hissed.

"Get back!" Gretchen hollered. "Go back to the Big House, all of you. Sandra, Emily, Jonas, let's get those godsdamned protection circles back up and working again. Today!"

"Beech," Josie murmured. "Do you know how to use that bow?"

"Oh man, Josie-slice," he said, voice trembling. "What the fuck?"

"You're going to kill it?" Allison asked. "You can't—"

"Allison, come back here." Nancy's voice was taut. "Now."

Josie started to step forward, but Judah's hand clamped down on her shoulder, preventing her. She dropped the scabbard to the ground. Without looking back, her hand touched his. She squeezed it until he released her.

She inched closer, eyes leaving the Wolf only long enough to see that Gretchen had succeeded in clearing off the stragglers. Judah and Beech remained, along with Nancy and Allison who stood farther behind, Nancy holding Allison's arm like she feared Allison might try to run at the god.

Beech nocked an arrow and drew back the string, aiming at the Wolf.

The Wolf God growled again. Russell's limbs began to twitch and jerk. The air was saturated with the metallic tang of blood.

"Drop him," Josie said, trying to restrain the trembling of her voice.

She didn't want to fight a god. Not this god. Not any god. Not really. But she would if left with no other choice.

The Wolf sank onto its haunches, its ears folding back against its head, upper lip curling.

Every muscle in Josie's body strained, taut and electrified. She wasn't a warrior. If the Wolf pounced, she had little hope of surviving. Her mother had taught her to deal with the gods through force of will, not force of fist. But that was before Josie had freed them.

When you are Triune, you wear many masks, Josie, she heard her mother's husky voice whispering from some distant place in her mind, *but fear can never be one of them.*

The Wolf growled again. It took a moment for her to pick out the word it had spoken from within the menacing guttural noise. "Coward."

She frowned. Name-calling? Did the god think that was going to provoke her?

But the Wolf continued, "A gift. Blood of the coward."

Then she realized. The god wasn't calling her a coward.

Russell's spasms were slowing. His fingers continued to flex, rivulets of red draining between them.

Was the Wolf presenting Russell as a gift? Like the Forest Goddess's bow or the Lake God's scabbard? Josie's stomach heaved.

Why would the Wolf think that Russell was a coward, and why would the god think that Josie would want him dead?

"Leave him," Josie said.

Russell's fingers stopped moving. His drooping head was turned away from her. A small favor. If she had to stand there staring into his lifeless eyes, she might forget how to be brave.

The Wolf growled at Josie. Its eyes left her.

Josie glanced over at Judah. He was watching her from the corner of his eyes. Brow read: *Now what?*

Good question. Russell hung motionless in the Wolf's mouth. As soon as she'd seen all the blood she'd known that Russell wouldn't survive. Time for guilt was later. She had to figure out what to do with the Wolf.

"Must remove the mark," the Wolf said. "The Profane Mother uses it to seed her demons. To build her army. To begin the war. To end the Core. Must repay the lonely one. Must repay Death."

"Repay Death?" she asked.

The gold chargers of the Wolf's eyes rolled back to her. "For bringing forth the one who bound us, the blood of his daughter. For bringing forth the one who freed us, the blood of his daughter. Your blood, demigod."

Russell jerked upright suddenly—alive, somehow—screaming and clawing at the Wolf's snout. The Wolf snarled and shook Russell back and forth violently. Bones crunched and snapped. Blood flew through the air, splattering across Josie's face and chest.

"Dear gods," Nancy cried.

Josie heard a deep twang as Beech let his arrow fly.

Kuso.

Allison screamed.

The arrow planted into the Wolf's right eye. He dropped Russell's body, threw back his head, and roar-howled—a half-god, half-animal sound that jarred Josie to action. She met Judah's gaze for a split second. Warning him.

Furious brow. Wanting to argue with her brow. About to tell her not to . . .

Too late. She rushed at the Wolf, to its right, hoping to be able to get in close enough, fast enough, without being noticed.

Its head whipped around towards her, snapping. She leapt back. Blood and saliva spattered her as the Wolf's fangs clacked deafeningly together, missing her. She tripped over Russell's body, slipping on the slick of his blood. She scrambled to her feet again. In the Wolf's remaining eye, she saw her own pale reflection.

Another arrow twanged as it flew. The Wolf jerked as the arrow struck, lodging deep into the Wolf's side.

She lifted the sword and charged at the Wolf again, leaping over Russell's body. The Wolf's eye flashed. The white curves of fangs, long as her forearms, stained crimson, lunged to meet her.

"Judah!" Beech shouted.

Judah slammed into the Wolf, tackling the god's neck. The Wolf was knocked off target, missing Josie again. Josie gasped as the sword, which she'd been thrusting towards the Wolf's throat, swung a hair's breadth from Judah's side. He and the Wolf crashed to the ground.

Josie drew the sword back as Judah was thrown by his own momentum, head over heels, onto his back. The Wolf snarled and snapped wildly at the air where Judah had been moments before.

Josie swept in before the Wolf could right himself. She plunged the sword into the Wolf's chest, surprised and unnerved by how easily it slid through the god's mortal form.

The Wolf stiffened and then went limp. He didn't make a sound.

Josie slid the sword free. It suddenly felt very heavy, though there was no blood, no trace of the wound it had inflicted.

Judah picked himself up, glaring at Josie with such fury that she had to look away. This wasn't exactly the reunion she'd been hoping for.

Beech touched her shoulder.

"Jos . . . gods. What did you do?"

"Allison!" Nancy shouted.

Allison raced up to the scene. Her Siberian princess face was the cold color of melting ice, her lips red as the blood pooled on the ground. She stood between Russell's body and the Wolf, clawing at her cheeks, shaking her head, sobbing.

Josie turned away. She'd known that Allison had had feelings for Russell, but she hadn't realized that she still had them or that they'd been like this.

Gretchen and Roxy appeared behind Nancy, then Josie's dad and Caroline and Tessa.

Josie strode over to the scabbard she'd dropped on the ground and picked it up, slipping the sword into the fitted silvery case. She slung the belt over her shoulder.

Gretchen approached her, leaving the others gaping behind her. "Josie, is that—?" She pointed towards the fallen god. Allison had dropped to her knees, rocking back and forth with her face buried in her hands.

"Yes," Josie said, eyes skimming over the wounds on Gretchen's chest. The wounds left by the Wolf and his summoner. "The Wolf."

Roxy, cat-eyed and full-lipped, slipped up beside Gretchen. "You killed a god?"

Josie fastened the lower belt around her waist, cinching it tight and adjusted the one that crossed over her chest. Blood dried on her shirt, sticking to her skin, tacky on her face. Her stomach heaved, but she sealed her lips and forced her breath through her nostrils until the queasiness passed.

She had killed a god.

"Allison," Beech said gently, kneeling beside her.

Judah remained on the other side of the Wolf, staring down at the dead god. When she looked at him, his eyes lifted, like he could sense her gaze.

For Judah, she would do it—all of it—again.

Only one question was nagging at her.

Why had the Wolf called her a demigod?

CHAPTER 12

AUGUST 30TH

"YOU WERE DEAD?" Caroline asked Judah.

Judah stopped pacing and looked down at his mom, who was seated next to Josie's dad.

"I guess," he said after a moment.

"What was that like?" Kai asked from the opposite side of the room, where he was tied to a chair.

Allison smacked his face. "Shut up, traitor, or you'll find out."

"Don't touch him," Josie said.

She stood in front of the hearth where Tessa had earlier stood. They'd reopened the blinds and turned on the lights, yet the room seemed darker than it had before.

Allison bared her teeth at Josie, the same way the Wolf had.

"I don't know why you're not tied up with him," Nancy said. She stood guard on the other side of Kai, like he might escape from the thirty feet of horse rope cinched around him.

"I don't know why you're here at all," Josie said to Nancy.

"She's here," Caroline said, taking a measured breath, "because we need to maintain some sense of stability." She gave Josie an unusually cold look.

Josie guessed she deserved it. After all, she'd just spent the last half hour recounting the events that had led up to this moment—the moment in which she'd shattered the mask of the Tripartite and changed the world for all of them. It would've taken her much less time if they hadn't been constantly interrupting. She knew they needed answers, but she had some questions of her own that felt far more pressing than clarifying the backstory.

Judah prowled around like a caged lion, not looking at her. His brow furrowed deeper and deeper as she explained her decision to deal with Death and to destroy the Covenant— saving Judah, saving Tessa, stopping Lily. He didn't look happy. No one looked happy or entirely convinced that what she'd done was right. Tessa glared at the floor the whole time. Their dad looked at Josie as if he didn't know who she was.

Not even Simone, curled up on the loveseat next to Gretchen, offered any support. She kept fiddling with her bracelets, not meeting Josie's eye.

Gretchen ran her ring-studded fingers through her hair. All of their rings were now, effectively, useless. The charm would still allow them to access their stashes, but the masks that had been in stored in them were gone.

"You should've told us the truth—" she started.

"Damn straight." Dad's eyes sharpened with sudden fury. "What were you thinking keeping this from us? From me? From your sister? What part of your brain told you it was okay for you to make a decision of this magnitude on your own?"

Josie turned her gaze away. The bird clock above the desk was about to strike Red-winged Blackbird. Nine. Only two hours had passed since they'd last been in this room and Tessa had stood where Josie did now. Daisuke and Allison behind her. But Daisuke was dead. And no one was standing behind Josie. Not even Judah.

He'd reached the far side of the room, near the door, and had stopped his restless pacing. Turning his back to the wall, he crossed his arms over his chest, face in shadow, his eyes sharp and glittering. Sapphires. Since his soul had been returned, she hadn't seen the faintest flicker of flame, even though she knew the Fire God was trapped inside Judah's body somewhere.

Unlike the other gods, the Fire God couldn't walk free again until Judah died.

She needed to give Judah the quartz pendant to assure his complete control over the god. But for the time being, he didn't seem to need it.

She shouldn't have been surprised he was silent. Typical Judah. If he thought she deserved to be grilled or reprimanded, he wouldn't intercede. Forget that it was his soul she'd been saving.

She didn't care if no one else thought that what she'd done had been right. There had been no right way, as far she could see. But that Judah was keeping his distance ... That hurt, more than her father's anger or Gretchen's disappointment or Simone's silence—far more.

"I should've known," Tessa spat. Her eyes were bloodshot, her face strained. "I should've known when I started having the visions of Death walking the earth in Judah's form. I told you about them, and you didn't say anything!"

Tessa punched the couch as she sprung to her feet. "Just like you didn't say anything about traveling the pathways or meeting Death or the Fire God becoming manifest or about your relationship with Judah! My boyfriend!" Her hands balled at her sides. "You know what I think? I think you were jealous."

Josie took a deep breath. A part of her wanted to jump up and scream at Tessa the same way Tessa was screaming at her, but she couldn't let things get any more off track.

One more deep breath.

"You were dying, Tessa," she said as calmly as she could. "I wasn't going to let that happen. You think... what? I saved your life out of jealousy?"

Tessa crossed her arms. "I wasn't dying."

"That's not what Death said."

"He tricked you."

"And Daisuke? Was he tricking me too?"

"Don't talk about him!" Tessa's tears started flowing again. "It's your fault he's dead!"

Tears pressed against Josie's eyes, but she held them back. "You're right. It is."

"I don't suppose you're going to make a deal with Death to bring him back too," Tessa said.

"I don't think Death is interested in making any more deals with me," Josie said. "He got what he wanted. Besides, Daisuke made it pretty clear what he thought about bringing back the souls of the dead."

Tessa frowned. "He knew? I don't believe that—he would never keep something like that from—"

"He figured it out a couple days ago. He didn't know exactly what I was going to do, because I didn't know myself until this morning. But he told me that if I didn't tell you the truth, he would. You're right. He would never have kept anything from you."

Tessa glared at her. "I hate you. I hate you so much."

"At the peril of being smacked again," Kai said, "is anyone interested in why I risked my neck to come back here?"

"Because you don't have any place else to go?" Allison sneered. "And you knew Josie was going to destroy the Tripartite and leave us all powerless which would prevent us from tearing you up into tiny little Emo shreds."

Kai sneered. "Emo?"

Allison raised her hand again to hit him.

"I wouldn't do that," Josie said.

Allison's lip curled. Her clothes were caked in blood, like Josie's. They hadn't been given a chance to change before they'd been herded upstairs, away from the gathering crowd of Core members, all of whom wanted answers. Nancy had assured them that they would get the answers. But she didn't look particularly satisfied now that she had received them.

"Why did you come back, Kai?" Gretchen asked.

"Did you find Lily?" Josie asked.

"I wish," Kai said, speaking almost solely to Josie, though he glanced over at Simone every other second. "But I did find a certain god of granite." He waggled the fingers of his left hand, which the Granite God had broken when Kai had been pretending to be Lily's prisoner. Josie was choosing to forget about Kai's duplicity for the moment. He seemed to be the only one in the room on her side. "Did you know water beats rock? I was thinking about adding it to the game: water, rock, paper—"

"Get on with it," Nancy said.

"Seems like Mom knew what was about to go down. Old Rock Face told me she'd warned them the gods were going to be freed. She had it all set up. When she got her mask back last month, one of the first things she did was make everyone take the goddess's mark. Apparently, she took it herself first."

"So instead of forcing the goddess to serve her, she's been serving the goddess—"

"It was always that way," he said. "You think she came up with this crazy-ass plan all on her own?"

"No," Nancy said, "she had your help with that."

"Well ... yeah, a little bit, but only in the details. The master plan was all the goddess and that started way before I came around."

"What does a goddess need with a bunch of human slaves?" Josie asked.

Kai lifted his shoulder "Snack food? You know the only reason the goddess is half as powerful as she is, is because my mom's been feeding her lots of juicy humans every chance she got."

"And I don't suppose you had anything to do with that either," Nancy said.

"Hey, lady, I don't even eat meat."

Simone was crying again, silently. Josie could only imagine how painful it was for her to know her boyfriend was the traitor who'd been terrorizing them.

"So the only thing that's really changed," Caroline said, "is now we're powerless. The goddess is still going to try to destroy us, she still has an army; only now, there's nothing we can do to stop her."

"Not true." Josie rose to her feet though every muscle in her body begged her to stay sitting, or better yet, lie down and go to sleep—something she hadn't done since the Fire God had taken her to the hotel in Hokkaido. "I happen to have the only weapon ever forged that can kill a goddess. A gift from our traitorous friend over there."

"You're welcome," Kai said without enthusiasm. He still seemed to be trying to catch Simone's eye, but she was plucking at her bracelets, sniffling. "But as I was saying, there's something else—"

Nancy sneered at Josie. "Does your megalomania know no bounds? I knew you were dangerous, but this—" Her eyes narrowed at Josie. "From the first moment you returned to our tribe, you displayed an alarming degree of disrespect for both your elders and the Eye. You flouted the rules at every turn and continued to act as though you were the Triune, which you were not. I warned you, Caroline, and you, Gretchen. That girl is unstable, I told you. She cannot to be trusted. She has no respect for the laws, but even I could not have imagined the depths of your mental instability. You don't think yourself the

Triune; you think yourself above the Triune. You think yourself a god! It's just—just—insanity! I can't believe we're even standing here listening to you."

A god. Josie turned to her father. The moment Nancy took a breath, Josie asked him, "Am I?"

Her dad looked up at her startled. "Are you what?"

"The Wolf called me a demigod."

"This is absurd," Nancy said. "I don't believe what I'm hearing—she actually believes it."

"All heirs of Lu-Ji carry the blood of the gods," her dad said. "That is what makes them heirs to the Triune."

"A myth—" Nancy said.

"It's not a myth," Josie said. "Ask Death. He's still pretty bitter about his daughter stealing his gauntlet and making him a slave to humanity."

"Thousands of years ago," Nancy persisted. "Any blood you might share with the first Triune would be so diluted—"

"There might be more to it than that," Dad said, rubbing his hands together like he was trying to warm them.

Nancy's mouth hung open like a fish.

Dad let out a breath and ran his hands over his sweat-dappled scalp. The welt on his face looked even worse, blacker and more swollen. In all the confusion, Josie hadn't even asked him what had happened.

"I don't know how much I can tell you," he said, finally looking at Josie, "because I don't recall the exact events, but . . ." He pursed his lips for a moment. "It is possible that you are a demigod."

CHAPTER 13

AUGUST 30TH

CAROLINE'S HAND TOUCHED HIS LEG. "What do you mean, possible? How is that possible?"

"It's not possible," Nancy said. "The demigods died out after the gods ceased to walk the mortal plane. Everyone knows that."

"Well..." he said. "Melinda and I weren't exactly on the mortal plane the night that Josie was conceived."

"Not exactly?" Gretchen asked.

"Melinda was struggling with Death," he said. "She always had. He never let up on her. She was exhausted all the time." He rubbed the bridge of his nose. "She invoked the Fates."

"She never told me that," Josie said.

Her dad looked up at her, grim. "Of course not. In hindsight, I never should've let her ... I should've tried harder to stop her, but she was desperate. She was afraid that Death would seize control of her and that ..."—he glanced over at

Tessa and then quickly away—"eventually, his power would overwhelm and kill her." He fixed his gaze on Josie again. "I don't know exactly what the Fates told her or what price they exacted from her, but I do know that when she came back, she was different."

"Different how?" Tessa asked softly.

He bowed his head again. "It's only something you would've noticed if you'd known her well and . . . no one knew Melinda well. She was so guarded. There were times when I felt like I didn't know her at all, and I knew her better than anyone." Emotion swelled in his voice. "You remind me so much of her, Josie. I never thought that you might be the way you are because . . ."

Caroline gripped his arm supportively.

Her dad cleared his throat and looked at Josie again. "There was a ritual. All I knew and all I know was the Fates told her it was the only way she'd survive another year. At the time, that's all I cared about."

"What kind of ritual?" Josie asked.

"The kind that required the both of us to traverse the pathways . . . into the outer realms of the Beyond."

Silence. The clock struck nine. Red-winged Blackbird. *Chee-a-whee. Chee-a-whee.*

"Well," Nancy said, "have we all lost our minds?"

"Traversing into the Beyond isn't possible," Caroline said gently. "Not for a mortal."

"That's what I thought too," he said. "And it's probably why I don't recall much of what happened, because at the time, I was in possession of Life."

"But Life is part of the Tripartite," Caroline said. "How could you—"

"I don't know," he said strongly. "I don't know how we traversed into the Beyond and survived. I don't know how Life was able to take possession of me. I'm not even sure that Melinda understood. But if it gave us more time . . ."

He gave Josie a lingering look. "Melinda told me that in the Outer Realms it was possible for her to take singular possession of Death. The reason I was there was to keep her in check. A counterweight. Life to her Death. The purpose was to allow her to gain some understanding, to get some purchase on that cold bastard. Tête-à-tête And it seemed to work. When we returned, she was clearer, focused, in control. She never complained about Death again. And . . . a couple of months later, we learned she was pregnant. She told me it happened while we were in the Beyond and I believed her, but I can't truthfully say that I remember it. And I can't say what it means that you were conceived in the godly realm, while your mother and I were . . . as much god as we were human. Does that make you . . . somehow, as much a child of Death and Life as of Melinda and I? Not in my book. You were always mine, Josie. That was never a question."

"No, the question is whether or not being conceived in that way makes her as much a god as a human," Gretchen said.

"That's why you can travel in the pathways of the gods," Kai said, arching his eyebrow at her, "because you are one."

"I'm not a god."

"Goddess," he corrected. "Sorry."

"Not funny."

"No, it was funny. Goddesses just have terrible senses of humor. Trust me."

Josie stared hard at the floor. Why hadn't her mom told her this? Why hadn't Death? But she wasn't sure she believed that the location of her conception made her anything. A demigod was a mortal with a few god-like powers, born to a mortal parent and an immortal one. In all her studies, she had never come across demigods created by two mortals in possession of gods. Of course, she'd never heard of mortals travelling into the Beyond and living to tell about it—no mortals but the demigods anyway. And she'd never known it was possible for Life to take possession of anyone outside of the Triune, at least not in the mortal realm.

She looked up and found Judah's eyes waiting for hers. Now that he was back, she missed him more than ever.

"What does the Fire God say?" she asked him.

His eyes darkened, like it was hurtful for her to ask, but she had to know. His gaze fell as if he were listening to a conversation in another room. Then his eyes tracked back up to hers, reluctantly. He didn't have to say anything. She knew what he was thinking.

"Great," she muttered.

Instead of anger, everyone seemed to be looking at her with some mix of awe and fear. Even Nancy and Allison, though they still displayed a healthy dose of incredulity, didn't seem as willing to voice it.

She guessed they weren't so keen to piss off a demigod.

"Is now the time to mention the demon army?" Kai asked. "Yes? No?"

"Demon army?" Gretchen repeated.

"Oh, yeah," Kai said. "See, if you round up a whole bunch of idiots willing to make themselves slaves to a psychotic goddess bent on destroying humanity, and she decides not to fill her belly with their blood, but instead trade their souls to a bunch of demons so they can take possession of the aforementioned idiots then, well . . . I don't know if you've ever read about what demons do when they have possession of a human body, but it's not baking cookies for the neighborhood daycare."

"I suppose this is one of those details you helped your mother with when you were plotting the end of the world?" Nancy asked.

"Actually, it was one of the details that the Granite God told me about after he admitted he was on the run. He'd been involved with my mother—in ways I prefer not to think about—and she confided in him the real plan. Mark up the followers, give them to the goddess, who, once she was free, would give them to the demons. Then let the demons do the dirty work."

"Give them to demons?" Allison said. "Can she do that?"

"Of all the things I've heard in the last hour, it's one of the least unbelievable," Nancy said.

Allison turned as gray as a corpse in a snow drift.

Someone knocked on the door.

Judah opened it.

Roxy came in holding a sheaf of paper that looked like it had been hastily torn out of a spiral notebook. Beech followed close behind. They both looked dead on their feet, their clothes splattered with blood.

"What's up?" Gretchen asked, standing.

Roxy sighed. "We moved Russell's body. We're getting him . . . cleaned up. We're sending a message to his parents at Outpost Three now. Some wolves, real ones I think, showed up and dragged the god away. Scared the—" Roxy shook the heavy fringe of her bangs off her eyebrows. "Anyway, you wouldn't believe the reports we're getting." She held the papers out towards Gretchen.

"Nothing about demon hordes? I hope," Kai said.

"Good gods," Roxy said, clutching her throat. "Please tell me you're joking."

"If only," Gretchen said, taking the papers from Roxy and kissing her briefly. Gretchen scanned the top page and sighed.

"Well?" Caroline asked.

Gretchen and Roxy exchanged a look.

"What's better?" Gretchen asked finally. "Mass destruction caused by a group of summoners in possession of ancient gods under the control of one truly crazy B, or mass destruction caused by thousands of recently freed gods under the control of no one but themselves?"

"I vote C, none of the above?" Beech offered, bouncing on his toes. "I missed some stuff again, didn't I?"

Gretchen continued to flip through the pages. She stopped and held one out for Roxy to see. "What's this?"

"Oh, that . . . accounting of who was on the island," Roxy said with a sad look. "Everyone seemed to have received the Triune's message—"

"I didn't send that message," Tessa said, shooting Josie a scathing glare.

"Oh," Roxy said. "Well, almost everyone left the island before they lost their masks—"

"What do you mean, almost?" Caroline asked.

"One person unaccounted for," Roxy said.

"Who?"

"Ty." Roxy reported, a tear sheen in her cat eyes. "I don't know how he got left behind, but it seems like he did—"

Kai rolled his eyes. "He was probably asleep on the toilet. Kid can fall asleep anywhere."

"So Ty's stuck there," Simone finally spoke up, worry-faced. "I mean, without the Triune and no summoners, no one can translocate back and Ty's—"

"Maybe we can find a god to do it?" Beech suggested. "How about the Forest Goddess?"

"At what cost?" Gretchen asked.

"We have a god," Josie said.

"You can't translocate," Tessa said, though she didn't look so certain.

"Not me," Josie said. "Judah. He can translocate to the island. He's still wearing a couple of Simone's access charms. He should be able to return and retrieve Ty."

Roxy and Gretchen turned towards him.

"Can you do that?" Gretchen asked.

"I think so," Judah replied, though he didn't sound happy about it. For someone whose soul had just been saved from the clutches of Death, he didn't look happy at all.

"I'm going back to the island too," she said.

CHAPTER 14

AUGUST 30TH

Now Judah looked really unhappy.

Her dad was frowning too. "Whatever you left there, it's not important—"

"I'm not going back for my stuff, Dad."

"Then why do you—?"

"I'm going to find a way end to this."

"Oh, so you're going to escape to the safety of an interdimensional island with your . . ."—Tessa made a pained face—"with Judah and leave the rest of us here to die, is that it? You think you're going to find a miracle in some moldy old book?"

"No, I don't," she said.

Judah stepped forward. "Why do you want to go back?"

She knew that look. She also knew it was no good to lie to him. But she didn't want to argue. Not now.

"Someone has to do something," she said. "There has to be a way—"

"Josie." Her dad stood up too. "I know what you're thinking and . . ."

"No way," Judah finished for him.

"Do you have a better idea? Because if you do, I'm open for suggestions."

"What am I missing here?" Roxy asked.

Gretchen dropped the stack of papers on a side table. "The Fates? That's a big risk, kiddo."

"Bigger than what?" Josie asked. "Dealing with Death? Destroying the mask of the Tripartite? Unleashing the gods? Waiting around here for Lily's goddess and her demon army?"

"What's this about a demon army?" Beech asked.

"You don't even know if you can find them," her dad said, taking her wrist gently. "You could die trying."

"I will find them," Josie told him. "And they will tell me—"

"Tell you what?" Nancy interjected. "How to turn back time? How to reinstitute the Covenant? Even if you could kill the goddess with that sword of yours, there are still tens of thousands of goddesses out there. Goddesses you released. And demons. Will you kill them all? One by one? Now that is one demigod myth I'd like to hear. I wonder how many of us would be left by the time such a tremendous task was completed."

"You're right," Josie said to her. "That's what I'll ask them."

Nancy snorted, shaking her head.

"What?" her dad asked, pulling on her arm slightly.

"How to reestablish the Covenant. How to send the gods back to the Beyond. Lu-Ji did it once, there has to be a way to do it again."

"But Lu-Ji was . . ."

"What, Dad? A demigod?"

"Let her go," Nancy said, flinging her hands at Josie like she was an unwanted solicitor on her doorstep. "She wants to live under the delusion she's a god, let her. She wants to get herself killed trying to undo what she's done. Well, it's not the kind of justice I was hoping for, but it will do."

"Nancy, really?" Caroline said.

Nancy stalked across the room. "I'm going downstairs to explain to our tribe that their powers have been stripped by a shortsighted, self-centered, mentally unstable young woman. And because of her, we will be defenseless when the gods, the Earth Goddess, the demons, all of them, come for our lives."

She stormed out.

Simone peeked up at Josie. "I don't like her."

"Nobody likes her," Gretchen said.

"Does someone want to untie me?" Kai asked.

Simone glanced around the room. When no one objected, she pushed off the couch and hurried to Kai, kissing him before she started to loosen his bounds.

"I really am sorry," he said to her softly.

"I know."

Josie ground her fingers against her forehead. "If I remember correctly, there are a couple hundred cases of salt in the supply warehouse," she said, looking at Gretchen and Roxy. "Pull some and distribute them to everyone here."

"Salt?" Beech asked.

"Wards off demons," Gretchen said.

"Add it to the new protection circles too. They'll strengthen them." Josie looked to her dad and Caroline. "In the meantime, start building some shrines. One for the Lake God and one for the Forest Goddess. They're our best hope of fending off any intruding gods right now."

Caroline nodded. Josie's dad took Caroline's hand

"And remember to spill blood before you start. Make it a good show for the Forest Goddess. But keep it low key for the Lake God. He mentioned something about an ox—"

"We're not really going to sacrifice animals are we?" Simone said in a whimper. "That is so wrong."

"We're functioning at primal levels here," Kai said to her as he tossed the last of the rope aside and stood up. "Kill or be killed."

"Where are we going to find an ox?" Beech asked.

"You're not," Josie said. "You're going to entertain a goddess."

"Wait a minute . . ." Gretchen said.

"She likes him," Josie said. "When a goddess likes a human, she'll do whatever she can to make them happy. And nothing would make you happier," she said to Beech, "than keeping your tribe safe right now."

"Absolutely," Beech agreed. "We all have to make sacrifices, right?" He grinned.

"I don't like the sound of this," Gretchen said. "As I recall, goddesses tend to be jealous lovers. Of the murderous variety."

"Don't give her the polyamorous speech," Josie warned Beech with a significant look. "And don't give her even the faintest idea that you're interested in anyone else."

Beech held up his hands. "Who said I was?"

"I mean now or ever. As far as she's concerned, you didn't exist until the day you met her. Flatter her. A lot. Everyone should start making sacrifices to her, the bloodier the better. We need her to be as powerful as possible. The Lake God too, but don't bug him. Leave him offerings, but don't make a lot of noise about it. I don't know how long it's going to take for me to contact the Fates or find them or . . ."

"Or if you'll survive," her dad said.

"Start making alliances," she said to him. "The Forest Goddess and the Lake God will have friends. Air gods, rock gods, river gods; find them, bring offerings, sleep with them, do whatever you have to do to make them want to protect you. Lily's goddess is powerful, but she's not invincible. As for her army . . . a dozen demons in human skin won't be able to stand up to one truly pissed off god. They won't want to. The Earth Goddess can't be killed by another god, but her power can be sapped if you gather enough gods willing to take her on."

"You have so much nerve," Tessa said. "You destroy the world, you change everything, and now you're giving orders?"

"The world was already being destroyed," Josie said. "We were outmatched, outnumbered, and overwhelmed."

"And now we're powerless too," Tessa said.

"No. Now you have one goddess bent on destroying everything and thousands of gods who are waiting to be told that they're your favorite. If they're wreaking havoc right now, it's probably because they're flexing their muscles. They're show offs. Contact the other tribes, tell them to do the same, build shrines, make sacrifices—not human ones. Before, we forced the gods to do our will. Now, we have to convince them that it's what they want to do. I'm not saying it's perfect and I'm not saying it will work, but as far as I'm concerned, it's better than the alternative."

"Better than having the gods under our control?" Tessa said.

"Better than you being dead."

"Oh, please—"

"Tessa, if you think I don't care about you, I'm sorry. What happened with Judah and me . . . we didn't plan it. We didn't want to hurt you. I haven't been the best sister or the best teacher . . . the only thing I seem to be good at is avoiding my emotions. But if you think that I was going to stand by and watch you die, then I guess I'm much better at hiding my emotions than I realized. I watched Mom die . . . I couldn't do anything. I'll be damned to Oblivion before I let anything happen to you—"

"You expect me to believe that?"

"After everything, I guess not." Josie tugged off the truth-charm and tossed it to Tessa. "But it's the truth."

Tessa caught the bracelet. She stared down at it, turning the beads between her thumb and forefinger.

"Nancy's going to go out there and get everyone more worked up and scared than they already are," Josie said. "I'm not giving you orders, Tessa. I'm asking you. Are you going to let her do that to your tribe? Are you going to let Lily's goddess charge in here and bury everyone? Are you the Triune or not?"

"There is no Triune," Tessa said.

"So all the trials, the battles, the losses, all the work and blood and sleeplessness nights, did that all disappear with the mask? Did the Tripartite do those things? Because if it was them, they had me fooled. I was sure it was you. Someone's going to step up and lead the Core. If not you, then I guess we'll let Nancy do it."

"Isn't that what you're doing?" Tessa said bitterly.

"I can't lead the Core, Tessa. I'm far too selfish. Everyone I care about is in this room, and I'd let the rest of the world rot before I would let something happen to any of you. I think I proved that by destroying the Covenant, didn't I?"

Tessa's shoulders rolled back. Some of the color had returned to her face. Though she remained too thin and hollow-eyed, the glitter was returning to her hazel eyes.

"Now you are lying," she said. "But I guess we don't have much choice." She pulled the elastic band from her hair and shook out the long blond locks. She'd been wearing it back for the last month. She tossed the elastic and the truth-charm onto the nearby desk. "You heard what my sister said. Let's get to work."

She started towards the door. "Roxy, let's put together a message for the Core, detailing my sister's instructions," she said. "How well are the radio signals coming through?"

"All right," Roxy said, following Tessa out the door.

"Guess I'll go find the goddess," Beech said, backing out.

"Hold your board there, Baby Bear." Gretchen picked up the stack of reports and then put her hand on his shoulder. "Let's discuss how one keeps himself from being disemboweled by a jealous goddess."

She led him out.

"When will you leave?" Josie's dad asked.

"Now," Josie said.

"Get some sleep before you start," her dad said. "It took your mother a full day to prepare and another to perform the Invocation of the Fates. It's not something you want to undertake sleep deprived. You can't risk misspeaking, not a single word."

"I know, Dad. I'll try."

"You don't have to try," Simone said. She took a bracelet off her arm and held it out to Judah. "Slip this on her when she's least expecting it." She gave Josie an impish grin. "You need to sleep."

"Thanks," Josie said, a smile tugged at the corners of her mouth, but didn't exert enough force for the expression to spread or stay.

Caroline turned to Judah and Simone. She hugged each of them, planting a kiss on Simone's forehead and Judah's cheek. She clasped Judah's face and peered into his eyes.

"I can't believe—" She glanced over at Josie. "No more secrets. Can we all agree to that much?"

"I can." Her dad hugged her, hard enough to realign her spine. "The moment you get back, find me."

She hugged him back, tighter than she ever had. She only hoped that by the time she returned, he was here to be found.

CHAPTER 15

AUGUST 30TH

"Here we are again, huh?" Kai said.

Judah's brow sharpened, deadly.

Simone backed into Kai. "We're all on the same side now. The side of living to see tomorrow?" She looked to Josie for support. "Right?"

Josie held Kai's gaze. Her own feelings about Kai's betrayal were muddled. Considering the current pressing circumstances, it hardly seemed to matter, but she could understand why Judah and the rest of the tribe might still think it did.

"It might be better for you," she said to Kai, "if you get some supplies together, a tent from the warehouse, and scout out the surrounding area. Try to find some other gods who seem amenable."

"In other words, lay low and try to do something useful," Kai said.

"If you're leaving, I'm going with you," Simone said.

"Don't stop making charms," Josie said to her. "They can still protect us. In fact, now that the masks are gone, people are going to wish they had been a bit nicer to the artisan drudges around here."

"How will you find us?" Simone asked.

"The locator charm," Kai said to Josie. "It works both ways. Give it to Fire Guy over there, and he'll be able to translocate right to us."

Simone wrung her hands and took a step towards Josie. "You're really going to consult the Fates?"

"I have to," Josie said. She glanced at Judah, waiting for the argument, but it didn't come. He stared at the floor, impassive-faced.

Pain. Everywhere.

Simone hurried across the room and gave Josie a quick hug. "Be safe."

"You too."

Simone returned to Judah. She hugged him too, for a long time. The sharp edge of his brow dulled until it had almost disappeared completely. Simone power.

Kai waited for Simone at the door. She looked back at Josie and Judah once more before she left.

They stood at opposite sides of the room. Not speaking.

This wasn't how Josie imagined it would be. Here he was. Yet she felt more alone than she had since he'd died.

Why didn't he say something? Why didn't she? Why couldn't she?

When the silence grew so stifling she could barely pull in a breath, she said,

"We have to go."

Judah closed his eyes. "I'm not sure I know how," he said. "I've never translocated without the mask."

"I can make it easier for you." She touched the quartz under her shirt. "Translocate us back to the Triune's Island."

His eyes flicked up, flaring.

With a whoosh, he was gone. Then, in another gust of air, he was behind her. His arm locked around her, slamming her against his chest, seemingly heedless of the sword.

In another buffeting blast of heat and air, through the paths of fire, they emerged, standing on the gray beach of the Triune's Island. Past the dunes rose the tumbling heap of the Triune's sanctuary. Gray sand, gray sky, gray water. For the first time in her life though, the primordial gods were silent. Gone.

All she could hear was the plaintive lapping of the water on the wide snaking strand of gray beach.

She supposed they were fortunate that the island continued to exist even though there was no longer a Triune. Not just for Ty's sake. If the island had disappeared, they would've had to travel the world over so she could gather all that was necessary to perform the Invocation of the Fates.

Judah's arms dropped from her, too quickly. She spun around to face him.

"Let's not do this, okay?" she said, pleading.

"You forced me to translocate—"

"The Chain forced you." She yanked her shirt up and unfastened the pendant from her piercings.

"When did you get your belly button pierced?" he said, frowning.

"When I had a fire god to keep in check." She slipped the mounting ring over his necklace and tightened the bead that secured it. "The Chain of the Gods. Si-Fa's Chain. It was strong enough to bend Death to Lu-Ji's will, so it should be enough to keep our fiery friend under your control." She gazed into his fierce blue eyes as his fingers ran over the pendant. "Just make sure you mean it."

"Mean what?"

Her fingertips lingered on his chest. "Please don't be angry."

"How can I not be angry?"

Her hands fell away from him. "For what?"

"You destroyed the Covenant. For me?"

"You would've done the same thing."

He looked away towards the flat expanse of surreal ocean. Stone-brow.

"Tell me I'm wrong," she said.

"I don't have that kind of power," he said. "What you did, I couldn't have done."

"You don't know what it's been like—"

"For you?"

"For the world. Portland is gone. Lily destroyed it. In less than a month. I wasn't lying to Tessa when I said we were outmatched and overwhelmed."

He gazed down at her. "You didn't make a deal with Death to stop Lily. You did it to get my soul back."

"And I'd do it again."

"Maybe I didn't want to come back."

She retreated from him. "You don't mean that."

"What did you bring me back for, Josie? The end of the world? Is that why you want me here? So we can die together?"

She quaked. "Do you remember why your soul left your body? It wasn't because the Fire God won the fight. You gave up. Remember?"

He frowned deeper, eyes flicking away as he seemed to try to recall what had happened before his death. Against the gray backdrop of the island, his eyes were so much bluer, his hair all the more golden. She ached to touch it, to kiss his lips that were redder than anything else in this bleak not-quite world. But she didn't move any closer.

"You gave up because you thought I was dead," she said. "So don't scold me for bringing you back, because as far as I'm concerned, you never should've left in the first place. If it's okay for you to surrender your soul, because of me, then I don't want to hear how what I did was any worse, or any crazier—"

Her hands fisted. She let out a guttural noise of frustration. "I should've known that even after all of this, after everything, after death and the end of the world and the end of the Covenant, that nothing would change. You're always going to question me, aren't you? You're always going to push me even when I'm standing right on the edge. Are you trying to see if I can fly? Because I can't. I'm falling, Judah. I've been falling since the day you died. And the only way I knew how to stop it was to bring you back. If I didn't do that then . . ."—she held up her hands in surrender—"I was going to give up too."

"You don't know how to give up," he said.

"I've been trying."

"Not very hard."

"Nothing's ever good enough for you."

"Not true."

"Hey!" Ty called, stumbling over the berm and down onto the beach.

He huffed as he came to a stop, pushing his horn-rimmed glasses up onto the bridge of his nose. "Josie, Judah! Gods, am I glad to see you. We've got problems."

Josie wanted to beat him over the head, but it wasn't his fault he'd interrupted.

"It's all right, Ty," she said. "I know you can't summon your mask—"

"Oh, yeah, there's that," he acknowledged. He turned and pointed back towards the crumbling cluster of buildings. "But I was talking about that—"

Another figure picked her way towards them across the grassy berm. Curvaceous and toned, in white yoga workout clothes, her skin silky ebony, her hair shorn close to her head, her eyes glowed white, blindingly.

Ty backpedalled as she approached.

Josie took a deep breath and drew her sword.

Life stopped where she was, at the edge of the berm.

Her smile was almost as white as her eyes. Her voice rich and pleasing, audible-decadence, a soft doughy pastry filled with cream and honey. "Is that how you treat your mother?"

CHAPTER 16

AUGUST 30TH

"YOU ARE NOT MY MOTHER," Josie said.

"No, I'm really more of your father, actually," Life said with a breezy gesture of her hand, like it all amounted to the same thing. "I'll admit, when Death started coming on to me, I was repelled, but he does have a certain charm ... wouldn't you say?" Her white eyes fixed on Josie.

Josie squinted, averting her gaze. Twin ghosts of the goddess eyes bounced across her vision.

"When he told me his little plan ... I honestly didn't see how it could work. But here you are a demigod, after all. He's really very clever."

"This is so messed up," Ty said, shifting further back, behind Judah. Judah watched with that impassive face of his, giving away nothing.

"What are you saying?" Josie said, glaring at the goddess from the corner of her eyes. "You want me to believe that Death planned this? My conception, making me a demigod, that he knew I would destroy the mask of the Tripartite?"

Life's hips swayed back and forth as if she was stretching before a run. "Death's mind has always been a mystery to me, but he did promise that if I took possession of your father and slept with your mother while he was in possession of her, then we could produce the first demigod since... oh, who knows how long? How could I resist an offer like that? Demigods really are the best of both worlds. And I do love children."

She seemed to look Judah over, though it was hard to tell since looking at her eyes for too long was sure to cause a person permanent retinal damage.

"Speaking of which, when can I expect grandchildren?" she asked. "You should hurry. Things are looking rather nasty back on the mortal plane." She crossed her arms. "I'm not pleased at all. Death is having far too much fun at my expense. I need everyone to procreate much faster if I'm to maintain any kind of balance." Her head tilted. "You're at the heights of fertility as we speak. Copulate now and you'll be pregnant in a snap. I shall bless the child myself, and she will grow to be the pride and delight of us all."

"Um..." Josie massaged her forehead, fumbling with her words. "Did you come to tell me that Death had my whole life planned out for me? That he orchestrated... all of this? How is that possible?"

Life lifted a shoulder. "How should I know? I'm only a god. Why don't you ask the Other? It usually has a better idea of what's going on with that mess Time. I really don't understand it myself. I'm not very interested. I only wanted to tell you that I'm not happy and I want you to fix it."

"Fix it?" Josie repeated.

"That's right. Do whatever you have to do. I'll even submit to returning to the Tripartite, if that's what it takes. I don't like Death's little minions trampling all over my work."

"You'll submit to the Tripartite?"

Life seemed to inspect her fingernails. "Well, submit might be too strong of a word. Certain details would have to be ironed out, of course. But if it will put Death back in his proper place, I'll be happy. He's jealous, you know. He always has been. Why not? I'm beautiful. I'm love and desire and happiness and all that is good. He is nothing but cold and rot and stench and grief. He's a slave to his work. And what a tedious job that is, escorting mortal souls through his realm to... wherever it is they go. I should've realized what it all meant when the Fates told your mother how she could save herself. Sometimes I think I'm far too trusting."

Josie lowered her sword. "What did they tell her?"

"Oh, lots of things. They gave her a charm enabling her to travel to the outer edges of the Beyond, where she and Death could be one and the same. Where they could deal without me, or the Other, intruding. They told her the day would come when Death would ask for something. If she wanted to save herself from him, she had to agree to give him whatever he asked for. She did."

"What did she give him?" Josie asked.

"Right before she died, the Other gave your mother a vision of her impending death and the many possible futures resulting from it. The Other told her she must choose one of her daughters to be Triune and one to be the mask-maker. Before your mother could make that decision, Death stepped in and demanded she give him that choice. She was bound to consent. Death chose you to be the mask-maker. I thought he was playing favorites."

Josie ached with rage. "He knew."

"I suppose, somehow, he must have," Life said. "Although the type of tedious machinations required to steer the course of the universe in such a way is simply too mind-numbing to consider, even for me. But that's Death for you. I'm sure he thought it was thrilling to pour through the infinite possible futures for hundreds of generations of human souls, tweaking and nudging them this way and that until he created one that might possibly free him, as if it was so terrible to share a bit of his power with a human or to allow mortals to manage things on their own. I actually found it quite freeing. Though I wasn't happy about everything you humans have done, there were so many wonderful new babies all the time. It made it nearly impossible to stay angry.

"Speaking of which, I'm more than happy to remove this one,"—she gestured towards Ty—"if he's going to distract you. I do find that these things happen much more efficiently when it's the two of you alone together. A third . . . well, I'm all for love in every form, and you humans really are very clever about creating new life in rather ingenious ways, but in my vast experience, I've found that the old-fashioned way works very well. Perhaps I'm a traditionalist. Of course, if you want to have the skinny one later, that's fine. You are part god and we do have voracious appetites, but have him first." Life pointed at Judah. "Having a manifest fire god within has altered him.

He's almost a demigod himself. I want my first granddaughter of the new age to be as much god as possible. Plus, the two of you will have such beautiful children. As soon as she's conceived I can influence any number of traits. Let's see, your hair and his eyes, and your lips and his nose ... oh gods, she's going to be gorgeous. I can't wait. I'm going to spoil her rotten."

Josie ignored the baby talk and focused instead on the fact that Death had planned everything. Her entire life. What did it mean that her very existence was part of Death's plot to destroy the Covenant? Were all the events that had lead up to this inevitable? Had she been a pawn, every move predetermined according to Death's plan? Did that mean any attempt she made to force him back into the Tripartite was already doomed to failure?

"Oh, you don't look well," Life said. "When was the last time you slept or ate? I know they seem like inconveniences but they really are necessary to sustaining your fragile living form, and if you're going to be carrying my granddaughter—"

"I'm *not* ..." Josie took a moment to measure her tone. She was talking to one of the Supreme deities. Even with the Sword of Eternity in her hand, she didn't want to risk annoying Life, especially since she seemed to be on Josie's side, for the moment. "I have a few other items on my agenda."

"Oh, yes, *that*. Well, you know the symptoms don't show up right away. You should have plenty of time to put Death back in his place before the morning sickness or any of that starts up. Besides, you won't have much longer before that disgusting sinkhole of a goddess opens her ugly face and devours you and all of your kind. So pregnant or not, you only have a short time to act. You might as well have something to look forward to should you succeed. And I've noted that women can be wonderfully fierce when the lives of their offspring are in danger. Knowing that the life of your daughter hangs in the balance might be the extra edge you need to assure your success. Not that I doubt it. I have complete faith in you. You are, after all, mine."

Gods, Josie had forgotten how dizzying Life could be.

"You can see the future," Josie said, maintaining her focus with all her might. "How long before the Earth Goddess devours us?"

"Yes, I can see many possible futures, popping up and floating all around the lot of you and disappearing again just as quickly, like tiny little bubbles. Your every thought creates another, as I said, all quite tedious. The future is of no concern to me so long as I'm still in it. That's all that matters. But I am quite set on having a granddaughter now. I think you know something about that, dear. Determination, I mean. You always struck me as godly in that manner—single-minded. Once you're set upon something, you will not be kept from it, regardless of whatever might stand in your way."

"You're right about that," Judah said.

"Oh, he speaks," Life said. "Well, that can be nice once in a while—so long as he says the right things. And remembers his place. Your soul is only here because my daughter wishes it. I shall not begrudge her in the slightest should you displease her and she decides to send you back."

"I would never do that," Josie said softly.

"Oh, it's like that, is it? Oh yes, of course. As I said, you do have the tendency to set your mind on one thing—very godly.

Well, that's just fine. After the daughter, there will be a son. Because it's always nice to have one and then the other, don't you think? And you're still young enough that there can be quite a lot. You would not believe the variations that can spring from the two of you, each of them unique and quite their own persons and with the powers of the gods to boot." Life pressed her hands to her chest. "With my blessings, they will become the queens and kings of the new age."

"Forgive me, but you never answered my question," Josie said. "How long?"

Life's glowing eyes skimmed over the three of them. "Oh, let me see. So many considerations, but it seems you may have..."—she popped her lips as if she was fixing her lipstick—"oh, something like a week."

"Something like?"

"Any number of things could push it back by days or weeks or speed it up or prevent it from happening altogether. As I said, speak to the Other. It understands these matters much more than I."

Josie let the tip of the sword fall into the sand. A week? It would take her hours to prepare the Invocation. And who knew how much longer for her to actually find the Fates and return—that is, if they let her return.

Life's voice seemed to grow richer, deeper, intoxicating. "To show you how much faith I have in you, I have a gift, for my one and only demigod daughter." Her long, graceful arm extended. In her fingers was a silver ring, plain and rather dull looking.

"What is it?"

"Ah-ah," Life said. "Do not offend me by asking what. Rather, you should ask, when?"

"When?"

"Only once," Life said. "This ring is like your summoners' rings. A key. What it opens, it will only open once. The question is when will you open it? Only you will be able to make that choice."

Life flicked the ring at her. It spun through the air. Josie's heart leapt. She snatched the ring from the air before it arced off over her shoulder and into the primordial waters.

When she looked back at the berm, Life was gone.

The silver band was thick, unadorned, dented, and nicked, like it'd been worn many times before. She slid it onto her finger. Perfect fit.

"Oh. My. Gods," Ty said, raking his hands back into his dirty-blond hair. "Really? You both got some serious explaining to do."

Josie had a hard time looking at Judah. After all the pregnant talk, she was feeling like it would be better if she didn't look at him again—ever.

"We'll explain everything," Josie said, swinging the sword back up over her shoulder and sliding it into its scabbard, "while we get ready."

Ty looked like he'd found a rotten egg in the fridge. "Ready for what?"

"I'm going to have a chat with the Fates."

CHAPTER 17

AUGUST 30TH

"**I**S THAT EVERYTHING?" Judah asked as Josie read over the list one more time.

She double checked her notes against the ancient text. The crumbling book was written in Core, and translation was one of her least favorite duties. The language of the Corpora wasn't spoken. It had been created by the gods so they could communicate with their chosen emissaries. And also, Josie was convinced, to give her a raging headache. In the instance of the Fates' Invocation, every other line was written backwards, upside down, and crammed in a series of spirals onto two ancient vellum pages. Dozens of vortexes, all sucking her down into the pits of aggravation.

"I think so," she said finally, falling back into the well-worn chair.

Judah took the notebook from Josie and pushed it against Ty's chest.

Judah had done his best to explain to Ty what had happened while Josie had changed clothes and scrubbed away Russell's blood. She'd stared into the basin of soapy pink water, listening to Judah's voice out in the hall, feeling raw and sore and on the verge of passing out.

Judah had continued his explanation to Ty as Josie had led them into the archives.

There, she'd written down all the necessary items and ingredients she would require for the Invocation. Ty brimmed with questions that neither Josie nor Judah could answer. How could Death plot all of this without the Other's knowledge? Why didn't Josie's mom see this future in her visions? Why hadn't Josie and Judah been able to admit their feelings for each other from the start so that they might've avoided this hot mess of the Fire God becoming manifest and pushing Judah's soul out, thus prompting Josie to destroy the Covenant and all the varied ramifications?

When he'd asked this, they'd both stared at him until he'd shrugged and said, "Just asking."

Now Ty was scanning the list of ingredients while Josie fought against the siren song of sleep.

"Find what you can," Judah said to Ty.

Ty chewed his lip. His eyes were summer sky blue, bright and clear.

"Will you let me stay?" he asked.

Josie rubbed the sleepless burn out of her eyes. "Stay?"

"For the Invocation," he said. "I want to be here. I want to help. 'Cause as far as I can see, this"—he held up the notebook—"is our best shot."

Josie felt like another ten tons had dropped onto her chest. "I don't know . . ."

"Oh, no, I'm telling you," he said tartly. "You remember that first day you showed up at the center? I was working the desk. You nearly ran me over. I wanted to take you down, but then Beech told me who you were. I'd heard about you, Josie Day. And now I understand why everyone was scared of you. I thought it was because you were supposed to be the Triune, but it wasn't that. You know what Kai told me once—I still can't believe he's such a backstabber. When I see him, he's going to get it. Anyway, he told me the reason you couldn't summon any gods, including the Tripartite, was because they were all too scared of that look."

He nodded at her. "Uh-huh, that one. It's one of those things people say that seems funny at first, but the more you think about it, the more you realize that it's true." He hugged the notebook to his chest. "I'll find what you need."

He strode out of the archive's reading room, which was two floors underground, though situated above the archives, which wound deep through seemingly endless tunnels and vaults.

Judah slid his hand under her arm and guided her to her feet.

"I should help him. Mom's storage rooms are a mess," she said as he led her out into the dim corridors, still packed with supplies for summoners who would never again be able to translocate to the island to retrieve them. Battery powered lights were stuck to the walls every few feet, casting an eerie pale glow over the boxes. "We should take these back to the mortal plane." She gestured at the crates marked *Bandages* and *Rubbing Alcohol.*

"I'll take back what I can," he said, nudging her ahead of him into the narrow stairwell.

"You're going back?" she asked, tripping on a broken edge of a step. Her hand caught the wall. His grip tightened on her arm. She regained her balance and turned back to look down at him. "Now?"

Even in the weak glow of the battery lights, his eyes shone. "Are you afraid I won't come back?"

The ceiling was low and arched, the walls close. Without any air moving around them, the only thing she could smell was him. Not the burning smoke stench that had surrounded his body while the Fire God had possession of it, but a living, pulsing scent. Warm and musky, but still clean somehow, like slept-in sheets.

"If you don't come back," she said, "I'll find you."

"Gods, Josie, why do you have to say shit like that?"

"What do you—?"

He stepped up and kissed her.

His lips tasted different than when the Fire God had kissed her—more real. Or maybe it was the way he was kissing her. Like he always had. Like he needed her. Like he loved her. The god had kissed her like it was a game, a challenge, like he was waiting to see how she would react, if he'd won. But Judah didn't wait to see how she would react, he pulled her closer and kissed her deeper, diving in. Getting carried away.

They stumbled down the steps, tangled up, falling back into the corridor, against a stack of boxes.

When he kissed her like this, she forgot about right and wrong. She forgot about the end of the world, the end of the Core, her family, herself. She forgot about everything but the thrum of his body against hers.

His mouth tore free from hers.

"We have to talk, Josie."

She kissed the edge of his jaw. His fingers caught in her hair and dug into the small of her back.

"Uh-huh." She snagged the collar of his shirt, wanting to rip it away. She kissed the hollow of his neck, wishing she could distill his smell and drink it.

He pushed back against her, jamming her into the slim bare space of stone wall between the boxes and the stairs. He grasped her face in his hands.

She gripped his wrists. "Really?"

"We need to get a few things cleared up—"

"Are you kidding?" Every layer of her skin seemed to be trembling at a different frequency. For a reckless, desperate moment she was sure that if he didn't kiss her again the layers would shake loose from each other and evaporate.

His hands remained on her face. Every throb of his pulse pushed her further towards dissolution.

"I don't want to be fair," he said. "I don't want to be rational or selfless."

She clung to his arms. "Then don't be."

"Are you going to the Fates?"

She sagged. "You know I am."

"I don't want you to."

"I have to."

"I know, but I don't want you to."

She was starting to draw back, to cool off, to close down.

"I'll kiss you again right now, Josie, but if I do, I'm not letting you go."

She released his arms. "You're not letting me?"

He hooked her waist and pressed her to him again. "You brought me back from the dead. Now you want me to sit here and watch while you charge off into the pathways—again? You're the demigod, the daughter of the gods. I'm only possessed by one. If I lose you, I can't bring you back. What am I supposed to do? It's hard enough. You want me to kiss you? You want me to be with you? Because I want to, but if you think I can do that without having something to say about what you do afterwards—"

"You're going to say something, regardless—"

"But I might not be able to stop myself from stopping you—"

"Yes, you will."

He shook his head. "Don't be so sure—"

"I am sure," she said. "Because you always do the right thing, Judah Goodwin. I know no matter what you feel, what you want for yourself, you'll do what has to be done."

He leaned so close they were almost kissing again. "I think you're talking about yourself."

"I haven't done what was right," she said. "I did what Death wanted. All along. I don't know how he did it, how he planned it, how it's possible, but he made all of this happen. He took my mother. He took you. He used me. Millions of people are dying right now. My dad, your mom, Simone . . . Tessa, they're all going to die too. And he planned all of it." Her hands curled, nails biting into her palms.

He shifted back. "So what, Josie? So what if we all die? It's going to happen. It already happened to me. You can't stop it forever."

"I don't want to stop it forever," she said. "Just this time."

"And what about next time?"

"Why are you always arguing with me?"

"Because somebody has to."

"You know—"

"I don't know anything and neither do you."

"You want me to do nothing?"

"Maybe that's what you're doing already."

"You don't believe that."

"What I believe and what I know are two different things. You've been following your gut this whole time and look where it's led us."

Pain.

He took a whole step back, disengaging completely. The shadows rushed to fill the space between them. The air chilled.

"This is what I know," he said. "The gods are back in the mortal realm. All the rest, demon armies, the end of our tribe, that's all speculation. I don't know much about the Fates, but I do know they only accept one form of payment. Our lives are short enough. You want to shorten yours even more for answers that may or may not help us? Or maybe you're only playing even deeper into Death's hand. Did that ever occur to you? If everything you've done has been what he wanted, then maybe that's what you're still doing. You don't stop and think, Josie. Not ever. And it's driving me effin' crazy."

"What am I supposed to do?"

"Why do you have to do anything? Frankly, I don't care anymore—"

"You don't mean that—"

"Josie, I was dead. I don't remember much about it, but I do remember having a sense that I'd spent a lot of time in life caring about things that didn't matter."

"You're saying that the end of our tribe doesn't matter? Your mom's life? Simone's?"

"Of course their lives matter. They're all that matter, but their lives and their deaths are separate." He stepped back again, as far as he could in the tight corridor. "You're too focused on Death. You're wasting time. Our lives are too short, whether it's seven days or seventy years. If you'd rather spend it trying to find a way to stop Death, then that's your choice."

"Why are you—?"

"Why did you bring me back? So I could watch you die again?"

"I didn't die—"

"I thought you did. Wasn't that enough? You just want to torture me or what?"

"How am I torturing—?"

"Because I don't know what you want, Josie. You bring me back and then you charge off into battle without a second thought. What am I supposed to do with that? It sucks. And if that's how it's going to be with you, then . . . maybe it's better if we . . . don't."

She stared. "You're not serious."

"Do I look like I'm not serious?"

He looked completely serious. Painfully so.

"I ended the Covenant for you—"

He closed in on her again. "I'm not saying I don't want to be with you. I do. More than . . . you gave me my soul back, but I can't do it this way anymore. I know myself. I tried to be with you and hold back at the same time. I couldn't. I lost my soul. There is no halfway for me. Either let me have everything or let me spend my last days with people who actually need me."

"I do need you."

"For what? A chauffeur?"

A slap to the face would've stung less.

"How can you say that? After everything—"

"After all the times I told you the truth and you didn't listen? After all the times I saved your life and you ignored me? After I lost my soul, because I thought you were mine and I thought I'd lost you, because you did what you wanted and you didn't care what I thought or what it would mean to me if you were gone? You haven't been thinking, Josie. Not about anything. Not about me." He drew back again, deeper into the shadows. "You're still treating me like another obstacle on your road to . . . wherever it is you're going. I honestly can't tell if you're being selfless or selfish anymore. But whoever you're doing this for, it's not me."

He stormed up the stairs.

"Judah—"

He didn't stop.

CHAPTER 18

AUGUST 30TH
EARLY EVENING

TY PLUNKED A BOX DOWN on the uneven pavers in the courtyard. He pulled a handkerchief from his back pocket and dabbed his forehead.

"That's about half." His voice carried, but didn't echo, falling flat against the tumbles of buildings. "What are you doing?"

Josie flung another armload of aluminum tent poles into the small hovel that had been used for storage while the Core had been there and had been empty, like most of the buildings, while Josie was growing up.

"I'll perform the Invocation here," she said.

Ty scrunched his nose, scanning the courtyard. "How much space do you need?"

The courtyard was an expansive area that seemed built for huge numbers of people—as if the Triune's Island had once hosted fairs or masquerades—easily as big as a professional soccer field.

She'd cleared a fifth of it, the part closest to the main building. But there were buildings all up and down the length. At the opposite end sat a huge mountain of stone, the ruins of a building that had probably been twice as big as any of the others. Sometimes the buildings would disappear altogether, leaving empty slabs of pavement where they'd once stood. Other times, they would be whole one day and crumbled the next. But the main house and the heaping ruin at the far end had stayed the same for as long as Josie could remember.

When she'd been younger, she'd asked her mother who had built all the buildings and what they'd all been for, since no one but the Triune could access the island. Her mother had said they were only reflections. When Josie had asked what that meant, her mother had replied, "Some things only appear the way we expect them to appear."

Then she'd told Josie to translate that sentence into every variation of Core she knew and write each a hundred times.

Josie hadn't asked about the architecture again.

Josie gathered up the orange and yellow nylon tent and pitched it inside with the others.

"I need as much space as I can get," she told Ty.

Ty arched his eyebrow. "Truer words."

She kicked aside a weighed bag of sand. "What does that mean?"

"You know Judah went back to the mortal plane, don't you?"

Josie stalked around the tent, kicking away the rest of the weights.

Ty came closer. "Lover's quarrel?"

"I don't think it's any of your business," she said.

Ty held up his hands. "Absolutely."

She removed the poles from their rings. The blue dome of fabric sighed as it collapsed. She tossed the pole down on top of the tent.

"What?" she said to him finally.

"What do you dream about, Josie?"

Josie's head had gone from aching to splitting to numb and back again so many times in the last hour that she was sure she was on the verge of blacking out, so when Ty asked her the question, she didn't know if she'd heard him correctly.

"Dream about?" she repeated.

"You don't, do you?" he asked.

"Huh?"

"When I was little and I saw that fairy tale movie for the first time, you know the one, at the end of it, I didn't want to be Prince Charming. I didn't even want to be the princess. I wanted to be the fairy godmother."

Josie gazed at him dully.

"Please, can you get past the irony? I don't tell this story to everyone because it actually means something to me. It has nothing to do with being gay. I genuinely wanted to be the one who could whisk in and wave my wand and make people's dreams come true. That was my dream. What could be better than finding some unfortunate little boy or girl and being able to make all their dreams reality?" He snapped his fingers. "Just like that. The real irony is that once I summoned my first god, I was so disappointed. Manipulating the elements is grunt work. Muddy, messy, ugly. I wanted the sparkly wand and the happy, singing mice. I wanted to feel like I was actually making a difference in someone's life. I got over it when I realized that you really can do good with an air or an earth god, if you're in the right place at the right time. And I started volunteering at the hospital too. Music classes for the kids."

She scooped up the downed tent and tossed it in with the others. "I'm sure the kids loved that."

"They did," he said. "And even though some of them were terminally ill, and everyone knew, including them, that they probably weren't going to survive, they still had dreams. Every one of them talked about what they wanted to do tomorrow."

Josie collected the little sacks of sand and lobbed them into the hovel with the rest. She went to the next tent, snagging the puffy sleeping bags, yanking them out, and wadding them up.

"So, what do you dream about, Josie?" he asked again.

"I don't know," she said, annoyed. "Getting these tents out of the way so I can prepare to summon the Fates and, maybe, find a way to save the world? Can you help me make that dream come true, fairy godfather?"

Ty folded his arms like an old woman preparing to listen to a long lecture by someone she already knew she wouldn't agree with.

"What do you think Judah dreams about?" he asked pointedly. "If I showed up with my magic wand and asked what wish I could grant him, what do you think he'd say?"

Josie scowled at him, lobbing the sleeping bags into the hovel. "What's your point?"

"I know exactly what he would say, Josie. It was written all over his face when Life was . . . well, Judah is just that type. You know? Cinderella isn't the only one who wanted the fairy tale ending. Prince Charming wanted it too. If he hadn't, then the whole story falls apart, you know what I mean? It's not for everyone, maybe it's not even possible, but that's why it's the dream. That's why you have to dream. And if you're going to dream, then you might as well dream big. Right? I know you want to save the world and all that, and I am behind you one hundred percent, believe me. But hello? What are you saving it for? What's the dream?"

"Isn't saving the world and my tribe and my family enough?"

Ty rolled his eyes. "No."

Josie frowned. "Why not?"

"My gods, Josie. Seriously? You got your Triune-for-Life card at birth and that was it? You did whatever you were told and never thought once about doing something else or being something else or wanting something else? For yourself?"

She pulled another pole loose from its tent. "I wanted Judah."

"Did you? From the way he described it, you didn't want him. Or you told yourself you didn't, for like . . . months."

"That's because he was my sister's boyfriend," she said.

"So? You're telling me you had all these hot achy feelings for him that you completely repressed? You didn't, even for a second, think about him . . . I don't know, shirtless? Sneaking into your room at night?"

"I thought about the Fire Summoner."

"What did you think about the Fire Summoner?"

"I thought about finding him, unmasking him."

"And then what?"

"What do you mean?"

"Judah was right. You really don't think, do you?"

"You were eavesdropping?"

"You two were fighting, rather loudly. I didn't have to do anything but have ears to hear you," Ty replied. "But don't try to change the subject. I'm trying to help you now because you're obviously clueless. Did you even hear what Judah was telling you? I mean, you were so focused on getting him back that you didn't think about what you were going to do once he was actually back, did you? You knew you wanted him, but did you think about, did you dream about, what was going to happen once he was here?"

She tugged apart the interlocking segments of the pole. "You mean did I dream about having sex with him?"

"I mean bigger than that, Josie. I mean long-term. That's what I'm saying. Judah is a long-term planner. He thinks ahead. He prepares. If I asked him what he wanted for tomorrow, he'd have an answer. And it wouldn't have anything to do with the immediate crisis we're facing. It'd be about the long-term aspirations and desires. And I'm certain it would involve you. But you are all about the short-term. You want Judah, but you don't know what to do with him because you haven't thought that far ahead. You don't know what you want. I'm not talking about what you need to do, like save all our asses, because that *is* what you need to do. I'm talking about what you want, princess. Is it the fairy tale? Do you want the castle and the whole bit, or what?"

Josie stared at him. "I don't have time to think about that—"

"Well then, it's no wonder that he left, isn't it?"

"What do you mean?"

"You have got to be kidding me. That boy wants to spend the rest of his life with you, for however long that is, and you can't even let him have that much. He can't have your past, that's done. He can't have your present, because you're too busy saving the world. And he can't have your future, because you refuse to even dream that it might happen. So what does he have? You say you want him, but if it's not now and it's not later, then when? And what exactly is it you want from him? Or for him? Have you thought about that? That's what he meant when he said you're not doing any of this for him. That you're not thinking, not listening, that he doesn't know what you want. Because you're not thinking, you're not listening, and you don't know what you want."

Ty flourished his hand like he held a magic wand. "So, I am here, Cinderella. I'm your fairy godfather. Not the world's, not the Core's, not your family's, yours. What do you want? What is the impossible dream, so impossible, it seems like it would take a miracle to make it happen? Hmm?"

She gazed at him. Her mind blank.

He dropped his arm, shaking his head. "Maybe it's part of the curse of being a demigod. You don't think anything is impossible, do you? Once the next crisis arises, you rush right at it and don't think about anything else or let yourself believe that anything will stop you."

For a moment, he looked put out. Then he shrugged. "Well, let me attempt to plant a seed for you. A very simple one. You and Judah, together. Living life. A house. College? A regular old job. No gods. No apocalypses. No jumping from one emergency to the next. A simple, mortal, everyday life that so many people until very recently took for granted. I promise you, those of us who've survived, we would give anything for that everyday life back. That dull routine, that crappy job, for morning coffee and stupid TV shows and sitting on the couch with someone, anyone, being bored and comfortable. Gods, I want that back so much I really wish I did have a magic wand. There you go, Josie. You didn't have a dream? I just gave you one. Now make it your own. Fairy godfather, out."

CHAPTER 19

AUGUST 31ST
EARLY MORNING

HER FAIRY GODFATHER WAS SLUMPED against a wall, mouth hanging open, snoring.

Josie's eyes burned. Her back and knees ached. She'd spent hours drawing the Invocation circle. When she finally stood up, her head swam.

But time for exhaustion was later.

She tapped the thick hunk of chalk against her thigh as she inspected the circle, which was easily as big as an amusement park Ferris wheel tipped on its side. Within it were more circles, like the ring of a tree. The rings were divided as well, by various shapes. In these were symbols. Each set of symbols answered a series of questions. Some had been easy to answer. Others had taken more thought than she'd anticipated.

Who are you?

Josie Day, daughter of Melinda Day, the Triune, and Marc Day (formerly Marc Rivers, because he'd changed his name to his wife's, as was Core tradition.) But then she'd sat there for a long while, finally adding: daughter of Death and of Life. She'd enclosed the symbols in an octagon, protected by more symbols for family and blood.

What do you seek?

The Fates. But was that enough? Or should she include the question she wanted answered once she found the Fates? Since she hadn't come to a firm decision on what that question should be, she wrote simply: guidance and clarity.

One of the most tasking elements had been diagraming her entire astrological birth chart. Showing what planet had been in what sign and where each planet and sign had been located in each of the houses at the time of her birth . . . tedious.

Fortunately, her mother had made her memorize these facts, along with the entire ritual, but Josie double and triple-checked as much as she could against her lifebook, which she'd pulled from the Triune's archives.

Josie rubbed her forehead. The signs for Pluto in the first house, Sagittarius on the second house cusp, blurred and doubled.

"Are you done?" Judah asked.

She jumped. The chalk fell, clattered, and rolled away. Luckily, it didn't damage the circle; otherwise, she would've had to redraw anything that had been marred.

Covered in chalk and dust and days of grime and sweat, she was truly exhausted. Judah looked more like a Grecian god of beauty than ever. His skin was clean and glowing, his eyes bright and clear, his hair gold and carelessly perfect.

Though she'd avoided thinking about it all day, Ty's words crept into her head. What would it be like to live a normal life . . . with Judah? She pushed the thought back into the lightless cellar where she banished all distracting thoughts. Distractions could be fatal during the Invocation, but the tension that lingered between her and Judah was more distracting than any errant thought she'd ever had.

"I think so." She wiped her chalky hands on her jeans. She noticed two bunches of bracelets in his hand. "Please say those aren't for me."

"I tried to tell my sister they wouldn't help much against the Fates, but she wouldn't listen."

"How is she?"

"Alive," he said. "She and Kai have located three other gods, two of whom didn't try to kill them outright. In other interesting news, two more traitors turned up."

"What happened?"

Judah's cool façade wavered a bit. "Steve West and Joanna Bell, they were a couple of years older than me. Steve and I used to run track together . . ."

She was about to reach for him, but before she could, the emotion vanished from his face again.

"Turns out Lily made them take the goddess's mark. They were possessed by demons during lunch and they attacked. Luckily, Beech and the Forest Goddess were there. Beech took out Steve with his bow and the Forest Goddess took care of Joanna . . . So Kai's demon army information was true after all."

Josie wondered if Joanna had been the Wolf's summoner. Now that the masks were gone, they might never know who had been in possession of the Wolf.

"Was anyone hurt?" she asked.

"A few people. Nothing major, unless you count Steve and Joanna. They're dead." He crossed his arms, his tone brusque. "Most of the disaster-level activity has subsided. The tribes are doing everything they can to appease the gods and explain to the rest of the world that the gods are, in fact, gods. Some people aren't taking it so well, but it seems like Armageddon is on hold for now. There are reports of problems at nuclear facilities, two in California, some on the East Coast, Europe, and a few in India. It's hard to tell what's happening. Everything we're getting is word of mouth via radio. Sketchy."

"Thanks for the report, Lieutenant."

"Lieutenant? I'm at least a colonel in this army, General."

She licked her lips. Chalk coated her tongue and stuck in her throat. Her words came out choked and barely audible. But she had to say something.

"What do you want?" she asked.

"Are you actually asking me that question?"

She gazed into those gem-hard eyes. Their faceted sparks were the only traces of the fire within. "You want me to give up, is that it?"

He looked away.

"You don't want me to go the Fates?" she asked.

His brow hardened. His eyes darkened.

She hated it when he went into blackout mode.

A wild, dizzy sensation whipped through her. It might have been nothing more than the usual Judah-inspired anger and frustration, except it kept growing.

"I can't do this anymore," she said. "I can't be at odds with you like this all of the time. I need you on my side."

"I've always been on your side, Josie," he said. "You're the one who refused to see it."

"This? Still? I'm sorry I didn't see it was you behind the Fire God's guise, okay? I'm sorry. It was stupid and crazy and—"

"I don't care about that anymore, Josie."

"Then why are you bringing it up?"

A storm was building inside of her. A fever-and-nausea-inducing cyclone. Two fronts, battling. Everything she'd been taught straining against everything she'd never let herself feel.

His nostrils flared as he took a deep breath. "Sometimes I think I know you better than anyone, Josie, and other times . . . I don't get you at all."

Her words started spilling out, past the carefully guarded barriers. "What don't you get? What do you want to know? Do you want to know why I didn't see you behind the Fire God's guise? Because I wasn't supposed to. You don't get that? I didn't see you because it wasn't right, Judah. You were Tessa's boyfriend—"

Judah shook his head. "That's a lame excuse—"

"Maybe! Maybe it doesn't make sense to you or the rest of the world, because people don't seem to give a shit about honor or loyalty or doing the right thing anymore! But I do. I did." Tears burned her eyes as they collected against the rims. "Do you get that? It's important to me. Duty to the Covenant. Duty to the Core. Duty to family. That was my life."

"You're not the only one who thinks that duty and family are important—"

She stepped back, throwing her arms out wide.

"This is where I grew up, Judah. No sun. No trees. No neighbors. No friends. No electricity or plumbing. And you know what? I didn't miss those things. My mom trained me to live without them. She taught me to live with only what was necessary, to do only what was right … to feel only what I needed to feel and nothing else. If I felt something that jeopardized my duty, or went against what was right, then I banished it. Into the cellar, into the darkness. And I locked the door. Because that's what my mom told me to do—"

His eyes blazed, not with godly fire, but with anger—Judah's anger. "It wasn't your mom who shut me out, Josie."

"You're right."

He winced, like she'd slapped him.

"It was me," she said, the inner storm raging, lashing against her windows, shaking her foundations. "I did what I thought I had to do. You want to *get* me, Judah? Then get that. A Triune doesn't betray her sister, no more than she betrays the Core or the Covenant."

"You're not the Triune, Josie."

"I know that!"

"Do you?"

"I destroyed the Covenant. There is no Triune anymore because of me. I gave up everything—"

"What did you give up?" He finally let his arms fall away from his chest. "You think destroying the Covenant means you're different? You're not different, Josie. You brought me back and then you ran right back to who you used to be—right back to pushing everyone away, keeping everyone out, keeping me out. You're still locking your emotions up—"

"Of course I am!" she said, hands curling into fists, trying to stop the trembling. "Do you know what this is like? Everything I was, everything I was supposed to be—gone." Her fingers splayed open as if throwing her words to the wind. "Like that. And everyone expects me to suddenly become this normal teenaged girl, who just feels whatever she feels and says whatever she thinks and has dreams—"

Her gaze flicked over to where Ty was napping, but he had slipped away at some point.

"It's not that easy," she said.

"I know—"

"No," she cut in, "you don't."

"If I don't know, Josie, it's because you haven't told me. You haven't told anyone, but you know what? It's all bullshit anyway. You were never able to control your emotions like you thought. If you had, you wouldn't have made the mask for me. You did that because you couldn't be who you thought you should be. Being loyal, doing your duty, doesn't mean you have to blind yourself to who you really are—"

"And who is that?"

"That's what I want to know, Josie. That's what I want you to tell me."

"You want me to be someone I'm not—"

"Because I want you to talk to me?" He dug his hands into his hair. "Gods, Josie. Look at us. Look at that!" He flung his hand out towards the circle of the Fates behind her. "Do you think I expect you to be a 'normal' girl? I have an ancient volcanic god trapped inside my body. Who's normal around here? Everyone I know is busy preparing to battle an earth goddess and her demon army. They're not doing it because they want to. They're doing it because they have to. We're Core. We understand duty. We understand sacrifice."

"Then why are you trying to stop me from going to the Fates?"

"Damn it, Josie! I'm not trying to stop you—"

"You said you didn't want—"

"That's right, want. I don't *want* you to go, Josie. Is that okay with you?"

Inside the twister was tearing her apart, ripping her house up from the ground and busting open that cellar door. Out and away, all of the emotions she'd never felt spun free.

"You want me to choose between you and the rest of the world?" she asked.

"You already did that, didn't you?"

She fumbled for a response.

He plowed ahead. "Do you think I would ask you to make that choice?"

The tears finally broke from the edges of her eyes, rolling down her face. "I don't know—"

"That's right. You don't know what I think, because you never ask."

Up and up, spinning and spinning, faster and faster.

"You're not alone anymore, Josie," he said. "That's what I want you to see. I'm here, but you have to let me be here. You have to let me in. And that's not something I want, Josie, it's something I need. You think I want you to be normal? There's a whole planet full of normal girls back there. You think I want you to stop being who you are? Who you are is exactly why I'm here. Because you're not normal. Because you're willing to put everything aside to do what's right, to take the chance to save the world or save my soul. How could I not want that? But gods, Josie, is it so much to ask that you talk to me? Tell me what you're thinking. Tell me what you want? Tell me... anything. I don't care. I just need to feel like you trust me a little bit more than not at all."

Suddenly, the tornado ceased, and she was flung out into a Technicolor world full of wand wavers and undreamt dreams. She felt bruised and lost and scared out of her mind. All she wanted was to run back to that black-and-white world. She might've been miserable there, but at least she'd understood it.

Judah's voice was gentle. "Josie—"

She swiped the tears from her cheeks. Her voice was weak and trembling.

"I don't know how." More tears fell from her eyes.

All the grief, all the anger, all the ... everything she had never felt. Finally, she could cry. Finally, she could feel.

And it was awful.

"It's not that I don't trust you, Judah. I do. I'm sorry that you don't feel it. I'm sorry that I don't know how to make you feel it or what to say to make you believe it—"

Judah held up his hands, tears shone in his eyes too, but the fire in them continued to burn. "Just tell me ... something, Josie. Something you've never told anyone else. I don't care what it is. How small or trivial, just ... tell me."

She remembered then something her dad had told her once, when she'd been younger, and they'd still lived together. One night after dinner, for some reason she couldn't remember, he'd tried to teach her how to waltz. She'd been so frustrated by stepping on his toes and not being able to pick up the sequence. He'd said, with a smile that reached all the way to his eyes, "It's better to misstep, Josie, than to not take a step at all. One small step at a time."

It was one of those memories she'd buried in the darkness because it had made her miss her dad, whom she'd never really known after her parents had split. And it had filled her with knotted, miserable feelings that were of no use to anyone, especially not a Triune.

Had her dad been right? Was one small step better than no step at all?

And she remembered what Ty had said about giving Judah some part of her, some place in her life.

When she was finally able to speak again, her voice sounded far-off and tremulous.

"I want to go running on the beach with you. I wanted to say yes when you offered before. I'm sorry I didn't. I want to do that . . . sometime. Okay?"

Tears streaked his cheeks. "What else?"

She was surprised how easily the answer came. "I want a party."

"A party?" he asked like he hadn't heard her right.

"A birthday party. I'll be eighteen in three weeks. The last time I had a birthday party was when I was six, before my parents split up. After that, Mom always took me to some fancy restaurant somewhere—Paris, New York, Hong Kong— for lunch or dinner. I hated it."

Her feet felt firmer on the ground now. Her headache retreated slightly. Though she was saying things that she'd barely allowed herself to think—because they were useless thoughts that would only weaken her—now that she was speaking them, her voice grew stronger.

"I want a cake," she said. "And I want candles. And I want people to sing. I want all those dumb things, streamers and balloons. The last time I blew out the candles, the last time I made a wish, I wished for my parents to stay together. It didn't come true. I stopped making wishes after that. But . . . I want to start again."

"What are you going to wish for?"

"I can't tell you that, or it won't come true."

The corner of his mouth twitched, a little.

"I'm sorry," she said. "I'm sorry for being so . . . if you don't want me to go to the Fates, then . . ."

He wiped the wetness from his cheeks. "Then what? You won't go? Don't start lying to me, okay? Of course, I don't want you to go and, of course, you're going anyway. It doesn't mean I have to like it. But at least . . . you thought about me. I don't want to stop you from saving the world, Josie. I just want you to remember that you have a reason to come back to it. I'm here, okay?"

She nodded, but still felt stunned and raw and uncertain.

He held open his arms.

She went to him. His arms closed around her and held her tight. He was warm and solid and alive and so . . . Judah. He felt right. He smelled right. He was, as always, right.

He kissed her.

She wanted to kiss him. She tried, but tilting her head back to receive his kiss made her knees wobble and her head foggy. She could barely cling to his shoulder for support.

When his lips left hers, her head dropped against his chest. She fought to keep her eyes open, to stay conscious. He held her up and against him.

"Don't shut me out any more," he said into her hair.

"Okay," she murmured.

He slipped one bunch of bracelets onto her wrist. "Whatever happens, we're doing this together, right?"

"Right," she said, forcing her eyes open again so she could look up at him. She rubbed her forehead. "I still have to cleanse the . . ."

He slipped the second group of bracelets over her hand. "Sweet dreams, Josie."

"Wait . . . wha—?"

She sank away into sleep.

CHAPTER 20

August 31st
Late

"YOU ARE SUCH A JERK," she groaned as she focused on Judah, who was hunched over her desk, reading.

He glanced over his shoulder and smiled. "Now we're even."

"That's not funny," she said, pushing aside her quilt, blinking away the hazy film of sleep. Her mouth tasted terrible, and her stomach ached from not having eaten since . . . When was the last time she'd eaten?

"How long did I sleep?" she asked.

He checked his watch. "Ten hours."

She sprung off the bed. "What?"

"Relax."

She looked down, realizing she was in her underwear. He'd removed her shoes and dirty clothes after he'd slipped on the sleep charm and put her to bed. Had it been any other guy in the world, she might've been creeped out, but mostly she felt warm and strangely self-conscious.

She tugged open her dresser drawers, which were pretty much empty since she hadn't owned many clothes in the first place and what she did have, she'd taken with her to Outpost One.

"How could you let me sleep for ten hours?"

Besides a few ratty T-shirts that didn't fit anymore, all she found were a couple of pairs of socks and some stretch pants.

"Your clothes are over there," he said, pointing to her duffle leaning near the door. "And I let you sleep because you needed to sleep."

As she un-cinched the top of her duffle, she couldn't help but notice how much she stank. She supposed if she'd already lost ten hours, she might as well take ten minutes to shower. She bent over to dig out some clean clothes.

"I would've been fine with five," she said, shooting him an irritated look. But his gaze was fixed on parts of her body other than her face. She stood up, forcing his eyes off her posterior. "What happened while I was asleep?"

He looked sheepish for a moment. He leaned back in the desk chair. "You know, the usual, murder, mayhem, mass destruction."

"You sound like Kai. Please tell me it's not that bad."

"Bad is much more relative than it used to be."

"Where do murder and mass destruction fall on this relative scale of badness?" Guilt swelled within her. Here she'd been deeply sleeping, dreamless, peaceful, safe from all the turmoil that she had helped create, while countless others suffered. It was beyond unacceptable. Her mother would've been ashamed and furious—

"If it makes you feel better, most of the deaths seem to be humans killing other humans," he said. "Governments can't keep the peace since many of them don't exist anymore. Last I checked, there's everything from revolution in Venezuela to riots in St. Petersburg to random shootings in Denver."

He seemed to read her distress. "This isn't something you can change by restoring the Covenant," he said, "or by banishing the gods. Unless you're planning on asking the Fates how you can finish off humanity, there's nothing you can do. It happened before. It'll continue to happen." He crossed his arms, grim-browed.

"I can't believe you let me sleep this long—"

"Then you're going to be really upset when I make you eat."

At the mention of eating, her stomach let out a low, mean-sounding growl. She returned her attention to finding a clean pair of jeans. Again she felt the weight of his gaze on her rear. She ignored the flush spreading across the back of her thighs.

Normally, she wasn't bashful about people looking at her—naked or otherwise. Triune training had required her to go nude from time to time. Wherever she went, a Triune was expected to respect the local customs. If that meant wearing nothing, then that's what she did.

Judah's attentions made her, for the first time in a long time, conscious about how little she was wearing. Though they'd been practically naked together more than once, it had always been in the heat of the moment, never . . . casually. Was this one of those "normal" experiences Ty had been talking about? Waking up in the morning, getting dressed . . . discussing the end of the world . . .

Well, she told herself as she tugged a towel out from the bottom of the bag, this was probably as close to normal as she and Judah would get as a couple, under the circumstances.

She stopped cold, hugging her clean clothes and her toiletry bag to her chest. She'd never thought of herself and Judah as a couple before.

Couple. The word brought goose bumps out on her arms.

And it bolstered her determination. Finding the Fates and discovering how to restore the Covenant seemed more important than ever.

It seemed wrong that wanting something so basely selfish, like a normal relationship with Judah, would strengthen her resolve—as if saving her life and Judah's life and the lives of their families and friends and what was left of humanity wasn't enough. Yet, somehow, it did. She guessed Ty had been right.

So much for duty and altruism.

"What's wrong?" he asked.

She shook her head. "Anything else I should know?"

"I think you have enough to worry about, don't you?"

"I'm going to take a shower," she said, moving towards the door-curtain.

"And then eat," he said.

"And then eat," she affirmed, lifting the curtain.

"Do you know yet?" he asked.

She stepped back from the door, letting the curtain fall. "You mean what I'm going to ask the Fates?"

He nodded. She could tell he was trying to be supportive. If only she could figure out how to tell him how much that meant to her.

"I haven't made my final decision yet," she said.

"I've been reading up on them," he said, gesturing over his shoulder to the open book on the desk.

"Anything interesting?"

For the first time she could remember, fear weakened Judah's ever-strong brow. She stepped closer and leaned a hand on the arm of his chair, eye to eye with him.

"I'm coming back," she said.

"That's what you said the last time."

"And I did come back." She poked his chest. "You were too impatient."

"I'll wait this time."

"You'd better."

She kissed him, briefly—too aware of how long it had been since she'd brushed her teeth. It seemed a silly thought, but she didn't try to stuff it into the darkness. She simply let it come and pass. She was surprised at how easy it was. All these years she'd been tamping down every idle thought, afraid that if she allowed too many to flourish, they'd multiply and fill her head like cockroaches. Instead, it simply drifted away and vanished.

She kissed him again, a bit longer. "If you're not here, who's going to chauffeur me back to the mortal plane?"

He smiled a little.

She straightened up and moved towards the door. "Besides, I still want my cake."

"What kind of cake?" he asked.

She paused in thought. "Good question."

"Maybe you should ask the Fates."

She grinned. "Don't tempt me."

"Josie—"

"That was what? Twenty whole seconds of an almost smile?" She pushed aside the curtain. "I'll take it. But I want a real one soon."

All the sacred objects had been cleansed with sage smoke and placed in their appropriate places within the circle: stones carved with Core marks, a pitch bowl poured a thousand years before, feathers of extinct birds, and the scrolls of the Fates, amongst many others.

"A cell phone?" Ty asked as Josie set her phone down in the circle.

The screen was dark. She hadn't charged it in weeks. Not that she would've gotten service on an interdimensional island or even on the mortal plane for that matter because there was virtually no service anywhere.

"I need a marker of my generation," she said. "That seemed about as good as anything."

She scanned the circle again. Everything looked right. Everything seemed to be ready.

She turned to Ty and Judah. "This is it."

Ty pressed his hands to his flat navel. "Oh gods, I'm going to be sick."

"You're not going to be sick," she said. "Once I start the Invocation, you cannot interrupt. If you do, I'll have to clear all of this and start over."

"Or you'll die," Judah added.

He had been standing as still as stone, arms crossed, emanating discontent for the last hour as she'd made the final preparations. Even after she'd eaten two packets of instant oatmeal and a whole can of syrup-laden fruit and had spent more than a few minutes letting him kiss all the syrup from her lips, his mood had continued to darken.

She couldn't blame him for worrying, but she wasn't afraid that she would fail to find the Fates or be killed in the attempt. She was all too sure she would find them and that's what scared her.

Not because they might take years off her life.

No, she was afraid the Fates would tell her there was nothing she could do.

If they told her it was hopeless, that she should go back and wait to die... she didn't think she could bear that. She might beg them to kill her. Except... Judah.

No matter what the Fates told her, she would come back for him.

"Or I might die," she acknowledged. "Like you said, it's going to happen someday."

He winced.

She moved closer to him. "There's nothing I can say that's going to make you feel any better."

"You're right."

"I'll give you two a moment alone," Ty said, turning away.

"Don't bother," Josie said.

She kissed Judah fully but quickly, not lingering—too long. Then she stepped back.

She wasn't going to say goodbye. Everything else seemed too weak or inappropriate to the moment. So she simply turned, treading carefully along the narrow path she had drawn into the circle—from the outer edge to the center.

She picked up the lighter she'd left in the middle, needing to light a few candles and a bowl of herbs, but before her thumb touched the flint wheel, the candles and bowl flared. Aromatic smoke wafted up from the bowl of sage and lavender, clouding her view of Judah. She smiled at him anyway.

"Thanks," she said, not sure if he could hear her.

She knelt.

The first half of the Invocation would take two hours to recite. She'd been timing herself, practicing as she prepared. If it worked, it would open the pathways to the Fates. Then she would face a series of obstacles. The specifics were vague because each was tailored to the individual requesting an audience.

If she survived the tests, then she would have to recite the second half of the Invocation. About ninety minutes, if she said it quickly and left out the clapping. Almost two, if she clapped. More than one Triune claimed that the long breaks filled with rhythmic sets of claps were essential to success. Others said it was unnecessary. She'd probably clap. She didn't want to fail because she was rushing. After that, more trials. Then, possibly, the third stanza of the Invocation. If she were really unlucky, more tests. And if she were *really* unlucky—the process would start all over again.

One Triune had gone through the cycle ten times before she'd been granted an audience. Josie didn't want to think about the possibility.

Smoke unfurled in thin ribbons around her. Focusing her gaze on the nearest candle flame, she took a long moment to breathe and clear her mind.

The flame rose and ebbed, a tiny orange heart of fire. Josie let out another breath and then began the Invocation.

"I summon thee, Fates—"

The world shifted around her.

One moment the Triune's Island—gray ruins, gray sky, gray stones.

In the next moment, she was kneeling in her driveway, facing the street. Her dad's driveway, back in Portland.

A clear blue sky arched over the peak of the green craftsman-style bungalow. The scents of lavender and sage hung in the air, but not burnt in an offering bowl. Rather the fragrances were fresh and green, alive. She looked over to see the aromatic plants growing in tidy rows along the fence—just like she remembered. Underneath her, the concrete was sun-warmed, no trace of the chalked Invocation circle.

A dove cooed from the cedar tree in the neighbor's backyard.

She knew she wasn't supposed to stop the Invocation, but she was so stunned by the change in scenery that she was afraid she'd passed out or been killed before she'd even started.

Portland didn't exist anymore. Her dad's house was gone, burned, flooded, and sunk into a hole in the ground. But everything seemed so real, Josie's heart ached at the sight of it.

"Are you going to sit there all day?" a pleasant voice called to her.

She turned. From where she knelt, she could just peek back into the yard. On the deck, three women sat around a table.

One of them held up a pair of scissors and smiled. "Time's a wastin' you know."

CHAPTER 21

AUGUST 31ST

JOSIE PUSHED UP TO HER FEET and approached the women, stopping shy of joining them on the deck. They sat at a circular, folding card table piled with papers and pictures, glue sticks and stamps...

"You're making scrapbooks?" Josie murmured. She'd meant to think it, but it had slipped out.

The blonde one, who had an old shoe box in her lap from which she was pulling glossy photos, nodded. "It's a wonderful way to preserve memories."

Seated in the middle facing Josie, the dark-haired one dabbed glue on a piece of paper and pressed a photo onto it. "And fun too."

The third wore a bright, floral headdress. "But let's face it; we don't do it for the memories or the fun."

The women shared a quiet look and then each took up their margarita glasses and clinked them together. "We do it for the drinks!"

They fell back in their chairs, giggling.

Josie stared. She kept trying to fix on their faces, to find some detail or feature that might help her remember them, but their faces seemed to defy all attempts at being remembered. The moment Josie looked away from one to the other she forgot what the first had looked like. When she looked back again, it was as if she was seeing the woman's face for the first time. It made her head spin. Their hair color or headdress—in the case of the third—was the only thing she could hold onto to keep her brain from spinning itself into a margarita-like slush.

The middle one, the brunette, looked up at her. "Don't hurt yourself, hon." The blonde handed the brunette a photo. She looked at it, grim. She waved it at Josie. "You have enough problems, believe me."

Josie tried to clear her shock, but it hung on. "I didn't finish the Invocation."

"Oh that." The brunette brushed aside the thought with a wave of her hand.

"I hate all that clapping," the blonde said.

"Who was it that started that?"

"Oh, that Triune with the pretty red hair," the blonde said.

"And that terrible foot problem," the headdressed one said.

They all cringed.

"She really should've bathed more often," the blonde said. "A little hygiene goes a long way."

The headdressed one tapped the handle of her scissors against the table. "She learned it in the end."

"They all learn it in the end, don't they?"

While they chattered, Josie tried to fix on their eyes. She wanted to say the blonde had blue eyes or green or black, but she couldn't. When she tried, her brain simply failed, as if it had forgotten what colors were or what eyes were.

"Now, where are we?" The brunette tilted her head as she inspected the pages spread out in front of her.

She sprinkled some pink glitter on the paper and then shook off the excess. Picking up the page, she examined it. Finally, she turned it so Josie could see. On the pink paper, framed in a layered heart of purple, edged with lace, surrounded by little flaming, glittering hearts all around, was a picture of Judah.

"True love?"

"No, we're past that already," the blonde said. "You're behind. As usual."

The brunette handed the pink page off to the headdressed woman. She looked it over and then winked at Josie.

"Not bad." She 3-hole punched the page and placed it into a binder.

"Okay, okay," the brunette said, looking over the pages, frowning. "Now, wait a minute." She shuffled pages around in front of her.

Josie lifted off her heels, trying to catch a glimpse, but the deck was too high.

"Here he is and then he's gone, but he's here again. Didn't he die?" the brunette asked.

"Yes, she's already brought him back," the blonde said, rolling her eyes.

The brunette scowled. "Oh yes, that."

The three of them looked at Josie in unison. Josie dropped back onto her heels.

"We allowed that?" the brunette asked the others.

"You insisted we give her the chance," the headdressed one said. "If you recall, which I know you don't, because you drink too much." She picked up her own glass and finished off her margarita. Or seemed to finish it. By the time she'd set it down on the table, it was full of lime green liquid again, with a freshly crusted rim of dyed-pink salt. She crossed her leg, pumping it. "And you are a sentimental fool when you are drunk."

"What is wrong with wanting a happy twist now and then? How often do we do get to offer an opportunity like that? You have to admit this book's been much more exciting than usual," the brunette said. "Does it all have to be gloom and doom with you?"

"I am not gloomy or doomy. I am realistic. You were the one who came up with this whole crazy scheme, and I must've been drunk too because I let you get away with it."

"Well, it's not over yet," the brunette said.

"If you had it your way, it would never be over," the headdressed one said.

The brunette sighed. "I do enjoy a good love story. And I know you enjoy this." She picked up another page and showed it to the headdressed one.

The headdressed one's eyebrows peaked. She picked up her margarita glass again, grinning behind the rim. "Now that is what makes a good book."

They all laughed together.

The headdressed one reached for the page. Josie craned for a look at it, but the brunette laid it back on the table.

"It's not done yet," the brunette said.

"What's taking so long?" the headdressed one asked.

"Ask her."

They all looked at Josie again.

"She has a little trouble opening up emotionally," the blonde said with sympathy. "What do you expect from the daughter of Death?"

"And Melinda," the headdressed one said, sitting back in her chair. "You needed a crowbar to pry an honest emotion out of that girl."

"Um . . ." The sound escaped Josie's mouth before she knew what she was going to follow it up with.

They looked down at her. Every time they did, her mind experienced rolling blackouts. She had to look away, towards her dad's manicured patch of mini-lawn. Everything seemed so real. She had to keep reminding herself that she wasn't actually in Portland and that these three giggling women were, in fact, the Fates.

"Okay, okay," the brunette said. "Let's see. Where are we?" She ran her hands over the papers in front of her. "Ah, here it is. Margs with the Sisters." She held up a bright green page with a giant margarita glass drawn on it. She laid it down with care. "I won't know which page to finish until after this happens. This is such a pivotal moment for her."

"Isn't it always pivotal?" the blonde one said.

"That depends entirely on her," the headdressed one said.

They gazed at her again.

Again, Josie was dumbstruck. Why was she here? She felt like she was supposed to be doing something, but she couldn't remember what. She could barely remember her own name.

"Now, Josie," the brunette said with a smile.

Josie. Right. That was her name. Josie Day.

"You have a problem," the brunette continued. "Truth is, we all have a problem."

Josie's voice was weak, but since the middle sister had said her name, her thoughts were becoming illuminated again. "You have a problem?"

The blonde nodded vehemently. The headdressed one pursed her lips.

"Yes, sadly, we do," the brunette said. "You see, every so often we're forced to . . . oh, how do I put it in a way you might understand?" She seemed to think. "To restart. You know, like a computer. Something's not right, so what's the first the thing you do? Switch it off and switch it back on again."

"It's more like an upgrade," the headdressed sister said.

"Oh, yes, much better analogy," the brunette said. "An upgrade to the latest version. But first we have to remove the old operating system, so we can install the new one. And hope it works."

"Hope what works?"

"Well, in this case, it's you."

"Me?"

"Right. See, we have a basic operating system, the Triune system. We like it, but there have been problems. We had to shut it down. When I say shut it down, well, it's not as simple as hitting the power button. We are still shutting it down. And if it's not done properly, then when things start up again, they might not be as . . . ideal as we would prefer."

"We like margaritas," the blonde said.

"Hear, hear," the headdressed one said.

"We like humanity," the brunette said. "And like I said, we liked the Triune. Not all of them, really, but the system worked well for us."

"We don't have a lot of free time," the blonde added.

"And we depended on the Triune to help us manage," the brunette said. "Losing the Triune would be like our whole system crashing—fried. Useless."

"Pain in the ass," the headdressed one said.

Josie's chest constricted. If she understood what they were saying, and she wasn't sure she did, they were telling her they'd liked having a Triune. And she was the one who'd destroyed the Triune's mask. "Please forgive me—"

The headdressed one laughed.

The blonde smiled.

The brunette brushed Josie's remark away again. "You don't have anything to apologize for. Thus far, you're doing . . ."—she exchanged a look with the headdressed one—"okay. You began the system shut down for us by destroying the mask. That's what we wanted."

"It was?"

"You don't want to know what would've happened if Death had overcome your sister and another had been Triune chosen," the blonde said.

"Ugly," the headdressed one added.

The blonde nodded.

"It would've prolonged the entire process and made it nearly impossible for us to salvage the Triune system," the brunette said.

"But the Triune is gone."

The sisters exchanged a look. The brunette folded her hands on top of the scattered papers—pages filled with the events of Josie's life.

Again, she wished she could get a peek at what they contained.

"For now," the brunette said. "Like I said, we're shutting it down in the hopes that we can restart with a new version. Not the same, mind you, but . . . we'll have to wait and see. You've begun the process by destroying the mask, but it's not complete. Like your computers, there's an order to things that must be respected. If you try to bypass the order, you risk the whole thing freezing up and making matters worse."

The headdressed one picked up her glass again. "Hardly seems possible."

"Unfortunately, it's all too possible," the brunette said.

"Forgive me . . . Fates," Josie said, as if she was addressing a tribe's Eye, "but why do you care so much? I thought the Triune was the intermediary for the gods. You're not gods . . ."

She stopped herself, realizing that she didn't know exactly what the Fates were.

The Fates existed outside of the gods' realm—beyond it. Their power wasn't tied to the mortal realm like the gods', which would have made them more like the Other, the root of whose power was a mystery. The Fates supposedly held sway over the destinies of the gods too. Did that mean they had power over the Other?

She remembered then what Death had said about being a mere gatekeeper—about there being a beyond the Beyond. It reminded her that though the scenery was comfortably familiar and the sisters seemed friendly, sympathetic even, she was not actually in Portland. Portland was gone. These women were not the neighborhood scrapbooking club, but beings of power far greater than anything she had ever encountered.

Josie's stomach curled back in on itself.

They were watching her, as if they were reading her deepest thoughts—maybe they were.

The brunette tapped her glass with her fingernails. "Who does the Triune serve, Josie?"

"Um . . . the Core? Humanity?"

"In a sense, yes, I suppose that's true," the brunette said. "But in another, greater sense, the Triune serves us." She gestured around to her sisters. "We needed someone to manage things between the gods and humanity. We tried to let the gods do it, but they failed, miserably."

"And the alcohol back then—" The headdressed sister stuck out her tongue, gagging.

The blonde nodded.

"We're very busy," the brunette said. "Back then, the gods and the demigods and the occasional apt mortal would wander in here, whining and begging. It was maddening. We weren't making any progress on our project, and the mortal realm was, frankly, a mess. So when it came to our attention that there was a demigod capable of managing the gods, well . . . we invested heavily."

"Lu-Ji," Josie said.

"Fierce, that one," the headdressed sister said.

"Um-hm," the blonde agreed.

"Lu-Ji was a savior. Not just for humanity. After she became the Triune, well . . . it was like I had nothing to do anymore. Such a relief. I want that feeling back," the brunette said.

"Hear, hear."

"Now, Josie, this is why we've brought you here and why we've . . . bent a few of the rules to give you the leeway you need to get us back up and running as quickly as possible."

"But don't you make the rules?"

"Don't we wish," the headdressed one said.

"So . . . you want me to restore the Covenant?"

"In a way," the brunette said.

"Okay. How?"

The brunette smiled. "Wonderful question. Here's the funny thing. There's no one way. The steps that must be taken cannot be changed, but the details are, more or less, up to you. And, as always, the devil's in the details, isn't it?"

"There's no such thing as the devil."

"Well, she's confident, I'll give her that much," the headdressed one said. "Even when she's wrong."

"There's a devil?"

"Oh, don't confuse her," the blonde sister said. "That doesn't have anything to do with her."

The headdressed sister shrugged. She eyed the middle sister who had pulled a big plastic box into her lap from somewhere (Josie hadn't noticed it before) and was digging through it.

"Careful there," the headdressed sister said. "It's not like we can ask for new ones."

The brunette waved her hand dismissively. "Most of them are redundant anyway." She pulled out what appeared to be a wood block attached to a handle—a stamper—and set it on the table. After a few more minutes of digging, she retrieved two more. Then she closed the box and it vanished.

"Now," she said, scooting her chair closer to the table, "let's get down to brass tacks, as they say, shall we?"

"Please," the headdressed one said.

"Ink?"

The blonde handed her sister a slim stack of ink pads.

"Paper?"

The blonde slid a sheet of silvery paper onto the table.

"Normally,"—the brunette clacked the plastic cases of the ink pads between her hands, like she was airing out a new card deck—"all we're allowed to do is point the petitioner— that's you—in the general direction of the answer she seeks. But in this instance, we're far more concerned about achieving a favorable outcome."

"So we're going to be straight with you," the headdressed sister added.

"In doing so, we're going to incur a hefty penalty," the brunette said.

"We already have," the blonde said.

"But we're hoping it's worth it, for everyone involved."

"What kind of penalty?"

"No one, neither god nor human, shall be able to invoke us so long as you live."

Josie was sure this was more dire than she realized, but all she could think to say was,

"Okay."

The brunette spread the ink pads out in front of her, one each for the three stampers.

"Three sacrifices must be made. One to the Earth Goddess who wants you dead, one to Death, and one to the Other."

"In that order," the headressed sister said.

Josie hated to ask, but knew she had no other choice. "Sacrifices?"

"Three people must take the god's marks. One person, one mark." The metallic aroma of wet ink drifted to Josie as the brunette flipped opened each of the cases. "They must do so willingly."

"The god's marks . . . no one knows the mark of the Other," Josie said.

"Is that right?" the headdressed one asked with a smile.

The brunette picked up one of the stampers, a squat chunk of wood with no handle. She rolled the stamp across an ink pad. She crinkled her nose as red ink dripped onto the table. She pressed the mark firmly to the paper, like a customs agent stamping a passport.

"We're not just giving you the mortal marks for the gods," she said. "We're giving you their godly marks."

Josie's hands caught each other, squeezing hard. "You—I—no." She shifted, fully expecting lightning to strike her dead or something. Some force to intervene. "You can't do that."

The sisters gave her a shared frown of irritation.

The godly marks. The true names of the gods. Marks that contained more power than their masks. The names written in the Book of the Other, which no mortal could read, lest their soul be liquefied and stricken from existence. A one way ticket to Oblivion.

"Of course you can do that," Josie recanted. Her eyes scanned the serene sky. No cracks of skull-splintering power, yet. "But godly marks are . . . they're not . . . why can't we use the mortal equivalents? Won't seeing the true names of gods melt my eyes in their sockets?"

"Very colorful," the brunette said, setting the first stamper aside and picking up the next. A black one with an elegantly carved handle.

"The average mortal would suffer grave consequences for meddling with the true names of the gods," the brunette said, "but in this instance, we are giving them to you. You will not have to worry about your eyes melting, because you will not be able to see them truly. All you need to do is transfer them to those willing to take them." She pressed the stamp onto the paper.

"How is one sacrifice going to stop the Earth Goddess? Or Death?"

"Stop is an interesting word," the headdressed one said, as if she were talking to herself. "It can mean so many things."

The blonde picked photos out of her shoe box. "Like end?"

"Like quell," the headdressed one said.

"Or arrest," the blonde said.

"Arrest, another interesting word."

"Enough." The brunette said.

The other two fell silent.

The brunette picked up the third stamper. It might've been silver or crystal, Josie couldn't tell. The light played off it in strange ways—casting prisms into Josie's eyes if she looked too hard.

"So, I need to find three people to take the marks. One for the Earth Goddess, one for Death, and one for the Other?" she asked.

"Three willing people," the headdressed one said.

"Why the Earth Goddess?" Josie asked. "If I'm trying to restart the Triune system, shouldn't I be taking Life's mark back with me?"

"No, you're trying to shut down the old system so that we can install a new, different one. Life has already stepped aside. She does not need to be placated. Think of the Earth Goddess as a virus. She must be dealt with before we can proceed with installing the new system. She, Death, and the Other, they are the forces in play now. They are the ones who must be satiated."

"By three willing . . ."—victims—"people."

"Three willing people who satisfy the Order. If they do not satisfy the Order, the mark won't transfer to them and someone else must take it instead."

"The Order?" Josie asked.

The sisters glanced away.

"As we said," the brunette replied after a pause, pushing the third stamp against the pad, "there's an order that must be respected, or all will be lost."

All will be lost.

The words echoed in Josie's mind. It was the first time they'd said something that remotely sounded like what she'd expected. Despite her inability to fix on their faces, she felt all too comfortable with these three entities of unimaginable power. Her comfort made her uncomfortable. It felt like a trick.

"And if I do that, then the Covenant will be restored? The gods will be returned to the Beyond?"

The sisters shared a look.

"There are many possible outcomes," the brunette said finally. "Some would be more favorable than others, and the one we might find most favorable might not be the one you would prefer, but . . . well, we'll just have to wait and see. We can promise you nothing."

She pressed the final stamp onto the paper. She blew on the ink. Lifting the paper off of the table, she examined it for a long moment and then flicked it in Josie's direction.

The silver sheet drifted towards Josie like it was caught on a gentle breeze. Josie's hands opened. The paper slipped onto her fingers and vanished. All she'd seen were three circles, red, black, and gray.

But then, a faint tint of red appeared on her left palm. She squinted at it. A circle. All other detail was lost under the lined layers of her skin. She had the urgent desire to wipe her hand on her jeans—to make the mark disappear. She didn't want it on her skin or under it.

"Your left hand into their right," the brunette instructed. "The mark will be passed. Then the next will appear. When all three have been given and accepted, the Order will be satisfied and we can get back to work."

"That's it?" Josie asked.

"That's it."

The sisters gazed at her.

"Go ahead," the blonde said. "Ask."

All the questions piled into Josie throat and stuck.

Had her mother known all along that Josie was a demigod? Had she known that Josie would never be the Triune? Had she known that the entire fate of the gods and humanity would come to rest on Josie's shoulders? And if she'd known, then why hadn't she told Josie?

"Don't be so hard on her," the blonde said, even though Josie hadn't spoken, "or on yourself. You're only human . . . well, partly human. And the gods are as flawed as humanity, in their own way."

"I wish I could speak to her again," Josie said.

"Of course you do," the blonde said.

"But you can't," the headdressed one said.

Josie frowned. "You're telling me there's no way—"

"There are ways," the brunette said. "But that's not what you came here to ask us. You have the answer you sought."

The headdressed one leaned towards Josie and winked. "Now go give 'em hell."

CHAPTER 22

AUGUST 31ST

JOSIE BLINKED. In front of her rose a gray stone heap of a building.

Portland was gone. The Fates, gone.

She glanced down. The candle flame burned in front of her. She looked over. Judah and Ty were right where she'd left them, watching her with frowns on their faces. Ty chewed his lip.

"How long?" she asked.

Ty and Judah exchanged a look.

"Oh no," Ty said. "Does this mean you have to wipe out the circle and start all over?"

She pushed up to her feet. "How long was I gone?"

"Gone?" Ty said. "You weren't gone. You haven't even started yet. All you said was, 'I summon thee, Fates . . .'"

Judah put a stalling hand on Ty's chest. "You saw them?"

She nodded and looked down at her palm. The red mark still showed on her skin, faintly, like an old ink stain. Her heart sank. She would have to ask three people in her tribe to sacrifice themselves to the gods. And she had the worst feeling that she knew who the most likely ones were to volunteer. She looked up at Judah.

"Not you," she said.

His brow plunged. "What?"

She strode towards him. "I'm not going to let you—" The look of confusion on his face stopped her. "Never mind. Ty, get whatever you need. Judah's taking you back."

Ty wrung his hands. "Now? I was hoping to get another nap—"

"Now," she said. "When you get there, tell my dad and Caroline that I need to get everybody together. We might be able to end this, but . . . just tell them."

Ty nodded. "I'll be right back." He turned and disappeared into the main building.

She turned to Judah. "As soon as yo—" Her words were cut off by his lips pressing against hers.

For a moment, she was stiff, mind stuck, unable to shift gears. The Fates, the Covenant, Death, the Earth Goddess . . . but the hammering of his heart against her chest pulverized each thought that rose against it. Before long she was returning his kiss, moving into him, even as he was moving her backwards, across the courtyard.

She ripped her mouth free from his. He took it as an opportunity to kiss her cheekbone, to bite at her jaw, to run his tongue beneath the hollow of her neck. Her knees almost buckled.

"This isn't a good time," she said breathlessly as he maneuvered her back into the ruined building where she'd tossed all the tents and sleeping bags.

"There will never be a good time for us, Josie," he said into her neck.

She caught his jaw, stopping him and holding his gaze. "Yes, there will."

The sapphires of his eyes had melted down into scintillating pools, and she was sinking into them.

His hands burned against the skin of her back, not with godly heat, but with his own thrumming pulse. He leaned in closer, lips brushing her ear. "I believe you."

Tears pricked at her eyes, remembering when he'd said it the first time, after he'd saved her from drowning, after he'd doubted that she really was a mask-maker.

"That's when I knew. That day at the beach," he said softly, like he was reading her thoughts. His arm tightened around her waist, his body melded against hers. "For sure."

"Knew what?"

He lowered her down to the floor. She sank beneath him into the silky piles of nylon, polyester, and down. Something hard pressed into the middle of her back, tent poles buried under the piles of fabric. She elbowed them away. Very romantic.

She pulled a face and he smiled a little, kissing her, pressing down against her.

"I knew that day, that my feelings for you were different, that they weren't going away," he said, lips grazing her face as he spoke. "When I pulled you out of the water,"—he drew back, suddenly somber—"when I thought you were gone . . . it was like I was drowning too."

She touched his chest lightly with her fingertips. "And Tessa?"

He bowed his head for a second. "What do you want me to say?"

"Did you?"

His brow furrowed. "No."

"But you were sleeping over—"

"We would fall asleep watching movies." His eyes hardened again, and she felt a stab of regret for bringing it up. "Would it make a difference if I had slept with her?"

"Only to her," she said.

"It wasn't going to happen, Josie, not when . . ."

"Not when what?"

He glanced away, like he was thinking about getting up.

She gripped the front of his T-shirt. The Chain was tucked beneath his collar. This close up she could see the surreal flecks of silver and gold running through the cord. It looked like leather, but it was something altogether different, something much more, something not of the mortal world. The closer she looked the more evident it became.

"It doesn't matter," she said. "I want to be with you. Nothing's going to change that."

"Not even knowing that I was using your sister?"

Her grip slackened. "Using her?"

"I liked her, don't get me wrong. She was fun and easy to be around and . . . she was the Triune's daughter. She's beautiful. She seemed perfect."

Josie's stomach squirmed. "Like a trophy."

"Don't think it wasn't the same for her. I know how girls in the tribe saw me because it was the way I wanted them to see me. It was a competition for them. Who gets to date Judah? She chased me for months before I finally agreed to go out with her."

She ran her fingers down his chest, hating that the heat between them was cooling.

"You think I'm a jerk," he said.

She smirked. "I've always thought that."

"So how does it feel, knowing you were right?"

"It sucks."

"Now you know how I feel when you're always telling me I'm right." He brushed her hair back from her temple, thumb resting against the hollow of it. "Dating Tessa, letting her use me the same way I was using her, didn't seem like a big deal until that day."

"The day I drowned?"

"The day you showed up at the center and told me to get the hell out of your way," he said, holding her gaze. "You were soaked, you were shivering, you didn't look like you'd slept in months. You looked like shit."

"Thanks a lot."

"And you looked incredible. You were incredible."

"You called me a bitch."

"You called me Fido."

Her eyes slid down his neck, resting on the pulse showing on his throat. "You really thought I was incredible?"

"I thought you hated me. And . . ."—he swallowed. She watched his Adam's apple move—"that's when I really started to use your sister."

"Use her how?"

"To get to you. To be close to you. To be in the same space with you. I kept waiting for you to give me ... something, anything. But you didn't. Not until I put on the Fire God's mask ..." He let out a breath through his nose, like he didn't know if he should keep talking. "Everything about you changed. Your face, your eyes, your voice. You let your guard down. I was angry you couldn't be that way with me, without the mask. Even after I left you, when I was fighting against the god and I thought you were a threat to my soul, when I was trying to convince myself I didn't really want you, I stayed with Tessa. If I left her, I wouldn't have had an excuse to see you."

She hated what he was saying. She knew that Tessa hadn't been using Judah the way that he thought. Tessa really thought she'd been in love with him. Maybe she had. She ached for her sister and hated herself for hurting Tessa. She was angry at Judah too. He really had been a jerk, but she couldn't hold onto her anger. She had tried to deny her feelings for Judah and it had almost cost him his soul. With everything they had yet to face, holding back from Judah wasn't going to happen. She couldn't do it, not even for Tessa.

"Why are you telling me this now?" she asked.

"I want you to know the truth," he said. "I don't want there to be anything unsaid between us. I don't want to die again knowing that I wasn't honest with you."

She ran her finger over the cord of the Chain, her thoughts returning to the task at hand. To the mark on her palm. To the three lives that would be sacrificed. "Anything else you need to be honest about?"

His forehead touched hers. "I'm going with you."

"With me where?"

"Wherever."

Judah's words tugged at her, but they weren't sweeping her up and away, like she wanted them to.

He drew back slightly. "It was pretty stupid of me to bring this up now, wasn't it?"

"It's never stupid for you to tell me the truth," she said.

"Well, it feels pretty stupid," he said. "Here I have you right where I want you, and I bring up your sister? What is wrong with me?"

"Maybe you're not as much of a jerk as you used to be."

"No . . . that's not it. I must be sick or something."

She smiled. "You're funny. Who knew? There's so much I don't know about you. I'm sorry I wasted so much time." She was starting to heat up beneath him again. "Are you doing that on purpose?"

His lips touched the corner of her mouth. "Doing what?" His words were caresses of steam on her skin.

Sweat dewed on her chest. Electrostatic fingers danced up and down her spine. She curled into the hard lines of his body, molding into him. His fingers dug into her hair, bringing her head to his. He kissed her in that way—the way that ignited a ring of fire around them. Each breath came shorter and the flames grew higher, until all she could feel was heat and all she could see was him.

She could think of a hundred reasons for them not to do this right now, but his lips on hers burned them down to cinders.

All that was left was the one good reason, the only reason, because they were here, now. And this might be the only chance they had. She didn't want to admit it. She never would've said it, but she couldn't deny the looming darkness. She couldn't deny the ugly, unhappy feeling she had when she looked at the mark on her hand. So she didn't look at it.

She looked at Judah. At his perfect face, with all its scars, and his perfect sapphire blue eyes, haunted by godly fire and fear—fear of losing her.

He pulled away for a breathless second. "Now?"

"Now." She caught his mouth with hers and pulled him back, into her.

She watched her hand, rising and falling on his chest. Her palm rested over his heart. On that palm was the mark of the Earth Goddess. She didn't want to think about it. She wanted to stay here with him, like this—burrowed against him, still short of breath, heart skipping beats, tingling, all over, feeling weak and wonderful. His arm was wrapped around her, thumb running idly along the back of hers. His other hand slid up her leg to her waist. He kissed her forehead. She could tell what he wanted—her, again.

She lifted her face to his, meeting his kiss halfway. His fingers skimmed down her stomach.

He knew her. When he'd been behind the Fire God's guise, they'd been close, had learned a little about each other. He'd learned quickly how to ignite her and leave her melting. He took her there and then further, again—until they were both sweat-soaked and trembling, clinging to each other.

His body remained plastered against hers. He dropped his head against the damp sleeping bag under her. She closed her eyes for a second, tasting him on her tongue, his sweat and scent, feeling his weight and his heart against her. She felt warmer and more vulnerable than ever, and yet, stronger. This was how it was supposed to be.

Her fingers ran through the wet waves of gold hair on the back of his head. She held him to her, wanting to keep his heat inside of her, but as thoughts shifted back to the mark on her hand, she began to grow chill.

He moved back, propped up on his elbow, gazing down at her. "Before you go, I want to tell you something—"

"I'm not going anywhere without—"

He took her hand from his shoulder, interlacing his fingers with hers. "That's not what I mean. Stay here with me for a few more seconds, before you start thinking about whatever the Fates told you and whatever shitstorm we're about to walk into."

She latched onto his gaze, returning her attention to him fully. "I'm here. What do you want to tell me?"

His eyes slid away, as if suddenly uncertain. "You said you wanted to go running. And you wanted a party."

"Tres leches," she said.

His brow quirked.

"Cake," she said. "Tres leches cake, the chocolate version, with strawberries."

He smiled. "I'll remember." The smile stayed. Her heart clenched, soaking in the expression. She couldn't remember ever seeing him smile like that. Tears snuck into her eyes.

His smile faded. "What's wrong?"

"Nothing. Everything's … perfect." A tear slipped, warm, across her temple, into her hair. "What did you want to tell me?"

His thumb stopped the next tear from falling. "Maybe I shouldn't."

"Tell me."

"I realized recently there's something I want, Josie."

"You mean, besides this?"

He smiled again. "This and more."

"More?"

"I want it all, Josie. Everything."

"Care to be more specific?"

"I don't just want to be with you, Josie. I want to *be* with you." He looked away again, bashful. "When Life started talking about the two of us and … kids. I realized … I want that. I want the whole thing. You, the house, the kids, the whole suburban lifestyle that everyone talks shit about. I want that."

She stared up at him, mind blank. "Oh."

"I'm not saying I'm ready for it now, I'm just saying … someday."

She came back to herself. Ty had been right. Judah really was a long-term planner. And all she'd asked for was cake.

She touched his cheek. "Okay."

He had not-quite-happy brow. "Okay?"

"House, kids, me." She smiled. "I'll remember."

"The order goes, you, house, kids."

Her smile fled.

He frowned. "What?"

"The order," she said, hand slipping away from him.

His eyes searched her face. "Time to save the world?"

She locked onto his gaze and nodded.

He kissed her, drawing her back into his world for one more moment. She wanted to stay there with him. Why not? Why not have the house and the kids? Like Ty had said. A normal, apocalypse-free life. What was wrong with that? The more she thought about it, the better it sounded. The more she wanted it too. Before the kiss had ended, Judah's dream had become hers.

He helped her up. They found their clothes and dressed. When they stepped into the courtyard, they found Ty passed out in the far corner, cuddling a backpack, filling the courtyard with resonant snores.

"I'm going to take a few more things back," Judah said over her shoulder. He squeezed her hand and disappeared inside. "It's probably not yet dawn there. Get whatever you need, and do me a favor, try to rest."

Josie nodded, marveling at Ty's ability to sleep anywhere, at any time. As much as she still wanted to kick Judah for slipping that sleep bracelet on her and letting her sleep as long as she had, she was grateful. She didn't know when she would sleep again. Not until after her task was completed.

She nudged Ty's foot with hers.

He snorted. His eyes opened and looked around. When he saw her, he grinned, stretching. "So?"

"So what?"

"So is Judah as good as I always imagined him to be?"

"Really?"

"So it's back to banging the tympani drums already?" He mimicked the ominous sound. "*Boom-boom, boom-boom.*"

His lighthearted expression melted when he looked back at up her. "Have you no sense of humor?"

"Not really."

Ty clapped his hands onto his thighs and stood up. "Well, then you and Judah really are perfect for each other. What next, my liege?"

"I need you to go down there and rally the troops for me. And bring back Kai and Simone."

His face fell. "Kai? He betrayed us. He was a freakin' liar. You can't trust him—"

"He loves Simone."

"So?"

"So, I trust that."

Ty shook his head, hands on his narrow hips. "People won't like it. They might try to do something to him—"

"No one's going to touch him."

"I can't stop them—"

"But I can. No one is going to touch him."

"Just because he loves Simone—"

"I ended the Covenant because I loved Judah. I brought him back from the dead and unleashed the gods and demons into the world because I loved him."

"Yeah, but . . . you're weird."

She slid her hands into her back pockets.

He held up his hands. "Don't give me *the* look, okay? All I mean to say is that, you take things to extremes that the rest of us . . . you didn't even think twice, did you? Judah was dead, and you just decided you were going to bring him back. Death made you a deal and you took it, no looking back. Gods, girl, I don't know if I should admire your determination or be terrified of it. Does it have something to do with you being a demigod or what?"

Josie didn't know how to answer that question. She hadn't really begun to think of herself as part ... god. She didn't even know what that meant. Was that why everyone thought she was so emotionless and difficult to read? Is that why she was able to cow her elders, even Nancy? She'd always thought it was her Triune training, but was it something else entirely? Ty was right. When Judah had been gone, she'd suffered. She'd doubted even. She'd despaired. And yet, she'd kept searching for a way to bring him back, because she hadn't known what else to do. Because nothing else had been acceptable.

She glanced down at the faded crimson circle on her hand. That terrible feeling filled her again. When she thought about asking three members of her tribe to sacrifices themselves ... her determination, godly or not, quailed. She knew she had to do it, but it filled her with foreboding.

Ty mussed his dark blond hair. "What did the Fates tell you to do, anyway?"

CHAPTER 23

September 1st
Early Morning

"I told Ty to gather the entire tribe," Josie said, shooting him a sharp look.

His face turned pink and he sank behind Gretchen.

"First you're going to tell us." Caroline sagged into one of the big patio chairs.

They were gathered on the Big House's screened porch which overlooked an open-air deck and the forest beyond. In spite of the chill overnight, the early morning air was warm. Ceiling fans cranked, moving the air without cooling it.

In the distance she could hear the buzz of a saw. The Forest Goddess's shrine was well underway. The stone altar was already in place. Beneath it, the blood of a deer had soaked the earth. The rest had gone to the kitchens, where the meat wouldn't be wasted. Judah reported that not everyone in the tribe had been onboard with slaughtering the deer. A fight had nearly broken out. Then the Forest Goddess had appeared, preening and flushed with new power, and the tribe had remembered that they were still fighting for their own lives. Old prayers had been dredged up, thanking the deer for its sacrifice, and new ones written, praising the Forest Goddess.

"Where is Judah?" Caroline asked.

"He's bringing Kai and Simone."

"So the traitor can be executed?" Nancy asked.

She stood by the doors that led into the house, trying to chill the room without success. Like everyone else, her eyes were half open, her face glistening with sweat and her silk shirt smeared with dirt. Josie was impressed. She hadn't expected Nancy to get her hands dirty, let alone her shirt.

Josie's scowled at her. "Are you really that eager for people to start dying?"

"Start?" Nancy repeated, holding Josie's gaze. "I suppose I'm not surprised by your ignorance, since you've been safe and sound on the Triune's Island, but the dying has already begun."

Josie ground her teeth. Her face grew hotter.

"Did you find the Fates?" her dad asked. His lean face was flushed and sweat-dappled from working on the Lake God's shrine. He sat on the arm of Caroline's chair, looking like he was ready for a long nap.

"I'm here," Beech said, yanking open the screen door and bounding in with a grin. He wore the Forest Goddess's bow and quiver across his bare chest. Over his numerous tattoos, faintly glittering symbols had been drawn on his torso. Tessa sidestepped away from the door where she'd been stationed, far from Josie. Allison was with her, looking almost as pale and tired as Tessa. Allison gave Beech a once over, like she hadn't realized how good-looking he really was until that moment, and then took another step back from him.

"You're sparkling," she said.

His grin widened. He opened his mouth like he was about to tell the best story of his life, and then Gretchen stepped towards him. His face fell. He lifted his shoulder. "It's nothing. Just some . . . goddess stuff."

Gretchen's eyes narrowed. "Goddess stuff?"

Beech held up his hands. "Worry not, Mama Bear. I'm not marked or anything." He waved his hand at his chest. "Blessings and protection charms . . . mostly."

"Mostly?"

Josie turned her gaze past them as Gretchen continued to interrogate Beech about what the symbols were exactly. She scanned the forest, wishing Judah would reappear.

Roxy came up to her, smiling gently and holding out a glass of iced tea. Josie took it.

"Thanks."

Roxy's plump lips curled in a sympathetic smile. "If you need something to give it a little kick, let me know." She winked and patted Josie's arm.

Josie forced out a smile. She took a sip of the tea and then set it aside on one of the small tables. The furniture was scattered across the long porch, clusters of chairs positioned here and there. Caroline and Josie's dad were the only ones who'd taken advantage of any of them. Everyone else stood, mostly at the other side of the deck, facing Josie.

"Be glad, Mama," Beech said to Gretchen finally. "I've got serious godly backup here. Do you know what it would take for someone to bust through these? Go ahead, try to stab me."

Tessa's voice was a weak whisper. "They're here."

From the cover of the trees, Judah emerged, back straight, shoulders broad, striding with confidence. Josie wondered if he really felt it or if he was simply incapable of showing trepidation. Behind him Kai followed, a leaner, paler shadow, eyes darting like he fully expected to be attacked. And then Simone, holding, of all things, a spear that was at least a foot taller than she was.

Judah led them across the lawn and up the long stairway to the elevated deck. Beech and Gretchen moved aside as he opened the door. Caroline stood up and met Judah as he came in, hugging him. He hugged her back. Kai slid in behind him. Finally, the room seemed to cool. Kai moved away from the others, closer to Josie. His dark eyes met hers, but he didn't speak. Caroline embraced Simone too, sparing Kai a hostile look over Simone's shoulder.

"What is this?" Caroline pulled back from the hug, touching the spear.

Judah joined Josie, touching her arm lightly. Josie ached to be back in his arms again, but she only gave him a small smile. She could feel Tessa's gaze on them.

"The Forest Goddess gave it to me," Simone said of the spear. "We ran into her on our way here. She said she's going to give one to all the women of the tribe. They're blessed. She said it's powerful enough to take out a demon."

"She's psyched about the shrine," Beech said, still grinning. "And the sacrifices and . . ." He shrugged. "You know."

"Oh, we get it," Ty said from the corner.

"What about the other gods?" Josie asked Kai, who was watching the others warily.

"A river god and two air gods," Kai said. "The river god pretended like he couldn't hear us. One of the air gods sent a gust so strong Simone was thrown fifteen feet—"

"Are you all right?" Caroline asked Simone softly.

"I'm fine," she said to her mom.

"And the other one wanted to know where her shrine was and if we had any blood we were interested in losing," Kai finished.

Josie frowned. Not a promising report.

"What about you?" Kai asked. "See any Fates around lately?"

Everyone turned to look at her.

Judah's hand skimmed her back supportively, and then he resumed his bodyguard pose at her side. Josie glanced at her sister. Although Tessa looked stronger and more alert than she had when she was the Triune, she was as gaunt and ashen as before, as if she hadn't eaten or slept since being freed of the Tripartite. She was glaring at Josie, hurt shining and anger burning in her eyes. Vaguely, Josie wondered if Tessa would ever forgive her.

Josie pushed this thought aside. Begging Tessa for forgiveness would have to wait.

"I did." She scrubbed her marked hand along the seam of her jeans.

"So quickly?" her dad said. The wound on his face showed rotted yellow around the edges, still deep purple and black in the middle, but at least the swelling had gone down and he could wear his glasses again. "You don't look like—"

"They were anxious to see me," she said.

Her gaze swept the room, from Nancy to her far left, over to Kai to her immediate right. In between was every person she cared about. Dad, Roxy, Gretchen, Beech, Ty, Tessa, Caroline, Simone, Kai . . . and Allison, who Josie didn't dislike so much that she'd wish any harm to come to her. The poor girl looked so tense and white-faced with fear that Josie felt a protective surge, even for her. Even for Nancy.

"I still think I should tell this to the whole tribe," Josie said, glancing over at Judah, hoping he'd back her up.

He stood there, brow said, *Just spit it out.* He was as anxious as everyone else to hear what the Fates had told her.

She rubbed her thumb over her palm.

"I'm going to tell you," she said. "But it's not going to be any of you."

Gretchen frowned. "Not going to be any of us what?"

"I know you're all going to think I'm being completely selfish and I am," she said. "The Fates told me how to restore the Triune . . . sort of."

Tessa stepped forward, seeming to forget her anger for the moment. "How?"

Josie held up her hand, palm to them. She wasn't sure if any of them could see the red mark or not. "With this."

Nancy squinted. "With what? Your hand?"

Judah turned so he could see her palm. "What is that?"

She lowered her hand. "The mark of the Earth Goddess. *The* Earth Goddess."

They all seemed to recoil.

"You're marked by the Earth Goddess?" Allison whimpered. "You're going to be possessed by a demon?"

"No," Josie said. "This isn't her mortal mark. It's her godly name. And it's not actually mine, I'm . . . holding onto it."

"Her godly name?" Caroline repeated.

"That's not possible," Nancy said, though she looked about ready to shove open the patio door and race back into the house.

"Why are you holding onto it?" Judah asked.

"So I can give it to someone else," she said, giving him a look she hoped he understood—NOT YOU. "I need three willing . . ."—sacrifices—"volunteers. One to take the mark of the Earth Goddess. One to take the mark of Death. And one to take the mark of the Other."

Silence greeted her. No one was jumping up to volunteer, and she was glad.

"And then?" Gretchen asked finally.

"And then . . . maybe . . . 'the Order' will be satisfied. The Triune will be restored, the gods and the demons will be gone, and we can start picking up the pieces."

"Maybe?" Beech said.

Josie sighed. "The Fates told me as much as they could. More, I guess, than they were supposed to."

"Why would they do that?" her dad asked.

"Because they want me to succeed," she said. "They want us to succeed."

More silence, heavier this time.

"What happens?" Caroline asked. "To the ones who take the marks?"

Josie shook her head. "I guess that's for the gods to decide."

Josie expected more thoughtful silence. Instead, she heard a soft voice, from her right.

"I'll do it."

She looked over at Kai. Heart sinking.

"No way," Simone said, banging her spear on the deck. But he didn't look at her. His dark eyes remained on Josie. She could see that he was serious.

Her hands fisted as if she could hide the mark from him. "I'm not letting anyone take the mark until after I've told the entire tribe."

Kai didn't back down. "You know it has to be me."

"No, it doesn't," Simone said in a reedy-high voice. She seized his arm and forced him to look at her. "You're not doing this. You'll be killed."

He grasped her arms. "I should've stopped this a long time ago," he said.

Simone stiffened. "Josie won't let you." She turned to Josie. "Will you?" Simone's eyes were pleading and demanding at the same time.

"I don't want anyone in this room to take the mark."

"That *is* selfish," Judah said softly behind her.

"I know." She glared at him. "I don't care."

He scowled.

"It seems entirely just to me," Nancy said. "Let the boy pay for his betrayal. I can't think of a more fitting punishment."

"It's not a punishment." Josie broke from Judah's judgmental glare. "No one can be forced to take the marks. Whoever does must do so willingly. And whoever it is, in the end, will be saving us all. It's not a sentence; it's a sacrifice."

"Sounds like a death sentence to me," Allison muttered.

No one argued with her. Just looking at a godly mark was supposed to kill a mortal. She couldn't imagine what it would do for someone to take it.

"Josie's right," Caroline said. "We should bring this to the tribe. Everyone should be allowed to consider it. We'll do it before lunch."

"On the front lawn?" Gretchen suggested.

Caroline gave a weary nod.

"Is that all?" Nancy asked. "I want to stop by the radio room before I return to the perimeter." She gave Josie a harsh glance. "Most of the protective circles have yet to be re-established since your last foray in here with that thing." She gestured to the Sword of Eternity on Josie's back.

Josie thought it better if she didn't respond.

"I guess that's all," Caroline said.

"I'll go with you," Roxy said to Nancy. She gave Gretchen a kiss and then followed Nancy back into the house.

"Allison, Ty, would you spread the word for us?" Gretchen asked.

"Sure thing." Ty hooked Allison's arm and dragged her to the outside door. Allison was green-lipped and gray-skinned, like she might puke. Ty propelled her out the door. "Happy to."

The tension around Simone and Kai was building. Simone stood there, hands wrapped around her spear like she might use it.

"I'll go too," Beech said, close at Ty's heels.

"Let's talk a little bit," Gretchen said, following him out onto the deck.

"Come on, Mama Bear," Beech said. "Since when have you gotten so uptight?"

"Sometime between the end of the world and when my son started sleeping with a goddess." The screen door closed behind her.

"Don't stress. It's not like I'm going to marry her—Ow! What's with the physical violence?"

"It's either me smacking you now or the goddess ripping out your testes when she hears you say something like that. I gave you more than good looks, Baby Bear, think—"

"All right . . ."

Josie turned to Judah, about to suggest that they take their own imminent argument some place more private, but was cut off by a shout and a cry.

Through the screen Josie saw Gretchen and Beech race down the steps and out of view.

"Oh, hell no!" Beech cried.

Caroline ripped open the screen door. Judah rushed after her. They, too, disappeared down the deck's stairs.

"Mom! Watch out!" Judah shouted.

"Judah, no!" Caroline screamed.

Josie collided with her dad at the door.

He gripped her arm. "Stay here."

She drew her sword. "You stay."

She pushed by him, onto the deck, blinded by the sudden brightness of the day.

"Josie!" Caroline cried in warning.

Allison, eyes blood red, face contorted in a grotesque mask of its former self, came bounding up the steps onto the deck and straight at Josie.

Crack!

Josie wasn't sure if the sound she heard was Allison's fist slamming into her face or her skull hitting the deck. Either way, she blacked out for a second.

When she came to, Allison—the drooling demon that possessed Allison—stood over her with the Sword of Eternity. Allison lifted the blade, ready to plunge it into Josie's chest.

Judah grabbed Allison from behind. An inhuman shriek issued from her throat that split Josie's already ringing ears. Fire laced Judah's arms, igniting Allison's clothes. Allison howled, thrashing. They stumbled back toward the far end of the deck. Allison wrenched her arm free from Judah's hold. Her elbow smashed into his face. He dropped her as he staggered into the deck's railing.

The left side of Josie's face was throbbing and wet. She forced herself to sit up. Allison's clothes were burning. The stink of melting flesh and burnt cotton filled the air, but Allison didn't seem to notice. She turned on Judah, swinging the sword at him wildly.

Allison had been taken over by a demon. She was a traitor. She'd been working for Lily the whole time.

Judah dodged away from the sword as it sliced towards him and slid straight through the deck's railing. Allison jerked the sword back and came at him again. He ducked, slamming a flaming fist into her stomach.

Josie searched the wide deck around her for a weapon. Simone and Tessa were pulling Josie's dad, who appeared to be unconscious, into the porch.

Kai grabbed Simone's fallen spear. He glanced over his shoulder at Josie.

"You okay?"

The Allison-demon swung again at Judah, even as she was burning alive. Except she wasn't alive, not since she'd been taken over by the demon. Her soul was gone. The demon didn't seem to mind having its new body charred. Flames had eaten away at her shirt, leaving them smoldering scraps. Beneath, her skin was blistered, red and purple.

Josie's head was still swimming when Gretchen appeared at the top of the steps, her chest heaving.

"Give that to me," Gretchen said, gesturing for the spear. Kai tossed it to her.

Judah caught Allison's arm as she brought the sword arcing down, stopping her from slicing open his skull. But she didn't stop coming. She snapped and tore at him, forcing him back. He hit the railing. The wood groaned and cracked, weakened from where the sword had severed it. Allison shoved. The railing snapped, and Judah fell from the deck.

"Judah!" Josie shouted. Kai gripped her arm, helping her to her feet. How far was it to the ground? Ten, twenty feet?

"He'll be okay," Kai said to her as she swayed, trying to get her head to stop spinning.

At that moment, Gretchen charged at Allison, spear raised. Allison turned, knocking the spear aside with the sword.

Gretchen stumbled. Her spear fell, clattering.

Allison was barely recognizable. Her hair curdled as the fire melted it to her skull, putrid smoke curling off her skin as it burned.

Gretchen swung at Allison with her fist. Allison seized Gretchen's hair and yanked her head back. Allison tore into Gretchen's throat with her teeth.

"No!" Josie screamed, lurching forward. Kai hooked her waist and held her back.

Gretchen dropped to the deck. Bleeding.

Smoke swirled around Allison's limbs. Fire ate away at her skin. She snarled at Josie, mouth a reddened smear, and lifted the Sword of Eternity.

An arrow sang through the air and struck Allison in the chest. Right in the heart. True, just as the goddess had said.

The demon's crimson eyes rolled. She staggered back, gurgling. Blood gushed from her mouth. Then she collapsed next to Gretchen. The sword fell with a clang.

Beech bounded up the steps, bow readied, arrow aimed. His gaze fell to Gretchen. His arrow dropped and rolled across the deck. Then over the edge. Gone.

CHAPTER 24

SEPTEMBER 1ST

KAI HELD JOSIE UPRIGHT. Her knees didn't seem to be working.

"Oh, hell no," Beech murmured.

He dropped his bow too.

He ran to Gretchen, falling to his knees next to her, lifting her in his arms, cradling her. "Come on, Mama Bear, wake up. Please."

Simone pushed open the screen door next to Kai. "What—?" Her gaze tracked over to Beech and Gretchen. Tears sprung into her eyes. She rushed to Beech's side, wrapping her arms around him.

Questioning voices were calling from beyond the deck. Judah appeared on the top of the steps. Josie was about to pull herself free of Kai and go to him, but stopped herself. His hair was almost as black as his eyes. Not Judah after all.

"What are you doing here?" she asked Death.

He leaned against the deck railing. "Don't you know?" His all-black gaze slid away from Josie. Tessa was in the doorway, glaring at Death. "Miss me?" He winked at Tessa.

Beech tore free of Simone. "Son of a bitch." He barreled towards Death.

Josie threw herself in front of him. He slammed into her. They both spun and stumbled down the deck steps.

Josie caught the railing, halting their descent. She hung onto Beech even as he pulled against her, ready to go back at Death, who watched from above with a vague look of amusement.

"Get off!" Beech shoved her, slamming her into the wooden rail. Pain shattered across her lower back. Beech started up the stairs again.

She grabbed his arm with both of her hands. "You can't fight Death!"

He ripped away from her. "Fuck you!"

"He'll kill you!"

Another cry of pain echoed from the deck. Beech tore free and raced back up the stairs. Josie chased him, catching up with him at the top, where he'd come to an abrupt halt—unnaturally still, especially for Beech.

Death was gone.

Roxy had taken Beech's place at Gretchen's side. She turned towards them, eyes overflowing and so pain-filled that Josie had to look away. Roxy pushed to her feet. Beech hung his head. Tears splattered the wood planks. Roxy wrapped her arms around him. He covered his face with his hands and sobbed.

Josie turned away. A crowd had gathered in the grassy lawn at the bottom of the steps. A few of them glanced up at her. They were circled around Ty. Blood ran from a wound on his head, but he was conscious. His hands moved as he talked.

Caroline sat on the ground near him, blood on her hands and head too, but at least they were both alive. People surrounded them both, tending their injuries. Judah appeared at the bottom of the steps, the real Judah. He looked up at her, meeting her eye.

Brow concerned, asking, *Okay?*

No. She wasn't okay. Ty and Caroline were injured. And Gretchen was dead.

His eyes darkened, and then he turned and knelt next to his mom.

Josie sat down hard on the top step. On the deck behind her, smoke and blood and tears, but she kept her back to it. She couldn't look. She couldn't start grieving. Not now. Not yet. Not until she'd finished what she'd started, not until this was all over.

Kai crouched at her shoulder. "Give it to me," he said softly.

She glanced back at him. Behind Kai, Roxy was still sobbing with Beech.

"My dad?" she asked.

"He's okay," Kai said. "Just knocked out. Simone and Tessa are with him."

Faint wisps of smoke swirled around them—Allison's body smoldering.

"It was her," Josie murmured.

"The Wolf?" he asked.

Josie nodded.

"Maybe." Kai's eyes were deep, dark, and full of the kind of determination that Josie hated to see in anyone she cared about. Now she knew how Judah felt. "Give me the mark."

She held her marked hand in a tight fist. "I don't want to do that to you."

His half-smile returned, no longer amused, only rueful. "You don't want to do that to Simone, you mean."

"I said what I meant."

His smile shriveled. "You should hate me."

"You stopped her."

"My mom? I helped her. I kidnapped you, remember? I cut you. I almost killed Beech."

"You stopped her from killing me. You stopped her from torturing me. You let yourself be tortured instead—"

"Only because I knew it would make you do what we wanted—"

"You told me to run away. You let me escape that day my mom was murdered."

"Because you weren't of any use to us—"

"You love Simone."

"So?"

"So you're not evil."

He smirked. "Evil? Really, Josie? Is that how you think the world works?"

"You're my friend."

"Are you delusional? I'm the enemy, remember?"

"No, you're not."

"I'm a traitor. I lied to you. I lied to Simone. I lied to everyone. I used them. All of them. I'm the bad guy, Lady Day." He held out his hand. "Now give me the godsdamned mark."

"Do you love Simone?"

He bowed, his hand dropped.

"Are we friends?" she asked.

He didn't look at her.

She gripped his arm. "You're not the bad guy, Kai."

He lifted his head. "Let me prove it."

"You don't have to prove it."

He held her gaze for a long moment. "Yes, I do. Let me, Josie. Please."

"I can't."

His smile returned faint and genuine. "Are we friends?"

Simone would hate her. Simone would kill her.

Kai seemed to be reading her mind. "She'll forgive you."

"I wouldn't."

"She's a better person than you are, than either of us."

Josie almost laughed. "You're right. She is. I guess that's why we both love her, huh?"

He held out his hand again. "Let's end this." He leaned close again. "You know it's right."

She did. But she hated herself for it.

Her fist uncurled. Her hand slid into his, gripping it. "I'm sorry, Kai."

His smile stayed. "Me too, Josie."

She expected some feeling, some sense that mark had been passed, but she didn't receive it.

His hand pulled back from hers. On it, a wine red mark appeared for a moment, but faded before Josie could fix on it, like the faces of the Fates.

Screams echoed around them. One, then many more.

Josie surged to her feet. Head dizzied by the stink of Allison's smoking corpse and the taint of fresh blood in the air and the loss of Gretchen and what she'd done to Kai, and now the screams issuing from seemingly everywhere, Josie couldn't get her thoughts to sit still long enough to understand them.

Kai was craning his neck. "What is—"

"The perimeter!" someone shouted. "It's breached! She's here!"

The women with the spears hefted them and raced back towards the front of the house, leaving Ty and Caroline in the care of the men.

Josie glanced down at Kai's hand, heart plummeting, realizing her mistake. "*Kuso.*"

She pushed by him. Beech and Roxy wiped their faces.

She couldn't look at them or at Gretchen's body. Time for grief was later.

Tessa and Simone emerged from the porch.

"What's going on?" Simone asked.

Josie came up short, guilt seizing her. How could she tell Simone that she'd given Kai the Earth Goddess's mark? Before Josie had the chance, Kai seized Simone, kissed her full on the lips, tears running down his face, and then turned and raced down the steps.

"Kai, what are you—?"

But he was gone.

She turned back to Josie. "What . . .?"

Judah translocated onto the deck with Caroline in his arms. She had a bloody wound to her head and seemed to be having trouble focusing.

He gave Josie a dark look. "You gave him the mark, didn't you?"

Simone dug her hands into her hair. "You what?"

Josie cringed.

Judah's eyes were burning. "What were you thinking?"

"I wasn't! Obviously!"

No, because if she'd been thinking, she would've remembered that giving Kai the goddess's mark would allow the goddess to cross any protective circles around him, including the few that were protecting the camp.

Simone was red-cheeked and white-faced. "Josie! How could you?"

"Simone, I'm sorry—"

Simone darted past Josie and grabbed the sword from the spreading slick of blood and gore between Allison and Gretchen's bodies. Then she raced after Kai.

Josie stared, stunned. Fire filled Judah's eyes as his little sister disappeared from view.

"Open the door," he barked at Tessa.

Tessa complied. Judah carried Caroline into the porch, where Tessa and Simone had left Josie's dad. She hoped he was still unconscious and would stay that way for whatever was about to happen. She didn't think she could handle watching anything happen to him.

"What do we do?" Roxy asked.

"We go after her," Josie said, picking up Gretchen's fallen spear from the deck. Beech nodded, scooped up the bow, and bounded down the steps.

Josie spared her sister a look, hoping it wouldn't be the last. "Stay with Dad."

"And wait to die?" Tessa said scathingly.

So much for crisis-inspired reconciliation.

Judah shoved open the porch door, forcing Tessa to step aside. Ghostly blue flames twined around his body.

Josie stepped back, not sure if Judah was in control or if the Fire God had somehow seized the moment and overtaken his body again.

"When this is over," he said to her in his own voice, not the Fire God's hissing rumble, thankfully, "we're going to have a conversation about impulsive decision making."

"Let's just go," she said, starting towards the steps.

He grabbed her arm and slammed her back to his chest. "This way."

Through the paths of fire. Into the battle.

CHAPTER 25

SEPTEMBER 1ST

O R SLAUGHTER.

Judah translocated them to the front of the house. The lawn sloped down before them. At the bottom, near the lake, was the Earth Goddess. Old sinkhole face herself.

Josie clutched the spear to her chest.

The Earth Goddess's body, tall as a water tower and twice as thick, was like a rotting tree, sloughing off putrid decay in thunderous hunks. Demons in human bodies clawed their way free from the root-tangled muck that made up her lower half, like some twisted version of a Trojan Horse. The demons, blood-eyed and sharp-teethed, human faces contorted into painful smiles, shrieked and howled as they launched themselves at the spear-wielding tribe members who rushed to meet them.

Blood flew in arcs and rained down on the ground, disappearing. The more blood that fell, the bigger the Earth Goddess grew. Her head was a boulder of churning dirt. Where her face should've been was a spinning maw of mud and branches and blood.

Judah drew her closer. She knew what he was thinking. He wanted to get her out of here. A part of her wanted to let him.

For every member of the tribe there seemed to be two demons and more kept coming.

Then she saw Kai, a lone figure in black, slipping through the fray, untouched by the demon hoard, heading straight to the base of the goddess.

Far behind him, lost in the stomach-knotting carnage, Josie spied a flash of steel.

"There." Josie pointed across the lawn to Simone. Her pixie-framed friend hacked her way through the demon onslaught, following Kai.

Judah's eyes turned to her for half a breath. The ghostly flames grew brighter, stronger, licking away at the hard perfect edges of his features. But she could still read the tilt of his brow behind the fire.

"I love you too." She moved away from him.

He erupted in flames. At his feet the ground cracked, explosive and deafening. Broken lines etched in bent fingers towards the nearest demons, who were still many yards away. The fissures began to glow orange, filling with lava. Sulfur and heat swelled into the air.

The first demon fell into one of the molten crevices, screeching and clawing at the air. Then another. Core members scrambled away, but Judah held the paths of fire in tight control.

The cracks opened before him, chasing away the demons, and slammed shut behind him, shaking the ground and booming like thunderclaps. He waded through the demons, killing off each that stood between him and Simone.

But there were dozens still and more pouring forth from the Earth Goddess's folds.

How could Josie have been so thoughtless? She was worse than impulsive, she was reckless.

A fierce shout drew her attention. On the opposite side of the lawn from Simone, Nancy had rallied a small knot of Core members together. She plunged her spear into one of the demons and then flung his limp body aside. Her gray silk blouse was splattered with blood. Nancy shouted again as she killed another demon and then rallied her fellow Core members to action.

Nancy was a pain in Josie's ass, but she was tough.

Josie lifted her spear. She started forward, but then saw another familiar figure appear at the far side of the main house some fifty feet away.

Tessa. She swept up a fallen spear and charged into the battle. She plunged the spear into the back of a demon that was tearing into the flesh of a shrieking member of the tribe. The demon jerked, spasmed, and then collapsed. Tessa ripped the spear free and went after the next.

Josie raced after her sister.

A demon charged at Josie. The body might once have been a woman. Josie couldn't tell since someone had slashed at its face, leaving flaps of skin hanging loose from the cheeks. The raw red wounds oozed blood.

Josie didn't have much experience with a spear. When she was younger she'd gone through a basic weapons training program which had included a sword and a spear, but at the time, hand-to-hand combat hadn't been a priority.

When the demon came at her, for a second, she froze. The spear felt clumsy and too heavy. Nothing like the Sword of Eternity, which had seemed to weigh nothing and move of its own accord.

"Blood of the gods!" the demon cried in spite of its facial wounds, charging right at her. Either it didn't see the spear or it didn't care.

Josie planted her feet, firmed her grip on the spear, and thrust it into the demon's gut.

Steam hissed around the wound. The demon groped at the spear and then the redness drained from its eyes. The body collapsed.

She yanked the spear free. Blood spilled and sank into the ground, absorbing as soon as it fell.

Josie glanced back at the ever-growing Earth Goddess. She hadn't moved. Her lower half, thankfully no longer spewing demons, was a bramble of thick black roots buried in the ground. The roots seemed to pulse and throb. She saw a body fall and a root burst from the earth and pull the corpse down into the hole. That was when Josie realized the Earth Goddess was drawing blood from the battle, using it to gain more power, to grow stronger.

Josie started towards Tessa again, but before she'd gone more than a few steps she was clotheslined by a demon and knocked flat on her back. Her head smacked against the ground. A dull rumble of pain rolled through her skull. The protective charms she wore popped as they vanished. Her vision blurred. The demon fell on her. Burning heat ripped across her cheek as the demon's claws tore across her skin. Then it struck her other cheek, sending her tumbling down the slope. Stars burst across her vision as she rolled. If she had a demigod power, it wasn't superhuman strength or genius in battle.

She collided with a dead body, staring at a thigh that was half torn away. Vomit pushed into her throat. Head throbbing, she shoved up to her feet, swaying. The demon barreled at her, screeching.

She swung the spear around like a bat. The wood cracked against the demon's head. It stumbled to the side, weaving and tripping over another body.

She barely had time to change her grip on the spear before the demon regained its balance. It leapt at her, snarling, eyes spilling blood. The demon tackled her, and at the same time, unwittingly impaled itself on her spear. Dead demon weight crushed down on her. Fetid shit stink and coppery rot of old blood choked her. She shoved the demon off and pushed up again, finding herself in the midst of the battle.

The demons were more voracious than she'd expected— probably driven to fight by some thrall the Earth Goddess held on them. Those tribe members who remained, Josie couldn't tell how many, though she could see they were outnumbered, seemed to be holding the demons back, for now.

Above the throngs, she could see fires igniting, singeing the blood-stained air with the stench of charred flesh and black smoke. She caught a glimpse of Judah. Demons were swarming him, like they wanted to be roasted. More likely the Earth Goddess recognized him as a real threat and had sent them to take him down.

She couldn't find Kai through the smoke and melee, but she saw the flash of a sword in the distance moving with surprising speed through the throngs of attacking demons, cutting them down like Simone had spent her entire life slicing and dicing former humans with godly swords. She was far closer to the goddess than Judah or Josie.

A battling tribe member bumped into Josie as she fought a demon. Josie stumbled, then whipped around and stabbed the demon. When it fell, Josie found herself face-to-face with Nancy. But the Future Eye didn't even blink. She simply gripped her spear and charged after the next one. Josie was about to do the same when a root snaked around her ankle and threw her face first onto the ground.

Not again.

The roots bit into the skin of her ankles, tightening their grip. She clung to the spear as she was ripped through the battle, over bodies, through the mud, slammed and banged and battered, to the base of the Earth Goddess.

Wrapped around her thighs and her waist, the thick roots flipped her over and lifted her upright, inches from the goddess's foul-stinking trunk. Josie thrashed against the squeezing tendrils as they tried to tear the spear from her hands.

"No use struggling, dear," a familiar nasal voice said.

Josie froze.

All she could see was a pulsing mash of black and red roots, big as pythons, twisting vein-like, up and up and up. Sinkhole face was taller than the hill and the Big House that stood atop it and still growing. Josie was an ant, looking up at an ancient rotting redwood.

Then the tangles shifted, a disgusting stink, sweet as a candy shop and thick as a mass grave, made Josie's stomach churn and lurch. Mud poured from the goddess's trunk, plopping to the ground, blood running through the black glops in sticky threads. Pink worms the size of pigs and purple beetles big as Josie's head skittered as they were set free, hurrying back into the trunk. From this horror show of earth gore, a pasty white face emerged.

Josie wanted to look away, but couldn't. "Lily?"

Cocooned in black roots and mud, Lily's dull green eyes rolled open, glassy and half dead. Her skin hung loose from her skull in rice-paper thin swags. When she opened her violet-hued lips, blood stained her teeth and dribbled down her chin.

"The Mother of the Earth would like to thank you." Her words were gasping and forced. "Daughter of Death. Destroyer of the Covenant."

More roots lashed around Josie's wrists. She wrenched away from them. "Nice way to thank me. The Forest Goddess gave me a gift. Try that instead."

Lily's thin lips stretched in a facsimile of a smile. "So I shall."

This wasn't Lily at all. Whatever was left of Lily had become a puppet for the Earth Goddess. Maybe, like Kai had said, Lily had been a puppet all along.

"The gift of sacrificing your blood to Mother Earth."

"No, thanks." The more Josie struggled, the tighter the vines' hold became until she couldn't feel her legs anymore and was having trouble drawing a full breath.

"But first, my son."

A ball of writhing roots dropped beside her. Peeking out from the gaps between them, Josie could see Kai's long black eyes, gazing down at her—tear-rimmed and resigned.

Josie's strength waned. Tears burned her eyes. "Kai—"

"Thank you for returning him to me," Lily said, more blood pouring from her lips. Her eyes losing focus.

Josie didn't think Lily was still really alive, but she screamed at the pale face anyway. "He's your son!"

"You are all my children."

The snake's nest of roots began to rise, reeling Kai up to the sinkhole of the goddess's face.

Josie regained her strength, tearing and elbowing at the roots, even as they pinned her arms to her sides.

"The Core shall be annihilated," the goddess intoned through Lily's rasping nasal throat. "Human civilization will be wiped out. Those who wish to survive will offer their children's lives to my earthly arms and then, perhaps, will humanity have paid its recompense for the crimes it has perpetrated against me."

Josie scrambled to find a way free. What did she have? The mark of Death on her hand? What good was that going to do her? The ring of Life? Also, not helpful. She didn't know what the Fates had in mind when they'd given her the marks of the gods, but she was sure that this was not it.

"A new age has begun," the goddess continued.

Josie turned her head, trying to spot Judah in the continuing battle behind her. But all she could see were smoke and demons.

"Judah!"

The vines clamped down, cutting off her air. They slithered across her lips, scraping and cold. Her head began to swim for lack of oxygen. Lily's pale face dimmed as shadows floated into Josie's vision—shadows of death.

Her heart banged against her chest—locked in, no escape. Her lungs burned, grasping onto what little air they could, clawing for it. But the vines kept squeezing. Two cracks, ribs breaking. Pain exploded through her. Her scream remained trapped in her throat. Blackness swooped in and carried her away.

CHAPTER 26

SEPTEMBER 1ST

S HE CAME TO CONSCIOUSNESS IN MID-FALL.

When she hit the ground, she screamed. This time the sound tore loose from her throat unhindered, dizzying her.

The roots dropped away around her.

Through the shadows and scintillating pain-flashes, she saw the gleam of metal. A pixie face and big manga eyes gazed down at her.

Simone grasped her wrist. "Are you okay?"

"Not really." Josie forced herself up, grimacing against the lightning strikes of pain lancing through her. Was it possible for someone to feel this much pain and live? She guessed she was about to find out.

"Charm-Maker, I will taste your blood—" Lily said.

"Fuck you!" Simone released Josie and plunged the Sword of Eternity into the soft mud below Lily's face.

Lily's eyes bulged. Blood gushed from her mouth. The planted trunk of the goddess groaned as it began to sway. Lily's body was spewed from the goddess. She toppled face-first into the muck, as small and limp as a discarded rag doll.

The earth beneath them undulated and broke open. Roots thick as elephant trunks burst from the ground, lunging at them. Josie ducked, swallowing a yelp of pain. Simone sliced the roots down again. The mutilated ends dropped, dead, around Josie.

Up until that point, the goddess had been mostly immobile, other than the swirling vortex of her face. But as Simone rendered the bloodsucking roots nothing but lifeless clods of compost, the goddess let out a low rumble. Her all-encompassing shadow shifted, loosing debris down on them. Josie cringed as a hard rain of dirt beat on her head. When she threw her arm up to protect herself, the pain in her ribs nearly made her black out. She doubled over, gasping.

A monkey's fist knot of a bramble swept down on them—the hand of the goddess—catching Simone and lifting her away.

"Simone!" Josie cried, blinking against the grit in her eyes.

Simone called back, but Josie couldn't make out the words over the clamor of battle and the rumble of the goddess.

Josie pushed to her feet again, stumbling as the ground continued to shake. The towering trunk of the goddess swayed and groaned against itself.

Josie backpedalled, clutching her side and spitting dirt. She craned her neck. Squinting through clouds of smoke and dust, she searched for any sign of Simone or Kai. But the goddess's body was a quaking jungle, and Josie's head was spinning.

She wiped the dirt from her face. Beneath the smears of blood and mud on her hand, she could make out a faint black circle. Death's mark. She could still end this. She had to find someone to take the last two marks.

As she turned back towards the battle, she murmured a prayer to whatever gods might be willing to accept it. Please let Simone and Kai survive, somehow.

The slope before her was a writhing tumult. She couldn't tell demon from Core.

Choking on pain and the acrid incense of charred flesh, she stumbled back. The Earth Goddess's body continued to sway and shed debris, like a mountain jarred by an earthquake. Josie didn't know much about the mortal forms of the gods—never having encountered them until she'd destroyed the mask of the Tripartite. But it seemed the goddess was encumbered by her own massive size, straining to slough off enough of her earthen weight to free herself from the ground.

The light was fading. Josie couldn't tell if it was from the smoke or the goddess's shadow or something else entirely. Regardless, through the gloaming, she spied a faint light glowing from one of the second floor windows of the Big House. The light seemed a lifetime away—a distant amber pinprick in the gathering darkness.

Were there people inside? Her dad? Caroline? Roxy? She hated herself for thinking it, but someone had to take the last two marks. She knew that if she could find them, they would help her end this.

First she had to cross the tangle of clashing bodies. It was a wonder to her that the fighting continued. But time was bending in strange ways. It seemed hours since she'd given Kai the mark. When, in fact, it might only have been twenty, maybe thirty minutes. As many bodies were fallen, it seemed there were hundreds still fighting on the hillside.

She tried to make sense of the tempest, to find a path through, or a friendly face, but her vision was dancing the tango with pain. Whenever she tried to pick one individual from the teeming mass, her head spun.

Underfoot, the ground broke as the goddess uprooted herself. Josie was pitched forward, knocking aside a demon who had been trying to wrest a spear from someone. Piercing claws dug into her arm as it grabbed her and yanked her down with it.

As she fell on top of the demon, she jammed the heel of her hand against its chin, snapping its head back. She tore from its grip and staggered to her feet. The demon lunged at her, grabbing her knees and dropping her flat on her back.

She screamed, not sure how she managed it. Her lungs felt like they were slowly suffocating. The demon bit into her thigh. Scalding hot pain flooded her.

"Josie!"

The demon's weight and teeth vanished—knocked away.

Against the backdrop of throbbing agony, screams and shouts of battle, rumbling earth and death's phantoms clouding the sky, her sister's face glowed angelic, even set in a fierce, sweat-and-dirt stained expression.

"Can you stand?" Tessa cried over the increasing grumble from the Earth Goddess.

Josie answered by gripping Tessa's arm and allowing her sister to pull her up to her feet. Her left leg wanted to fold. The shaking of the ground wasn't helping her. She clung to Tessa's shoulders, narrow and bony, but sturdy.

Tessa held her waist, keeping her upright. "We have to get you—"

Her words came to an abrupt halt as her body pitched forward. Her eyes bulged, the hazel hue intensifying suddenly. Her hands tightened around Josie's waist, grasping.

"Tessa?"

Amidst the raucous clamor of battle, Josie could hear a weak breath escape Tessa's lips. A sigh.

The end of a spear jutted from Tessa's stomach. Dark, wet. Then it was pulled free. Blood gushed from her body.

Tessa collapsed onto Josie. Under her sister's weight and her own blinding pain, Josie toppled.

A demon smiled down at them with those vicious pointed teeth, brandishing a spear. It seemed so strange that he wore a pastel pink button-down and khaki slacks, the crease still sharp in spite of the mud. Other than his blood-red eyes and inhumanly elongated teeth, he appeared a normal middle-aged guy. Blond hair thinning, beard trimmed close, he wore a silver medic alert bracelet. She stared up at the silver band imprinted with a red cross as he lifted the spear again, pointed at her face.

At this, her last moment, she wondered, did he have a heart condition? Was he a diabetic? Maybe an epileptic?

The spear drove towards her.

Then disappeared.

The demon's fist slammed into Tessa's back as it followed through with the motion, though the spear had been ripped from its hands.

Josie rolled her sister off of her, laying Tessa gently onto the trembling ground.

Tessa's hands groped for her. "Josie."

"Right here." Josie seized her sister's hand and held on, tight.

The demon whipped around, probably intending to gut whoever had taken its spear. Instead, it burst into flames.

Judah shoved the burning body aside. The fires encircling his body extinguished. He swept down, wrapping his arms around Josie. She grimaced, biting back against the pain of his embrace.

"Time to go," he said, lips against her temple.

Josie pushed her free hand against his shoulder weakly. "No," she said. "Tessa."

His eyes flicked down to Tessa, the fires in them dimmed, pain-dowsed. But his brow hardened. "There's nothing we can do."

"Yes, there is," Josie said, pulling her hand free of her sister's.

"Josie—"

"I'm here, Tessa. Right here." Josie ran her fingers over Life's ring, removing the muck. The gleam of silver shone, emanating its own light. She pushed the sick, rollercoaster swells and falls of pain aside and focused on the ring. The gift of Life. The key to a hidden stash. She only hoped it contained what she thought it did.

She poised her hand to flick her wrist and access the stash. A swell of dark movement over Judah's shoulder stopped her.

"Judah!"

He turned, pushing her away as three demons barreled into him.

She fell back next to Tessa.

The ground bucked under her, throwing her and Tessa over. She landed on her stomach, gasping, pain-inspired tears flowing freely down her face.

The earth shook in bursts, like a series of explosions. Stones and dirt, twigs and vines showered down on her. Somehow, she pushed to her knees and looked up.

The Earth Goddess had moved back into the silver waters of the lake. Her giant appendages looked less like tangled treetops and more like skinless hands—mud-muscles, root-veins, branch-bones. The goddess tore into her own chest, digging frantically. Whole trees and massive rocks tumbled out and splashed into the lake. The water turned black with dirt and blood.

Josie stared. The goddess was ripping herself apart.

"Josie—" Tessa's hand found her arm.

Josie snapped out of her daze.

Tessa was on her side now, half-sunk into the mud, too pale, eyes barely open. Josie reached for her and then heard a shout and a yell that pulled her attention away again.

Ten feet from them, six demons were engulfed in fire, falling into each other as they were incinerated. A figure rung in flickering blue flames stumbled back from them—Judah. He staggered slightly and fell to his knees. His hand was pressed to his chest. His fire sputtered and went out. His body convulsed. Dark liquid dripped from his lips—blood.

"Judah—"

He glanced towards her. His shirt was torn, blood spilling through his fingers. The fire in his eyes flared and then died.

CHAPTER 27

SEPTEMBER 1ST
TAKING CARE OF MOTHER EARTH WITH SIMONE

"RUN, JOSIE! GO!" Simone cried as the Earth Goddess's 'hand' closed around her, forcing her into a crouch.

Vines darted at her, attacking from every side. She hacked at them as the cage of branches grew smaller, the wedges of smoky light dissolving into slivers. One of the vines coiled around her sword arm.

"Bad plant," she said through her teeth, moving the sword to her left hand to slice the vine away from her right.

Her only experience with swords had been with the latex-covered foam variety. She'd spent a few years hanging out with kids who were involved in Live Action Role Play. But brandishing an actual sword—a sacred tool of the divine, no less—was nothing like bashing a kid dressed up as an ogre with a piece of foam.

This sword was bigger and heavier and seemed to have a mind of its own, which she appreciated to an extent. She was a bit unnerved by an inanimate object jerking on her arm, anticipating blows and dangers from every angle.

As she'd worked her way through the demons, the sword had moved smoothly, arcing and thrusting, shoring up her confidence. At the moment, it was slashing wildly, practically yanking her arm out of its socket as it tried to fend off every insidious little tendril and hack through the branches that made up her quickly shrinking cage.

Her main focus was keeping her breathing steady and remembering the words of her tae kwon do instructor: Breathe. Because you need to.

But as the gnarly branches pressed in on her, forcing her to tuck in and bow her head, it was getting harder to measure her breaths. Making things worse, her heart was bouncing around her chest like a Super Ball in a concrete room.

She could feel the ground getting further away. Humans must've come with some internal sensor for that sort of thing. All she could see were the tightly knotted branches closing around her. Yet, she was certain she was being lifted.

The sword kept moving. The blade kept most of the vines off her body, but it wasn't fast enough. She needed two swords.

She would've liked to have said that she wasn't afraid, but she was. Big time. Fear had set up an amusement park inside of her—the lights flashed, the roller coasters tore up the tracks, dizzy little kids puked up cotton candy, and big tough guys screamed like babies.

There had been times when she couldn't imagine how people like her mom and Judah and Josie could wear such brave faces when they were dealing with such terrifying forces of godly power, but now she knew—they didn't have any other choice.

She couldn't let anything happen to Kai.

Yes, he'd lied to her. And, yes, they'd been seriously epic, horrible lies. She had wanted to be angry and betrayed and cause a big scene and make him beg forgiveness, except there hadn't been time for that. When she'd overheard Daisuke talking about execution, she'd forgotten to be angry. She wasn't good at holding onto emotions like that, not like Judah and Josie who seemed to think that making each other miserable was some form of flirtation. She didn't want to be miserable. She didn't want to be angry.

When she'd come to warn Kai, he'd looked miserable enough for all of them. He'd tried to apologize, but she just hadn't cared. She only wanted him safe and alive. That was all that mattered to her.

While Tessa and the Eye had questioned her, she'd come to realize the scope of his lies. How he'd fooled them all, like his mom had. But instead of feeling like it called for some public trial and more public punishment, all she could think about were all the good things he'd done, how hard he'd been working this last month, how he'd saved Josie's life, and how he'd chosen Simone over his mom, risking his life.

The fact that he'd volunteered to take the goddess's mark proved it beyond any doubt. Whatever he'd done in the past, he was sorry now. But she hadn't needed him to prove anything. She'd known he wasn't the bad guy. She knew that whatever he'd done, it was because Lily had wanted him to do it. Simone knew that when Kai loved someone, he would do anything for them. Which was why he was sacrificing himself right now. Which was why she was going to save him. Because she would do anything for him.

Like be crushed by the Earth Goddess. This seemed to be imminent. Her cage had constricted so that her chin was now to her knees and her butt to her heels. The sword was still doing what it could, but there wasn't much room for either of them to move. The branches pressed against her back and closed in on her sides.

Had this happened to Kai? Had he been flattened like a bug?

The thought ignited something in her, a bright, hot feeling that surged through her limbs and seemed to give the sword a jolt. The blade swung upwards, spinning her around as it cut right through the branches bearing down on her.

The Earth Goddess's deep bellow shook Simone to her pores as the branches split above her and the smoke-filled sky appeared.

The sword pushed back. She gripped it with both hands as it sliced away another section of branches. She turned her face away as they fell on her. Shoving them aside, she pushed herself up to her feet, even as the sword continued hacking at the attacking plant-vipers. Simone was starting to love this sword, even though she knew it belonged to Josie. She was thinking about giving it a name. Little Jo.

As she rose through the splintered opening, the wind ripped at her. She was higher than the roof of the Big House and the surrounding trees. The battle below was shrouded by smoke, except for an occasional flare of blue flame. Judah. She wanted to scream to him, but a low rumble, like an oncoming freight train was vibrating her ears.

Little Jo jerked on her arm and she turned. She stumbled back, catching herself on a sliced stub of a branch, which was dripping with red sap that had a salty metallic scent.

In front of her was a vortex. A foul stinking pit of muck and gods-knew-what that was spinning fast as a cyclone, leading into emptiness. Icky bile burn pushed into her throat as she clung to what had once been her prison to keep from falling the couple hundred feet to the ground below.

Where was Kai? She'd seen the goddess lift him up in one of these same hand-branch-cage monstrosities, but she hadn't seen what had happened to him after that.

"Kai!" she screamed over the rumble of the goddess and the clangor of the battle below.

Her heart shuddered as she stared down into the gaping hole of the goddess's face. What if he were already dead?

She steadied herself. She had always been an optimist and she wasn't about to stop now. Kai was alive. She would find him. She would save him.

"Where is he, you bitch?"

She plunged the sword into the goddess's hand. The goddess let out a deep noise that could've been a groan or a laugh. Either way, it trembled in Simone's squishy insides and made her want to puke.

Then the hand began to tilt towards the black pit.

She gripped the stumps of bleeding wood as the cage tipped. Her boots scraped against the slick tangle, trying to gain purchase, but soon she was hanging, dangling above the vortex.

She'd lost her breath. It was way gone. She sucked air in panicked gulps, straining to keep hold of the branches. Little Jo wasn't helping—hard enough to keep a hold of it and try to save herself, but it kept tugging at her arm, like it was trying to get her to let go.

Gritting her teeth, she attempted to heave herself up, thinking maybe she could climb over the broken stubs, but the branches were wet, bleeding, and her hands were sweaty and she sucked at pull-ups. She couldn't climb a rope to save her life—clearly. Why hadn't she been more of a jock like Judah?

Little Jo suddenly wrenched her arm free. She screamed as she found herself hanging by one hand. The sword pointed down, into the vortex.

Simone's pulse and breath chafed inside her as she stared into the abyss. Was Little Jo trying to help her? Had Kai been dropped down that black hole? If so, could he have survived?

Simone firmed her grip on the sword. She would be an optimist. To the end.

She let go.

CHAPTER 28

SEPTEMBER 1ST

"JUDAH."

Josie had meant to scream, but couldn't get enough air in to manage more than a whimper.

When she tried to stand, Tessa's grip on her arm tightened. Josie turned back to her sister.

Tessa's eyes fluttered. She was still alive. Josie could save her.

Her lungs hardly seemed to be working anymore. She was drowning again. When she looked back at Judah's prone body, agony ripped through her and she nearly blacked out. Her hands sank into the mire. She gritted her teeth against the sobs and her body's treacherous attempts to give in to the darkness.

"Come along then, dear daughter," a smooth, seductive voice said.

She glanced up.

Death, dark-haired, black-eyed Judah, crouched on the other side of Tessa, smiling sadly. "Let go."

"Fuck off," she said, pushing herself back onto her heels.

His smile grew. "That's my girl."

Tessa's hand slipped away from Josie. She rolled onto her back and looked up at Death. "Judah?"

"No," he said, running his fingers down her cheek. "He never loved you, you know."

Tessa's eyes closed, her lips trembled.

"You son of a bitch," Josie said, turning back towards Judah. Was it the trembling of the earth or was his chest still moving? She looked down at Life's ring.

With a flick of her wrist, her fingertips closed around a rough stem of clay.

And there it was—a drab earthenware cup—the Chalice of Life. In its bowl, a sip of water. Just enough for one drink. The Waters of Life.

"Well, how nice of your father," Death said. "But who will you save? Your beautiful sister? Your love? Or yourself?"

Josie stared into the black pools of his eyes, expecting to see the howling emptiness of the abyss, the cold distance of the Beyond, but instead, all she saw was sadness. Weary loneliness.

"Tick, tock," he said softly.

Tessa's eyes cracked open. "Give it to me."

Josie was grateful to let Tessa make the decision. At least if Josie and Judah were going to die, then they could do it together. Tessa could live.

She moved the Chalice towards Tessa's mouth.

Tessa seized her wrist.

"No," she said, lips tight, straining, like the light in her eyes. "The mark."

"Mark?" Death tilted his head, eyes narrowing.

He didn't know. So this hadn't all been part of his plan.

"No, Tessa—" Josie tried to move the Chalice again, but for someone who was lying in Death's shadow, Tessa's grip was adamant.

"I can save you," Josie said.

"No," Tessa said.

"But—"

"Don't argue." Tessa's eyes fixed on Josie, suddenly sharp and clear. "Am I Triune? Or not?"

Josie's heart clenched, but her hand uncurled. "You are."

Tessa's right hand lay limp in the mud.

"I'm sorry, Tessa," Josie said. "I never wanted to hurt you."

Tessa's eyes softened. "I believe you."

Josie's fingers slid down Tessa's thin, cold wrist. She bent over Tessa, shaking from the pain. She kissed Tessa's forehead. "I love you."

"Love you too," Tessa murmured.

Tessa's hand closed around Josie's.

Josie pulled back, gazing into the green-gold rings of her sister's eyes.

"I'll tell Mom you said, hi," Tessa said with a small smile. "I can't wait to see her again."

Her hand clamped down on Josie's.

Death frowned, standing up quickly. "What have you done?"

Tessa's eyes slipped shut, her fingers slid from Josie's grasp.

"Bye, baby sister," Josie said, tears splashing into the Chalice of Life clutched to her chest.

A slender shadow grew between her and Death. He took a few steps back, scowl deepening. "What is this?"

Josie didn't know what the shadow was or what it meant. All her concentration was focused on gathering up every ounce of strength and pushing to her feet.

Huge chunks of the Earth Goddess were sloughing away, splashing into the serene surface of the lake. Water sprayed into the air, splattering against Josie as she staggered towards Judah.

All around her, the battle raged.

Josie limped to Judah's side and then fell to her knees, cradling the Chalice.

She pushed him over onto his back.

It looked like someone had tried to punch a hole through his chest to his heart. She swallowed a sob and searched his neck for a pulse. A faint thump greeted her.

She ran her hand over his cheek, smearing the mud caked to his skin.

She pressed her forehead to his. "Judah?"

His eyes cracked open—the faintest blue sparks appeared.

His voice was so thin she could barely hear him.

"Let me . . ."

She shook her head. "No way."

She knew what he was going to say. He wanted the last mark. She didn't even have to look at her palm to know it was there. But she wasn't going to give it to him.

A chill spread through her body, eating up the pain. Her breaths came shorter and shallower. Her heart was slowing, giving in. She knew what was happening. She was dying.

She kissed him. His lips tasted like iron and ash. "You're not going to die."

His brow hardened. "Josie—"

"I never wanted anything for myself until I met you," she said in fitful gasps. "This is what I want now."

Before he could argue, she tilted the cup to his mouth and poured the Waters of Life between his lips. He choked and sputtered, grabbing hold of her arm as his body jerked and spasmed. The black wound on his chest vanished, sealing before her eyes.

The Chalice disappeared from her hand.

His eyes rolled. He slipped into unconsciousness.

She laid her head to his chest. His heart beat was steady and strong.

"You've always tried to do what was right," she said. "Don't stop."

She brought her left hand to her right and clasped them together, taking the mark of the Other.

Her eyes closed.

And the mist came.

CHAPTER 29

SEPTEMBER 1ST

"HI, JOSIE."

Josie opened her eyes. They rolled, searching for something to focus on. All they found was diffuse grayish light, like a slowly developing picture.

She sat up. The ground beneath her was an indistinct gray mass like the thickest fog, though it seemed as solid as stone or wood.

Though she was dressed in her blood and mud-spattered clothes, her wounds were gone and she felt no pain. She could still taste Judah's blood on her lips, the wretched stink of burning flesh continued to poison her breath. But she could breathe. At least she thought she was breathing.

She stood up. "Hello?"

A figure emerged from the gray haze, slight, small—a child.

A young girl about seven or eight stepped forward, dressed in gray jeans and a gray T-shirt, her feet bare. Something about her was familiar.

"Hi," she said.

Josie stared at the girl's blue eyes, her long dark hair, her full lips and straight nose. "Who are you?"

The girl smiled a little. The expression struck Josie, hard as a fist. Josie's hands clutched at her abdomen. She knew that smile. Not that she'd seen it often. But she would've known it anywhere. It was Judah's smile.

The girl's sapphire blue eyes—Judah's eyes—tracked down to Josie's hand, pressed against her navel.

"Yep," the girl said. "That's me. I'm in there. Right now. Or I could be."

A ragged pain zigzagged through Josie from her throat to her belly. She was pregnant? Or she had been, before she'd come to wherever she was now? If Judah had known . . .

She swallowed back her tears, refocusing. "I'm dead."

The girl bobbled her head. "More or less."

"Then I'm not pregnant. I can't be. I'm not alive."

"Hmm . . ."

"And you're not . . ."—she swallowed again, painfully—"who you say you are."

The girl's eyes clouded and turned gray.

Josie stepped back. "You're the Other."

"More or less," the girl said.

"What do you want?"

"You're the one with my mark on your hand," the girl said. "What do you want?"

Josie glanced down at her palm. A grayish circle spun on her skin, changing shape as it moved, like a clock of mist.

"Did it work?" Josie asked. "Is the Triune restored?"

"Not quite," the girl said, rocking back and forth, heel to toe. "We're waiting."

"Waiting for what?"

"For you to decide," the girl said.

"Decide?"

"You're the daughter of Life and Death," the girl said. "You are the first demigod in a long time. Your power is unusual. You see and shape and bring forth the faces of the gods, but that's not all you could bring forth. That is not all you could see and shape. You are in a unique position; you have a unique opportunity." The girl's eyes slid down to Josie's navel.

Josie recoiled. "What do you want?" she asked.

"To live," the Other said. "That's all I've ever wanted."

Josie's fingers clutched possessively at her stomach. "You want..." She couldn't say it, she could hardly think it.

"That's right," the girl said. "I want to be born."

"You can't."

"Why not?"

"Because you're... you're a god. The gods aren't born. They just... aren't."

"Are you sure about that?"

No. Josie wasn't sure about anything, but she knew that gods didn't have mortal souls. Only those who were born mortal had souls. She couldn't fathom what it would mean for a god to have a mortal soul. She wasn't even sure if that was possible.

"Or . . ." the girl said with a sigh, "we can start all over again."

"Start what?"

"All of it," the girl said. "The Covenant will be restored, as it was. Life and Death and the Other bound up in a mask. A new Triune will be named. You'll die and your unborn child with you, but . . . things will go back to what they were before. More or less. And you can die knowing you made that happen."

"Or?"

"Or you can let me be born."

"And?"

The girl smiled again. It stung, seeing that smile. She ached to see it again on Judah's face.

"I don't know," the girl said. "I can't see my own future."

"What about the gods and the demons? What will happen to them?"

The girl shrugged.

"So my choice is a future that is known, the Covenant, the masks, humanity free of the gods, or . . ."

"Or," the girl said with a nod, "the unknown."

"But I'll be alive."

"Well, you'd have to be to give birth to me, wouldn't you? And you are marked by my godly name. I suspect that . . ." The girl's gray eyes shifted away thoughtfully.

"Suspect what?"

The girl looked back at her. "All kinds of things, but they're only guesses. It's exciting to think about." Tears shone in the girl's eyes, her voice dropped to a thrilled whisper. "Not knowing. Don't you think?"

Josie wasn't sure about that either. "But the gods might still be there on the mortal plane? The Earth Goddess? The demons? What kind of world is that for..."—her hand clenched against her navel—"anyone? Even if I do live long enough to give birth to you. How long will any of us survive?"

"I don't know," the girl said. "But I'm sure you and Judah will be wonderful parents."

Why didn't she just stick a knife in Josie's heart?

"How do you know that?" Josie asked.

The girl smiled. "Just a feeling."

Josie tried to imagine what Judah would say if he were here to make this choice. But he wasn't.

She fought with the selfish longing that only wanted to see him again, to live and do all the things she'd never gotten to do, go running on the beach, the birthday party, have a family. But how could she risk subjecting the world to a future that might be filled with godly torment and demonic incursions? Judah would say it was selfish. And yet . . . he would want her back.

Even now, she could feel the pull of him, deep down and far off. His pain, his grief, his anger, they called to her. His cries were like echoes issuing from a distant cliff across a vast sea, so soft that they sounded like sighs carried by the wind, but she knew they were screams. They would have to be to reach her wherever she was now. She glimpsed what it was like then, to be a god. To hear the agonized pleas of humanity, begging for some intercession, for some end, for some respite, for an answer. And yet she stood there, not acting. Racked by indecision. What was the right way? She didn't know.

All she knew was that she wanted to go back to Judah. She didn't know if it was right or wrong, good or bad, selfish or not, but she did know it was true. It was the only true thing she knew.

She eyed the girl with Judah's smile. "What will you be?"

"You mean will I be a doctor or a firefighter?"

"No, I mean will you be a human or a god? A demigod?"

The girl's eyes crinkled at the corners—it reminded Josie of her mom. She ached, wondering what her mom would have done in her place, wishing that her mom were here, pained that her mom would never see . . .

"I'll have a mortal soul." The Other tilted her head. "Like you. Simply because your soul is able to channel a bit more of the divine that doesn't make you any less human, does it?"

"That's all you want? To be human?"

"All? Josie, that's everything."

"But you're a god."

"Am I?

"You're the Other. *The* Other. Gods and demons bow to you. You hold the Book of Creation. You . . . you're it. You're the ultimate power."

The girl took the ends of her hair into her mouth, sucking on them a bit. "Hmm."

"Are you saying you're not?"

The girl ran her thumb over the damp ends of her hair. "I'm saying I want to live, Josie. That's all. I want to live and I want to die. And I want to find out."

"Find out what?"

The girl smiled. "I don't know. That's what I want to find out."

Josie pressed her fingers to her forehead. "I don't know if I can. Every choice I make ends up hurting people. Every decision I make seems to lead to death."

"Death is on his own journey, Josie."

Josie stared at the girl, the Other, who was taunting her with the form of this child—hers and Judah's.

She knew what she wanted, but she wasn't sure she could bring herself to take it.

"It's too selfish," she said softly.

"You think every time you get something you want it means you were selfish?"

"I can't do that to the world—"

"Do what?"

"Leave them to the gods—"

"Who said you would?"

"But you said—"

"I said the future is unknown. No matter what you choose. Even if you choose to restore the Covenant. You don't know what will happen after that."

"You just want to live."

"You're right. Do you think that makes me selfish?"

"You are a god."

The girl grinned. "Good point. Gods are selfish, aren't they? But if you give me this chance, Josie, you'll be helping me achieve something that I've longed for... for time beyond your reckoning. And in my book, that makes you the least selfish person who has ever walked any realm or any of the pathways between."

A book appeared in the girl's hand. A slim brown book, like a children's book of verse, unassuming, unadorned. But Josie knew better without knowing how she knew. It was the Book of Creation. The Book of Life, Death, the gods, Time, everything.

"I'm tired of reading about it, Josie," the girl said, holding up the book. "I'm tired of wondering. Please . . . I want to live. I want to feel. I want to scream. I want to suffer and to cry. I want to laugh. I want to sing. I want to love and I want to die too. I've read the book, Josie. Now I want to experience it for myself."

Josie looked down at her hand, still pressed to her belly. "I'm scared."

The girl gazed at her. The gray clouds in her eyes began to disperse, revealing the brilliant blue beneath. "I want to know what that feels like too."

"I'm afraid you will, too well."

"You've made your decision?"

Josie nodded.

"Will you know what you are?" she asked the girl, who would be her daughter, who was also the Other. "When you're born?"

"I don't know, but you won't."

"What?"

"You won't remember any of this."

"What . . . why?"

"I don't know," the girl said, fading into the gray haze around them. "There's so much I don't know, but I can't wait to find out."

CHAPTER 30

SEPTEMBER 1ST

SHE WOKE TO A WORLD FULL OF SCREAMING. Her lungs hitched, sucking in a full, deep breath—a smoke-filled, sulfurish breath. A gray film clouded her vision. All around her were screams and shouts.

"Judah! Stop!"

"I'm going to end this!"

"You're going to end all of us!"

"Then run."

She was shaking... no, the ground was shaking, and rupturing. Rumbles like thunder and cracks like lightning assaulted her ears. She felt thick all over as if she'd been asleep for weeks and her body had atrophied. Heat licked at her arms and legs. She drew another breath, blinking away the last of the fog. She tried to remember what had happened, where she was, but her mind was as sluggish as the rest of her.

Beech stood on the other side of a glowing rift—a wide crack in the earth choked with a slow burning lava flow. An ancient Core warrior painted in blood, his bow in hand.

"This isn't what Josie would want!" Beech screamed across the river of liquid fire.

Roxy appeared next to Beech, grabbing his arm. "We have to go!"

They both stumbled as the ground at their toes crumbled into the flames. Roxy yanked Beech back. Beech recovered his balance, hesitated at the other side of the fire-flow a moment longer, and then turned, but was brought up short. A glow showed through the smoke on their far side—more lava. They were hemmed in.

"We'll jump!" she heard Beech shout to Roxy.

"Jump where?" Roxy looked around, desperately searching, and then met Josie's eyes. Cat eyes squinted. Plump lips pulled into a frown. Josie blinked and struggled to move. Her arms were stuck in the ground like she'd fallen asleep in wet concrete.

Roxy's eyes widened. She rushed back to the other edge of her island, arm thrown across her face against the heat. "Judah!" she screamed.

"He won't listen!" Beech cried, tugging on Roxy's arm. "We have to bail! We'll—"

"No, Beech! Look!" Roxy pointed at Josie.

Josie lifted her hand, finally, and touched her head. A silver circle flashed on her palm. The Mark of the Other. She'd taken it. She remembered that. But she should've died, shouldn't she? Hadn't she? She couldn't remember. It was all a haze.

Beech's green eyes were bright even in the ash-filled world. "Josie? Josie! Oh shit . . . Judah! She's alive! She's alive! Stop!"

Slowly, her body became responsive again. She turned her head. A blinding blue fire towered over her. She jerked away, rolling to her side, barely catching herself. Inches from her nose, the stream of lava whispered in a low hissing voice, burning her vision.

"Josie!" Roxy cried, dropping to her knees on the other side of the flow, holding her hands up like she could keep Josie from falling into the lava with her force of will alone.

Josie clung to the burning ground. The earth was hard and brittle on the top and yet seemed to be melting underneath.

"Judah! Snap out of it, you chode!" Beech yelled. "She's alive! You're going to incinerate her!"

Josie pushed herself back from the edge and up onto her elbows.

Everything was on fire. The entire slope was fractured into chunks, traced by jagged lines of glowing, molten rock. Shadowy figures were fleeing in every direction. The forest was smoking, going up in flames. Others were trapped, surrounded on every side by burning lava. At the top of the hill, the Big House was wrapped in fire. Josie bolted upright.

"Dad!"

"Josie?"

She turned. Judah remained shrouded by sapphire blue flames. Somewhere beneath them, she could see his eyes, staring at her.

"Stop," she said.

The fires extinguished, Judah's and the trees and the house. They simply puffed out. Lava flows seized, darkened, and hardened. Steam and smoke ribboned up into the air. For a second, an eerie quiet surrounded them, as if the whole world was holding its breath.

Then an atmosphere rending scream—the scream of a god. Josie twisted around, grimacing at the stiffness of her limbs, but at least the pain was gone. Her ribs, her leg, the wounds on her face, they all seemed to be healed.

In the lake, the last of the giant goddess crumbled. A heap of tree limbs and dirt settled with a sigh.

Then Judah was there, on his knees, kissing her. He grasped at her hair, at her waist, gathering her to him.

"I am so pissed off at you right now," he said in the breathless gasps when his lips weren't pulling at hers.

This was pissed off? She was going to have to do it more often.

"Celebrating?" a low, hollow voice asked.

Judah broke from Josie, twisting around.

At the edge of the lake was a woman in a ragged gown of rotted brown. A corpse that had clawed itself out of its grave. A faceless woman. The Earth Goddess.

"Not yet," she said.

The ground shook and broke open underneath them. Josie scrambled to her feet, Judah at her side. They ran as the earth fell away into a gaping hole at their heels. Roxy and Beech ran ahead of them.

Screams began to echo around them again as the survivors, demon and Core alike, raced from the spreading sinkhole.

Josie glanced back and saw a silver-haired woman trip and fall, groping at the earth even as it disintegrated under her—Nancy.

"No!" Josie skidded to a halt.

"Josie!" Judah grabbed her arm. But she held her ground.

The sinkhole stopped growing. Nancy clung to the edge, feet dangling over an open black pit.

"What—how—?" The Earth Goddess's empty face turned towards Josie. The goddess's bony hands balled at her sides. The earth groaned. Clumps of dirt tumbled away into the darkness at Josie's toes. Judah's hand tightened around her arm, but Josie didn't move.

"No," Josie said again. The groaning stopped.

The Earth Goddess roared and plunged her hand into her stomach. The muddy flesh squelched around her wrist. She ripped it out again, a sucking pop sounded around her. In her hand was an hourglass. She turned it, stalking towards Josie. The sands within didn't move.

Josie could feel the air around her constrict. The earth bitch was using the same time bender on Josie as she had used Josie's mother—freezing her in time.

The Earth Goddess grabbed a spear from the ground and charged around the edge of the hole towards Josie.

Pressure built around her. She guessed that Judah, Beech, and Roxy were trapped in the time disruption too, since she couldn't hear them, though she could still hear shouts of the surviving tribe members, faint and muffled, as if through a concrete wall.

The Earth Goddess lifted the spear at her shoulder, gaining momentum as she approached.

"No." The word slipped from Josie's supposedly time-frozen lips.

The hourglass shattered.

The Earth Goddess staggered, halting.

The hourglass disintegrated into glittering sand and blew away. Time began to move forward again.

"Watch out!" Nancy cried from where she was still hanging above the massive hole.

Josie turned. Half a dozen demons rushed at her.

Beech loosed an arrow. The point planted between the brows of one of the demons. Behind her, Josie could feel Judah heating up.

Josie held up her hand. "Wait."

The demons skittered to a stop, blood-eyes widening.

"The Other, the Other." They mewled like frightened kittens, cowering and knocking each other over as they backed away. One fell shrieking into the bottomless pit.

Josie turned back to the Earth Goddess.

"It can't be," the Earth Goddess said, but she, too, was backing up.

She turned and ran right into Simone and the Sword of Eternity.

The Earth Goddess jerked, skewered by the sword. Then she cracked and crumbled, like dried mud. Before the chunks hit the ground, they evaporated and vanished.

The goddess was dead.

Simone, soaking wet, face streaked with muck, lowered the sword. Another figure came running up from the lake, lean and dark, shedding water. Kai.

He caught up with Simone and hooked his arms around her, hugging her tight. She buried her face against his heaving chest. The sword fell from her hand.

Kai's long, dark eyes met Josie's. Water dripped over his face, or maybe they were tears.

He inclined his head towards her. "Lady Day."

"I'm glad you're not dead," she said.

His half-smile returned. "Me too."

"Me three," Simone said.

She kissed Kai. Like she needed to. Like she loved him. And, clearly, she did.

"Would someone like to help me?" Nancy called, straining to pull herself up.

"That's one ugly hole," Kai said. And suddenly, the earth rose up and the hole was gone.

Nancy lay flat on her face. Huffing, she picked herself up.

Josie frowned at Kai. "Did you do that?"

Kai's mouth opened and then shut. He looked as surprised as Josie felt.

Josie looked down at her palm. The silvery symbol moved and flowed, like sunlight on the ocean. The symbol of the Other.

Judah's hand slid down her other arm. His fingers interlaced with hers.

His shirt was gone. Maroon smears of dried blood circled the white knotted fist of a scar at the center of his chest. Three more trails of scars marred his face, across his cheek, where a demon had clawed him. The Waters of Life had healed the wounds, but the scars were clear on his skin. Clods of mud clung to his hair. His eyes were half open, the flames in them faint. He was battered and scarred and filthy. He looked like he was about to pass out and fall over.

He was perfect.

He took her hand, tracing the symbol with his thumb. "What does it mean?"

She shook her head. "I don't know."

"Are we done fighting?"

"I don't know."

"What do we do now?"

Her fingertips skimmed the scar on his chest. "Ready for that run on the beach?"

He smiled. "How about tomorrow?"

Something stirred deep in Josie's core. A strange flutter. She touched her belly, thinking she might be sick.

His grip tightened. "Josie?"

She smiled.

"Tomorrow."

EPILOGUE

SEPTEMBER 22ND
ONE YEAR AND THREE WEEKS LATER

"You should've told him to suck it," Kai said.

The black chopper grew distant, turning into little more than a fly speck against the blue sky before disappearing entirely. Josie turned back towards the ocean. The gray water glittered in the afternoon sunlight. A warm breeze rustled the grass around them.

"He's the president."

"All the more reason."

She gestured to the mark on his hand. "I'm starting to worry this is going to your head."

"Come on, Josie. I had a bad attitude way before I got my godly power-up." Amusement glinted in his dark eyes, made longer and darker by eyeliner. "But if Your Supreme Otherness wants to take it away from me, you could, couldn't you?"

"Don't tempt me."

"You didn't answer."

"I don't know. And I'm not interested," she said. "I'm sure there's a reason that you acquired the Earth Goddess's powers after her death."

"Oh, yeah? Like what?"

"I don't know."

"You say that a lot these days."

"Because I don't."

"You're the Big Kahuna now. Leaders are supposed to act like they know everything, especially when they don't. You're not instilling a lot of confidence. No wonder that douchebag was trying to push you around."

"He's not a douchebag. He's scared."

Kai lifted an eyebrow.

"Okay, maybe he's a little bit of a douchebag."

"Just like all the others," Kai said grimly.

Josie nodded. The leaders of the world hadn't been particularly excited about having to deal with her, but she was the only one who could keep the gods and demons in check.

The gods and demons called her Mistress. Humans called her all kinds of things, including witch, devil, and tyrant. To her face, it was more often, Lady. She wasn't sure how that had started. The Core called her the new Triune, but she wasn't Triune. She didn't possess the power of the three gods. Only one god, the Other.

But it wasn't like it had been. There were no masks anymore. Now the Other's power flowed constantly into her, because of the mark, she assumed, since she and Kai were two of the three mortals still capable of using godly powers. The third was Judah, but he and the Fire God seemed to have melded somehow. He didn't wear the Chain anymore. He said the Fire God was silent, perhaps because of the Waters of Life. Josie wasn't entirely sure.

She wasn't sure of much these days actually. Some people seemed to think that since she had the Other's powers, she had the Other's knowledge too, but she didn't know anything more than she ever had. Now that the New Age had begun, she felt like she knew less. Everything was new. Everything was different. Everything was . . . unknown.

"We should get back," Josie said. "I need to feed Gretchen." She pressed her swollen breasts.

"Please,"—he held up his hands—"spare me."

"Get over it."

"Humanity and the gods may bow and scrape to Your Mightiness, but as far as I'm concerned, you're just another poster teen for irresponsible sexual behavior. Did it ever occur to you that you're a role-model? Do you want every young impressionable girl in the world to think it's okay to get pregnant at seventeen? For shame."

"Are you enjoying yourself?"

"Not so much. Considering that we wield all this superhuman power now," he said, "our lives have gotten pretty boring. Who knew that dealing with gods and presidents and demons would be so tedious?"

Josie rubbed her eyes. She hadn't slept a full night since Gretchen had been born two months before. The girl ate constantly and never seemed to sleep for longer than an hour at a time. The only reason Josie was able to put together a coherent sentence, let alone wrangle with the leaders of the world, was because of all the help she received from her family and tribe. And Judah. He'd pretty much become a single parent since she was always having to run off to mediate between the gods and humans, or the humans and the demons, or the demons and the gods.

"Is this what you imagined you were saving the world for? The salvation of bureaucracy?" he asked.

"Are you suffering a relapse?"

He cracked his knuckles. "Tell me you haven't wanted to take out a few of these tight-assed pricks in their pretentious power suits. After the way that guy just talked to you . . . he's lucky I've turned away from the dark side . . . for now."

Josie couldn't argue. She didn't have the energy, but he was right. The politicians could be as bad as the gods, worse because after the first few moments of pleasantries, their polite tone often reverted to condescension and patronization. Or they were just bullies.

One European prime minister had told her that if she couldn't persuade a mountain god to stop repeatedly caving in a train tunnel the government was trying to reconstruct, she should sleep with the god, since it seemed to be the only thing she had going for her. This when she was eight months pregnant. Kai had started the building shaking and had sent the minister's entire entourage screaming. Eventually, Josie had convinced the mountain god to allow the tunnel to be repaired, so long as a shrine was built at both ends in his honor. The prime minister had grudgingly agreed, but he'd never apologized to her for the insult. Kai swore he was going to open up a sinkhole under the guy the next chance he got. "A small one," Kai had said, when she'd given him a stern look. "I won't hurt him. I'll just drop him into a sewer."

Some people thought she was insane for depending on Kai so much. They still thought of him as a traitor. But she didn't know how she could've managed without him, especially since Judah was consumed by parental responsibilities. Without Kai keeping tabs on the gods and the demons and making all the sarcastic and semi-threatening remarks and shows of godly power to the mortals that wouldn't have been appropriate for her to make, she would've retreated to the island and let the mortal plane fend for itself.

Not really.

Kai's phone beeped. He pulled it out, scrolling through the screen.

"Is it Ty?" she asked.

Ty had become her mortal plane liaison. He really was a fairy godfather. He scheduled all her appointments, kept her up-to-date on everything mortal, coordinated her many assistants working around the world, and made sure she had a few moments to enjoy her life from time to time. He and Kai were the only reason she was still sane.

"Just an update on Portland reconstruction," he said, frowning.

"That is not a look that denotes just an update. What's wrong?"

"Some douche dumped sewage into the river. The river god is demanding his blood—"

"Again? What is wrong with people?

Kai slipped his phone into his pocket again. "Ty's got it under control for now."

"But—"

"Didn't you say something about some squalling brat who requires your attention?"

"Are we talking about the president again?"

Kai put his hand on her shoulder, turning her away from the ocean and the setting sun. "I love your meager attempts at humor. They remind me that you're not as omnipotent as you seem."

"*Urusai.*"

Kai smirked.

They stepped forward together. One moment on the grassy hills on Oregon's north coast and the next, her living room.

"Surprise!" a dozen or so people cried and then launched into an off-key rendition of a birthday song.

She gave Kai the I-am-going-to-kill-you look, but he just gave her that sideswiped grin.

Simone popped a pointy birthday hat on Josie's head and crushed her in a big hug.

Josie's dad ushered her forward as Caroline lit the nineteen candles on the cake. Red velvet this year, like she'd wanted. Judah had remembered, just like he had the year before. When the song was over, she blew out the candles.

Everyone clapped, and Caroline promptly cut into the cake.

Kai strolled away towards the kitchen with his arm wrapped around Simone. She dropped her head, cut in a sharp bob now, dyed acid green, onto his shoulder.

"I miss cake," Tessa said from beside her.

Josie didn't flinch like she had the first few times her sister had "popped" in.

"Tessa." She hugged her sister and gave Death—still a black-haired, black-eyed former Judah—a dark look. "Thanks for coming."

Death winked. Josie frowned at him, but straightened her face as Tessa pulled back from the hug.

"Of course I came," Tessa said with a flip of her hair. "Just because I don't have birthdays anymore, doesn't mean I can't celebrate yours."

"You do so have birthdays."

"Birthdays mean you're getting older, and the Goddess of Death doesn't get any older."

Josie pursed her lips. Tessa had died, but instead of passing through the gateway of death, she'd become Death's . . . well, girlfriend. And even though she was dead, she, like Kai and Josie, had taken possession of some of Death's powers, even though he continued to exist. Just one more thing Josie didn't quite understand. Though it had been rough at first, Tessa seemed to be content, in a way.

"I was going to get you something, but you're impossible to shop for," Tessa said. "Since you can just . . . poof whatever you want into existence." She gestured around the living room. "But you know that's not the same as it was, don't you?" Tessa pointed to the burgundy colored curtains over the front window.

Josie had recreated their dad's old house in Portland on the Triune's Island. All she'd had to do was think it and it had appeared. She and Judah lived in it now. Her dad stayed next door, with Caroline, in the house that was an exact match to Caroline's old one. Simone and Kai had their own place too, which Josie had created based on a few sketches Simone had given her, across the street.

"I like the curtains better than the blinds," Josie said.

Tessa shrugged. "I guess it's your house now."

Josie ignored the bitter tang of her sister's words and hugged her again. "Thanks again for coming. I have a gift for you."

She held out her hand. A plate with a slice of red velvet cake appeared on it.

"You know it's not the same—" Tessa started.

Josie pushed the plate into her sister's hands. "Try it."

Tessa took the plate and the fork perched on its edge. "I don't need to eat anyway, you know." She took a bite. Her eyes grew wide, gleaming with tears.

Josie put her hand on her sister's shoulder. "Whatever you want will appear on that plate, Tessa. It'll taste like you remember. Just think it and . . . poof."

Tessa nodded and hugged Josie again, tighter than before.

"I'm sorry I didn't think of it sooner," Josie said.

"What? No hug for me?" Beech asked.

She disengaged from Tessa.

"Where's . . . who is it this week, the ocean goddess?" Tessa asked as she cut herself another bite of cake.

The moment Josie turned, Beech swept her up in a hard, bearish hug. As always, he smelled like candy and boy musk. It only reminded her that her sister had no smell at all, now that she was a goddess.

"You know most goddesses are very open-minded," he told Tessa. "All you have to do is be honest with them. The two of you are definitely the exceptions." He planted a wet kiss on

Josie's temple, his arm still draped around her shoulders. "Where is Prince Chode anyway? And my baby girl? I am prepared for some serious cuddling."

"You're not cuddling my niece before I do," Tessa said between mouthfuls. "Where are they anyway?"

"Judah's next door with the baby," Caroline said, putting a plate into Beech's hands. "They'll be by later."

Roxy appeared behind her. "Beer?" She offered a bottle to Beech.

"This island is full of women I want to cuddle," he said, leaving Josie to gather Roxy in a hug.

Tessa and Josie exchanged an eye roll and a small smile.

The party moved into the backyard. Cake was followed by food on the deck. Josie slipped away across the driveway, which was only there because she remembered it being there, not because anyone drove on the island.

Overhead, the sky was ribboned in indigo and burnt orange—sunset. Never in her life on the island had Josie seen the sun or the moon or the stars. The sky had always been gray and empty. But she didn't want her own daughter to miss a single day or a single night, even while they lived on the island.

Josie slipped through the back door. Padding up the stairs, she followed the sound of Judah's soft humming. He was in what had been the guest room back in Portland, but was now the nursery in Grandma and Grandpa's. He stood at the window with a tightly wrapped baby, like a little pill bug, curled against his shoulder.

Josie leaned against the jamb and watched him.

The sun sank against the primordial ocean. A night sky that mirrored the one in Portland appeared. But this one was always clear. The one thing she hadn't brought from Portland to the island, the rain. She figured there would be enough of that when they finally moved back to the mortal plane.

Judah turned to lay the baby into her crib and finally noticed Josie. Even in the fading light, his eyes sparkled.

She crept back. All-powerful demigod or not, she still had to tiptoe to keep from waking the baby.

Judah eased the door almost closed.

She opened her mouth to ask if he thought Gretchen would actually stay asleep in her crib, but he put his finger to her lips, stopping her. He wrapped his arms around her waist and drew her to him. Kissing her. In that way.

He propelled her back down the hall, towards the room that had been Simone's, but was now another guest room.

"She'll wake up," Josie murmured as Judah pulled off his shirt.

"We'll ignore her," he said, taking off her shirt as well.

Josie arched an eyebrow at him.

"I'll ignore her. I promise." He kissed her again and then pulled back. "Did you get what you wanted for your birthday?"

She smiled. "Not yet."

Early the next morning, in that gray hour between night and dawn, Josie rocked on the porch swing. It creaked, just like she remembered it. Gretchen was fed and asleep in her arms. Her chubby little fingers curled around Josie's bigger slimmer one. Gretchen's big blue eyes—Judah's eyes—were closed, though Josie knew it wouldn't last long.

Simone came up the steps, smiling, carrying a clear dish in her arms.

"What are you doing here?" Josie whispered.

Simone set the dish down on the iron porch table and sat down next to Josie, holding out her arms. Josie, oh-so-carefully, passed the baby over to Simone.

"Eat up, Mama," Simone said, raising her eyebrows at the covered dish.

Josie opened the lid. Cinnamon and sugar wafted into the cool, damp air. Josie dug one of the cinnamon rolls out of the dish—still warm—and devoured it.

As she was licking the sticky sugar frosting from her fingers, she noticed Simone gazing down the lane at the Gray Beast, as Judah called it. What once had been a massive heap of stone, a ruin, was now a huge gray cloud. A swirling fog bank.

Josie had transformed almost everything on the island. She had left the main building as she remembered it. A crumbling stone mansion. But the courtyard was now a park, full of big, shady trees, blooming flower beds, and herringbone brickwork. On each side of the courtyard the crumbling buildings had been transformed into craftsman-style houses. She hadn't given many people access to the island. No one could come unless she, Kai, or Judah brought them anyway, so few of the houses were ever used. Still, she'd wanted a neighborhood, so that's what she'd created. But, at the far end of the oak and crabapple-lined street, the Gray Beast hung—a churning, impenetrable wall of fog.

Everyone wanted to know why she didn't get rid of it. Why she didn't turn it into something else, anything else.

Only Simone, Kai, and Judah knew the truth, although she guessed that the others suspected it.

She couldn't get rid of it. She'd tried. Over and over. The Gray Beast never moved. It never changed.

Josie helped herself to another cinnamon roll. She drew her knees to her chest, teasing apart the sweet pastry layers.

"What do you think it means?" Simone asked.

"I don't know," Josie said.

Simone shifted the baby in her arms, running her finger over Gretchen's cheek. "Kai thinks it's a reminder."

"A reminder of what?"

"That there's something out there more powerful than you."

"I already have a reminder of that." She touched the white swaddling blankets gently. "Her name's Gretchen Melinda."

Simone smiled down at the serene face of baby Gretchen. "She rules our little world, don't you, my sweet little baby?"

Josie sat back. The rhythmic sway and soft creak of the porch swing lulled her. Warm light slid over the peaks of the roofs, pushing through the filters of the treetops, scattering on the pavement like glowing autumn leaves. Sugar and cinnamon rolled over her tongue, but couldn't dispel the lingering taste, the ever-present scent, of Judah, who was asleep upstairs.

Her eyes slipped shut.

What she hadn't told Judah or Simone or anyone was that when she closed her eyes, it wasn't darkness that greeted her, but grayness. A churning, impenetrable gray cloud. And she knew what it meant.

Kai was right.

Something more was out there.

But for all the unanswered questions, for all the remaining mysteries, for all the great unknowns, she had so much more than she'd ever wanted, so much more than she'd ever imagined possible.

For Josie Day, this moment was enough. She didn't want anything more.

ACKNOWLEDGMENTS

I must first thank my editorial team. Renae, she is my first and best reader, fan, and friend. Chad A. Clark, fellow indie author, whose feedback and insights are invaluable. My proofreader, Kris, who wrestled my prose into submission with good humor, generosity, and grace. And my editor and partner-in-crime, Pam House Caster—she asked all the hard questions and always inspires me to get my butt back in the chair.

Thank you to all the family, friends, and teachers who have loved, encouraged, and guided me.

Finally, my boys. I had dreams before you came into my life, but it wasn't until you were in my life that my dreams actually started to come true.

WORKS BY
A.M. YATES

Summoners Series

Minor Gods: Book One
Lost Gods: Book Two
Fated Gods: Book Three

The Horizon Cycle

Shield and the Shadow
Stoneheart and the Axe
Sparrow and the Dagger

Stealer
Hunter (Stealer #2)
Unraveler (Stealer #3)

Find out more and sign up for the new release newsletter at www.amyates.com

Hear the playlists that inspired this book and the entire series by following amyates on Spotify

Read exclusive stories from AM Yates by following on Wattpad

AM Yates can also be found on facebook, tumblr, goodreads, and twitter